EXQUISITE CORPSE

POPPY Z. BRITE

Scribner Paperback Fiction
Published by Simon & Schuster

SCRIBNER PAPERBACK FICTION
Simon & Schuster Inc.
Rockefeller Center
1230 Avenue of the Americas
New York, NY 10020

First Scribner Paperback Fiction edition 1997

SCRIBNER PAPERBACK FICTION and design are trademarks
of Simon & Schuster Inc

Designed by Deirdre C. Amthor

Manufactured in the United States of America

3   5   7   9   10   8   6   4   2

The Library of Congress has cataloged the Simon & Schuster
edition as follows:
Brite, Poppy Z.
Exquisite corpse / Poppy Z. Brite.
p. cm.
1. Murderers—Psychology—Fiction. 2. Serial murders—Fiction.
3. Cannibalism—Fiction. I. Title.
PS3552.R4967E97   1996
813'.54—dc20   96-2455
CIP

ISBN 0-684-82254-7
0-684-83627-0 (Pbk)

To my mother,
Connie Burton Brite,
who gave me all the guts
I would ever need

Records of the 1994 autopsy of serial killer Jeffrey Dahmer reveal that officials kept Dahmer's body shackled at the feet during the entire procedure, "such was the fear of this man," according to pathologist Robert Huntington.

Milwaukee Journal–AP, March 17, 1995

1

Sometimes a man grows tired of carrying everything the world heaps upon his head. The shoulders sag, the spine bows cruelly, the muscles tremble with weariness. Hope of relief begins to die. And the man must decide whether to cast off his load or endure it until his neck snaps like a brittle twig in autumn.

Such was my situation late in my thirty-third year. Although I deserved everything the world had heaped on—and torments after death far worse than any the world could threaten: the torture of my skeleton, the rape and dismemberment of my immortal soul—though I deserved all that and more, I found that I could no longer bear the weight.

I realized I didn't *have* to bear it, you see. I came to understand that I had a choice. It must have been difficult for Christ himself to withstand the agonies of the cross—the filth, the thirst, the terrible spikes raping the jellied flesh of his hands—knowing he had a choice. And I am not Christ, not even by half.

My name is Andrew Compton. Between 1977 and 1988 I killed twenty-three boys and young men in London. I was seventeen years old when I began, twenty-eight when they caught me. All the time I was in prison, I knew that if they ever let me out I would continue killing boys. But I also knew they would never let me out.

My boys and young men were transients in the city: friend-less, hungry, drunk and strung out on the excellent Pakistani heroin that has coursed through the veins of London since the swinging sixties. I gave them good food, strong tea, a warm place in my bed, what few pleasures my body could provide. In return, all I asked was their lives. Sometimes they appeared to give those as readily as anything else.

I remember a sloe-eyed skinhead who went home with me because he said I was a nice white bloke, not a bleeding queer like most of these others that chatted him up in the pubs of Soho. (What he was doing in the pubs of Soho, I cannot tell you.) He did not seem inclined to revise his opinion even as I sucked his cock and slid two greased fingers into his anus. I noticed later that he had a dotted line tattooed in scarlet round his throat, along with the words CUT HERE. I had only to fol-low directions. ("You look like a bleeding queer," I'd told his headless corpse, but young Mr. White England had nothing to say for himself anymore.)

I killed most of the twenty-three by cutting. By severing their major arteries with a knife or a razor after they were in-sensible from drink. I killed them this way not out of cow-ardice or from a wish to avoid struggle; though I am not a large man, I could have overcome any of my half-starved, drug-addled waifs in a fair fight. I killed them by cutting be-cause I appreciated the beautiful objects that their bodies were, the bright ribbons of blood coursing over the velvet of their skin, the feel of their muscles parting like soft butter. I drowned two in the bath, and choked one with the laces of his own Dr. Marten boots as he lay in a drunken stupor. But mostly I killed them by cutting.

This is not to say that I took them to pieces for pleasure. I found no joy in gross mutilation or dismemberment, not then; it was the subtle whisper and slice of the razor that appealed to me. I liked my boys as they were, big dead dolls with an extra weeping crimson mouth or two. I would keep them with me for as much as a week, until the smell in my flat grew obvious. I did not find the odour of death unpleasant. It was rather like cut flowers left too long in stagnant water, a heavy sickish sweetness that coated the nostrils and curled into the back of the throat with every breath.

But the neighbours complained, and I would have to invent some excuse or other, something about my waste disposal backing up or my toilet having overflowed. (Humiliating, and ultimately futile, for it was a neighbour who called the police in the end.) I would leave a boy in my armchair when I went to work, and he would be waiting patiently for me when I came home. I would take him into my bed and cradle his creamy smoothness all night. For a day or two days or a week I wouldn't feel alone. Then it would be time to let another one go.

I would use a saw to cut him in half at the waist, to separate the arms from the torso, to bisect the legs at the knee. I would wrestle the segments into bulging bags of wet garbage, where their odd angles and powerful stench might be disguised, and leave them out for collection. I would drink whiskey until the flat spun. I would vomit in the basin and sob myself to sleep, having lost at love again. I did not come to appreciate the aesthetics of dismemberment until much later.

But for now I sat in a dank cell in Her Majesty's Prison Painswick, in Lower Slaughter near the industrial wasteland of Birmingham. These lurid appellations might seem designed to terrify and titillate the soul, and so they do. Look on any map of England and you'll find them, along with places called Grimsby, Kettle Crag, Fitful Head, Mousehole, Devil's Elbow, and Stool End Farm. England is a country that spares no resonance or descriptive colour in its place-names, forbidding though they may be.

I'd looked around my cell without much interest when they brought me in five years ago. I knew I was classed as a Category *A* prisoner. (*D* was the least dangerous sort; *C* and *B* types you mightn't want to turn your back on; *A* was, of course, the ravening killer.) The papers had dubbed me "The Eternal Host" and invested my unremarkable black-and-white visage with a dread that bordered on the talismanic. The contents of my flat had been lovingly inventoried a hundred times over. My trial was a legal circus of the vilest sort. The possibility of my escape was deemed highly dangerous to the public. I would remain Category *A* until the day I died with my eyes fixed on some bleak eternity beyond these four mouldering stone walls.

I could receive no visitors without approval from the prison governor and close supervision. I didn't care; everyone I had ever loved was dead. I could be denied education and recreation, but at that time there was nothing more in life I wanted to learn, no fun I wanted to have. I must endure a light burning constantly in my cell, all night, all day, until the outline of it was seared into my corneas. All the better, I thought then, to stare at these hands steeped in blood.

Aside from my blazing bulb and my guilty hands, I had an iron bed bolted to the wall and covered with a thin lumpy mattress, a rickety table and chair, and a pot to piss in. I often reminded myself that at least I had a pot to piss in, but this was cold comfort indeed—quite literally so on winter mornings in Painswick. I had all these things inside a stone box of a cell measuring three and a half by four metres.

I wondered how many of Her Majesty's prisoners realized the extra half-metre along one wall was a subtle form of torture. (As Oscar Wilde was being hounded in chains round the prison yard, he remarked that if this was how Her Majesty treated prisoners, she had no business having any.) When I looked at this wall for a long time, which was the only way I could look at it, the wrong geometry began to hurt my eyes.

For more than a year the imperfect square tormented me. I visualized all four walls grinding in, cutting off that dreadful extra half-metre, beginning to crumble around me. Then gradually I got used to it, and that chilled me as much as the torment had done. I've never liked getting used to things, especially when I am given no choice in the matter.

Once they realized I wasn't going to make trouble, I was given all the notebooks and pencils I wanted. I was seldom allowed out of my cell except for solitary exercise and showers; sodden joyless meals were brought to me by silent guards with faces like the judgement at the end of time. I could do no harm with my pencils save driving one into my own eye, and I wore them down too dull for that.

I filled twenty notebooks my first year, thirty-one my second, nineteen my third. At this time I was as close to true remorse as I ever came. It was as if I had been in a dream that lasted eleven years, and had woken from it into a world I barely recognized. How had I ever done twenty-three killings? What had made me want to? I attempted to plumb the depths of my soul with words. I dissected my childhood and family (stultifying but hardly traumatic), my sexual history (abortive), my career in various branches of the civil service (utterly without distinction, except for the number of times I was fired for insubordination to my superiors).

This done, and little learned, I began to write about the things that interested me now. I found myself with a great many descriptions of murders and sex acts performed upon dead boys. Small details began to return to me, such as the way a fingerprint would stay in the flesh of a corpse's thigh as if pressed into wax, or a cold thread of semen would sometimes leak out of a flaccid penis as I rolled it about on my tongue.

The only constant thread running through my prison notebooks was a pervasive loneliness with no discernible beginning and no conceivable end. But a corpse could never walk away.

I came to understand that these memories were my salvation. I no longer wanted to know why I had done such things if it meant I wouldn't want to do them anymore. I put my notebooks aside forever. I was different, and that was all. I had always known I was different; I could not trudge through life contentedly chewing whatever cud I found in my mouth, as those around me seemed to do. My boys were only another thing that set me apart from the rest.

Someone had loved my boys once upon a time, someone who did not have to steal their lives to show that love. Each had been someone's baby once. But so had I, and what good did it ever do me? By all accounts, I emerged from the womb quite blue, with the umbilical cord wrapped around my neck, and my state of life or death was disputed for several minutes before I sucked in a great gulp of air and began to breathe on my own. The boys I killed may have been strapping infants, but at the time of their deaths they were intravenous drug users who shared needles as if borrowing one another's pocket handkerchiefs, who often traded blowjobs for cash or a fix. Of those I took to bed with me while they were still alive, not one asked me to use a condom, and not one expressed concern when I swallowed his sperm. I suspected later that I might have actually saved lives by killing some of them.

I was never one to moralize, and how could I argue ethics now? There is no excuse for wanton, random murder. But I came to understand that I didn't need an excuse. I needed only a reason, and the terrible joy of the act was reason enough. I wanted to return to my art, to fulfill my obvious destiny. I wanted the rest of my life to do as I pleased, and I had no doubt what that would be. My hands itched for the blade, for the warmth of fresh blood, for the marble smoothness of flesh three days dead.

I decided to exercise my freedom of choice.

Before I began killing boys, and afterward when I couldn't find one or hadn't the energy to go looking, there was another thing I would sometimes do. It began as a crude masturbation technique and ended very near mysticism. At the trial they called me *necrophiliac* without considering the ancient roots of the word, or its profound resonance. I was friend of the dead, lover of the dead. And I was my own first friend and lover.

It first happened when I was thirteen. I would lie on my back and relax my muscles slowly, limb by limb, fibre by fibre. I would imagine my organs turning to a bitter soup, my brain beginning to liquefy inside my skull. Sometimes I drew a razor across my chest and let the blood run down the sides of my ribcage and pool in the hollow of my belly. Sometimes I enhanced my natural pallor with blue-white makeup, and later a trace of purple here and there, my own artistic interpretation of lividity and gaseous stain. I tried to escape what seemed a hateful prison of flesh; to imagine myself outside my body was the only way I could love it.

After doing this for a time, I began to feel certain changes in my body. I never managed to make my spirit separate completely from my flesh. If I had, I probably wouldn't have come back. But I achieved a hovering state between consciousness and void, a state where my lungs seemed to stop pulling in air and my heart to cease beating. I could still sense a subliminal murmur of bodily function, but no pulse, no breath. I thought I could feel my skin loosening from the connective tissues, my eyes drying out behind blue-tinged lids, my molten core beginning to cool.

I did this in prison from time to time, without the makeup or razors of course, remembering some boy or other, imagining my rancid living body to be his dear dead flesh. It took me five years to realize that my talent might be put to another use, one that would allow me to someday hold a real corpse again.

I spent most of my time lying on my bunk. I breathed the heady, meaty smell of hundreds of men eating and sweating and pissing and shitting and fucking and living together in cramped, dirty quarters, often with only one chance to shower each week. I closed my eyes and listened to the rhythms of my own body, the myriad paths of my blood, the sweat beading on my skin, the steady pull and release of my lungs, the soft electric hum of my brain and all its tributaries.

I wondered just how much I could slow it all down, how much of it I could stop entirely. And I wondered, if I was successful, whether I would be able to start it all up again. What I had in mind was much more advanced than my old game of playing dead. I would have to be dead enough to fool the guards, the nursing officer, and almost certainly a doctor. But I had read about Hindu fakirs who stopped their own hearts, who allowed themselves to be buried for weeks without oxygen. I knew it could be done. And I thought I could do it.

I halved the amount I ate, which had never been much in prison. On the outside I had been something of a gourmand. I often treated my boys to a restaurant meal before the evening's festivities, though the fare I chose was usually too exotic for them: lamb vindaloo with flaky nan bread, Chinese pork buns, jellied eels, stuffed grape leaves, Vietnamese emerald curry, Ethiopian steak tartare, and the like. Prison food was either gristly, starchy, or cabbagey. I had no trouble leaving half of it on the plate. I knew brains would serve me better than brawn anyway; they always had. And I felt an emaciated look would aid my task somehow.

("Off your feed then, Compton?" was the only comment I ever received on this matter from the guard who delivered and removed my trays. I managed a listless nod, aware that he was trying to be friendly in his fashion. Some of the guards would try to talk to me now and then, presumably so they could go home and tell the wife and kiddies the Eternal Host had spoken to them today. But I didn't want him to remember this particular exchange.)

One day I deliberately gashed my forehead open on the bars. Telling the guard I'd tripped and banged my skull earned me a trip to the infirmary. I was in handcuffs and leg irons the entire time, but I managed to have a look round as a garrulous nursing officer swabbed out my wound and stitched it up.

"Did you have Hummer in here?" I asked, referring to an A-wing prisoner who had died of heart failure the month before.

"Old Artie? No, we didn't know the cause of death, so they took him out in an ambulance. Autopsied him in Lower Slaughter and sent him home to his family, what was left of 'em. Artie was in for shooting his wife and son, you know, but there was a daughter away at school. I expect she was none too pleased to get Daddy back, eh?"

"What do they do with the organs after an autopsy?" I asked, partly so he wouldn't remember my asking only one question, partly out of honest curiosity.

"Toss 'em back in every which way and sew up the trench. Oh, and they save the brains for study. Murderers' brains in particular. I'll wager someone gets yours in a jar of spirits one day, Mr. Compton."

"Perhaps," I said. And perhaps someone would. But not a grinning sawbones in Lower Slaughter, not if I could help it.

The nursing officer took a vial of blood from my arm that day, though I didn't know why. A week later I was hauled off to the infirmary again, where I learned something that would help me more than I could fathom.

"HIV-positive?" I asked the pale, sweaty nursing officer. "What does that mean?"

"Well, Mr. Compton, maybe nothing." He pinched a slender pamphlet between the tips of his thumb and forefinger and gingerly passed it to me. I noticed that he was wearing rubber gloves. "But it means you could develop AIDS."

I studied the pamphlet with interest, then looked back at the officer's chagrined face. The whites of his eyes were webbed with red, and he looked as if he'd forgotten to shave for a few days. "It says here the virus can be transmitted by

sexual contact or through the blood," I noted. "You sewed up
my cut last week. Wasn't that dangerous for you?"

"We . . . I don't . . ." He stared at his gloved fingers and
shook his head, almost sobbing. "No one knows."

I brought my shackled wrists up and coughed into my hand
to hide a tiny wicked grin.

Back in my cell, I read the pamphlet twice and tried to remember what I had heard about this malady borne on the fluids of love. The odd news article had caught my interest back
before I was arrested, but I'd never been a great follower of
current events, and I hadn't seen a paper since my trial. There
were some in the prison library, but I spent my precious hours
there reading books. I didn't see how news of the world could
help me any longer.

Even so, I remembered a mind-boggling assortment of re-
ports: headlines shrilling HOMO PLAGUE, calm assertions that
it was all a Labour Party conspiracy, hysterical speculations
that anyone could catch it by almost any means. I'd managed
to ascertain that gay men and intravenous drug users were at
special risk. Though I wondered whether any of my boys
might have been exposed, I never dreamed I could catch it
myself. Most of my contact with them had occurred after
their deaths, and I assumed any virus would have died with
them. But now it looked as though viruses were hardier than
boys.

Well, Andrew, I told myself, *anyone who violates the sweet
sanctity of a dead boy's ass cannot expect to get away scot-
free. Now forget that you may become ill, for you are not ill
now, and remember only that this virus in your blood makes
people afraid of you. Any time someone is afraid of you, you
can use it to your own advantage.*

My supper tray arrived. I ate a sliver of boiled beef, a soggy
leaf of cabbage, and a few crumbs of dry bread. Then I lay on
my bunk, stared at the pale blue network of veins under the
skin of my arm, and plotted my leave of Painswick.

• • •

Compton...

I squeezed my eyes shut and turned my face toward the sound of the sea. The sunlight felt like liquid gold spilling over my cheeks, my chest, my skinny legs. My bare toes dug into the cool, rich soil of the bluff. I was ten years old, on holiday with my family in the Isle of Man.

Andrew Compton...

The bright yellow gorse and dusky purple heather made a shifting wall, tall enough to hide a small boy lying on his back, refusing to move, refusing to answer. No one in the world knew where I was, or even who I was. I began to feel as if I might fall off the earth and into the boundless blue sky. I would drown in it like a sea, flailing my arms and legs, straining to breathe, sucking in crystalline lungfuls of cloud. Cloud would taste of mint drops, I imagined, and would instantly turn my insides to ice.

I decided I wouldn't mind falling into the sky. I tried to let go, to stop believing in gravity. But the earth held me fast, as if it wanted to pull me in.

Fine, I thought. I would sink into the earth, I would release my body's nourishing juices into the roots of the heather, I would let the worms and beetles flake away the tender meat packed between my bones. But the earth would not take me either. I was trapped inside this vault of sky and earth and sea, separate from all of them, at one with nothing but my own wretched flesh.

COMP... TONNN...

The syllables were nonsense, as meaningless as the insistent clang that accompanied them. There was a box made of stone, and inside that box was a slab of metal covered with a thin cloth pad, and on top of the pad was an inert thing made of bone encased in meat. I was attached to that thing by an invisible tether, a fragile umbilical cord of ectoplasm and habit.

All times and all places seemed a constantly moving river, and while the inert thing lay on the shore of that river, I was immersed in its waters. Only the fragile umbilical cord kept me from being swept away on the current. I could sense the cord stretching, the ephemeral tissue beginning to disintegrate.

I heard the hollow rattle of metal against stone and recognized it as the door of my cell opening. A firearm cocked, and footsteps rang on cold stone. "Compton, you try anything funny and I'll put a bullet in your head. What the fuckin' 'ell are you playing at?"

Another voice. "Shoot 'im in the arse, Arnie, an' see if he moves." Raucous laughter, unechoed by the first guard. My muscles did not tense, my eyelids did not flutter. If the guard did shoot me, I wondered if I would feel the bullet tunnelling into my flesh.

Steel bracelets snapped round my wrists, a familiar sensation; then callused fingers checked my pulse. Something cold and smooth brushed my lips. The guard called Arnie spoke again, his voice hushed, almost awed.

"I think he's dead."

"Compton dead? Can't be; he's like a cat, only he's got twenty-three lives."

"Shut up, Blackie. He ain't breathin' an' I don't feel a pulse. We'd better ring the infirmary."

When one is an habitual murderer, one tends also to become a good actor. Now I had begun to pull off the greatest acting job of my life: my death. But it didn't feel like acting.

A blinding succession of cut-frame, stop-action memories: a gurney thundering down a long cinder-block hallway, my body strapped down tight, my wrists still cuffed, dangerous enough to merit bondage even in death. A smell of medicine and mildew that I recognized as the prison infirmary. A tiny needling pain in the crook of my arm, in the sole of my foot. A cold circle of metal on my chest, on my stomach. A tug on my right eyelid, and a ray of light as sharp and thin as a wire.

I remember hearing the voice of the prison governor, a man whose pale cold stare always drilled through me as if his first-born son had died at my hands. "Aren't you going to examine the body? We need to know what killed him before we can let him out of here."

"Sorry, sir." That was the nursing officer who'd sewn up my cut forehead, sounding more frightened than ever. "Andrew Compton recently tested HIV-positive. He may have died of an AIDS-related complication. I'm not qualified to examine him."

"Well, bloody hell, people don't just up and die of AIDS one fine morning, do they? They get lesions and things, don't they?"

"I don't know, sir. He'd be the first case who's died here. Most of the HIV-positive prisoners have been transferred to Wormwood Scrubs. Compton would have gone there eventually too."

My tethered soul gave a little shudder of delight. If I'd ended up in Wormwood Scrubs, I would have had little chance of getting out alive or dead. The prison there was the largest in England, with its own hospital and morgue.

"Well, we can't be messing about with communicable diseases here. He'll have to be autopsied in Lower Slaughter. Ring Dr. Masters to come sign his death certificate; they won't take him without one."

I had seen Dr. Masters exactly five times, once each year for the required physical exam. Now here he was again. His hands were as gentle and dry as ever; his breath still smelt of wintergreen and something rotten deep inside. "Poor old fellow," I heard him murmur, too low for anyone else to hear, as he took the key from the guard and uncuffed my wrists. He searched in vain for my pulse, removed my prison uniform, prodded my belly, rolled me over and slid the fragile glass stem of his thermometer into my cooling rectum. I loosed my tenuous grip on the world and let my soul go drifting beneath the black waves of oblivion.

"What killed him then?" was the last thing I heard, and Dr. Masters' soft voice answering, "I've really no idea."

A clatter of metal, then wheels thrumming on a paved road. There were no paved roads on the prison grounds. I couldn't risk opening my eyes, and even if I'd wanted to, the lids felt as though they had been weighted shut with sandbags. I heard the clink of tubes and bottles, the intermittent static of a scanner radio, the bleat and snarl of traffic answered by the rising wail of a siren. I was in an ambulance. I had made it out of Painswick; now all I had to do was come back to life. But not yet.

I was strapped to another gurney and sent racing down another hall, the sound of the wheels echoing more immensely somehow here, as if this hall were made of tile and glass instead of mouldering cinder block. Another cold metal table beneath my naked back, and all at once my body was swathed in heavy crackling plastic. A body bag.

If I had been breathing, the bag's interior would soon have grown unbearably hot and humid. Once I had used up the oxygen trapped inside, I might well have suffocated. But my lungs were closed off, soaked like two sponges with all the oxygen they would need for a while. I could enjoy the sensation of being zipped into a body bag, of my own flesh chilling. For all intents and purposes, the meat-filled envelope of skin called Andrew Compton was a lifeless corpse.

I thought of the plague years of London, of narrow muddy streets turned charnelhouses, of naked, slat-sided bodies heaped on carts and trundled through the city, pale limp bodies beginning to discolour, to distend. I imagined the smell of charred flesh, the smell of burning sickness everywhere, the sound of iron wheels trundling over broken cobblestones, the constant weary invocation *Bring out your dead.* I imagined myself tossed roughly onto a wooden cart atop a pile of my diseased brethren, a plague-swollen face thrust into mine, black pus dripping into my eyes, trickling into my mouth . . .

I feared I would get an erection and give myself away. But I was foolish to worry. I knew corpses were perfectly capable of getting lovely hard-ons. Surely the doctors would know it as well.

A harsh white light filtered through my eyelids, tracing the webwork of veins in electric red. Then there was not even that. I ceased to feel time passing. Words echoed through my head, meaning nothing; soon they too were gone. I could not remember my name or what was supposed to be happening to me. I might have been spinning in a void without feature or dimension, a blank universe of my own design.

This, then, was where the seed of consciousness was planted in the loam of existence. From here I sensed I might keep spinning away, might keep sinking. I needn't go back. I could barely remember why I had wanted to.

I believe I could have died then. Legally, medically, I already had. My heart had been listened for and not heard; my pulse had been felt for and not found. It would have been so easy to let go.

But within the seed of consciousness curls the germ of ego. I never doubted that ego was the last part of the organism to die. I had seen the last helpless fury in some of my boys' eyes as they realized they were really going: how could it happen to *them?* And what was a ghost but a leftover shred of ego, unable to believe it had been jilted by its own corruptible flesh?

Likewise my own ghost, ego, or soul—it never told me its preferred form of address—would not quite separate from from the dense gray bundle of nerves that had housed it for thirty-three years. In the manner of a wild animal kept too long in a cage, it feared to venture out even when the door was flung wide open.

So I hung suspended between life and death, unable to swing either way, twirling like a spider at the end of a taut gossamer line. Was I stuck here in the void of near-consciousness?

Was this the fate I had given myself over to, a necrophiliac trapped in his own decaying corpse?

There were fates I would welcome less. But not now, not when I had decided I wanted to live in the world and enjoy the fruits of my destiny. I knew I had enormous strength of will. I had used it to mimic charm when I had none, to put off neighbours complaining about the smell of my flat, to make a boy who broke away from me and ran for the door stop in his tracks simply by saying his name. (This was a memory I cherished. "Benjamin," I'd said, quietly but more firmly than anyone had spoken to him in his whole life; and he turned, terrible emotions warring in his face, desire and dread and a wish to just have it all over with, which I quickly fulfilled.)

With all that strength of will I tried to rise, to wake. At first I could not so much feel my body as sense its boundaries and the space it occupied, without having any control over these dimensions. Then my heart twitched and my brain seemed to convulse, and my flesh rose around me like the sides of a coffin. Indeed, a coffin could not have felt more claustrophobic.

I was back in, if indeed I had ever been out. But I still couldn't move.

Suddenly my body bag was unzipped and peeled away. I felt the metal table under me again; we were old friends by now, even if its reception was a bit chilly. The rush of air around my head smelled of formaldehyde, disinfectant, and the onions on someone's breath. I felt gloved palms like slices of boiled meat adhering to my chest, fingers like greasy sausages closing around my biceps.

"Lock that door," said an unfamiliar voice. "People keep popping round to have a look at him, and I won't be disturbed."

Not Dr. Masters, then. I was glad of it. I'd rather liked him.

I heard a click, and whoever was handling me began to speak as if into a tape recorder. "Five November . . . Dr. Martin Drummond assisted by junior doctor Waring . . . Subject of autopsy is Andrew Compton, white male aged thirty-three, incarcerated for the past five years . . . lividity of skin observed, but no pooling of blood. Rigor mortis may have already passed. Open his mouth, Waring." A finger swathed in foul-tasting rubber pried my jaws apart. "Teeth in good condition . . . Deceased tested positive for the HIV virus, but has exhibited no symptoms of AIDS. Cause of death remains unknown." If Drummond's odour and the feel of his hands had not been so repulsive, I might have imagined he was reading me love poetry.

Another thermometer up the bum. "Intestinal temperature is rising," Drummond recorded, "which would indicate the rapid onset of decomposition."

I heard Waring's voice, young and nervous: "Skinny little bloke, wasn't he? How could he ever kill twenty-three men?"

"They weren't men, they were teenage addicts." (A lie; most of them were over twenty.) "Punks and homosexual prostitutes. Reckon they put up much of a fight?"

"Perhaps when they knew they were going to die?" Waring suggested timidly.

"He drugged them. They never saw it coming." More lies. I only offered my guests a drink, then kept their glass filled as any host should do. And unfortunately, more than one of them did see it coming; it was just that none of them seemed to care much.

The doctors paused to write something. I knew that when they started up again they would mean business. I had read about autopsy procedure. They'd soon be coming at me with a scalpel, intending to make a Y-shaped incision that started at my collarbone, converged at my sternum, and ran straight down my stomach to the pubic bone. They would pry off my breastplate and crack open my ribs, after which they would remove, weigh, and examine my viscera. I'd heard somewhere that the organs of people who had died of long wasting diseases looked as if they'd been detonated, but of course mine were still ticking.

When my guts were bagged and catalogued, all that remained would be to peel my scalp down over my face, saw off the top of my skull, and remove my brain. This they would drop into a jar of spirits, where it ought to feel perfectly at home, and where it would have to marinate for a fortnight before it was firm enough to be sectioned and analyzed. The brain begins turning to mush at the moment of death, and by the time they finished doing all these things to me, I supposed I really would be dead.

I strained to plug back into my nervous system, to regain control of my muscles and skeleton. It all seemed an impossibly complicated tangle I had forgotten how to operate, if I had ever known. It was as though I had risen through murky fathoms of sentience and was now pressing against a cell-thin but very strong membrane stretched across the surface.

"Opening him up," said Drummond. The stainless steel blade sliced deep into the left pectoral muscle of my chest. The pain burst the membrane, sang through my nerves like an electric shock, and pulled me all the way out of death.

My eyes flew open, met Drummond's uncomprehending muddy-coloured ones. My left hand rose, grabbed Drummond by his sparse hair, and drew him down toward me. My right hand seized the scalpel and wrenched it from his grasp. The blade slipped out of my chest incision and whispered across the doctor's palm, laying open the rubber glove, then the greasy flesh clear to the bone. I watched his mouth fall open in amazement or agony, revealing two rows of yellow teeth, a meaty maw, a scabrous-looking pale pink tongue.

Before he could react further, I drew back the scalpel and plunged it into one of those muddy eyes—or, to be precise, I impaled his head on the scalpel. Hot bloody fluid spilled over my knuckles. Drummond sagged forward, driving the blade deep into his own brain. I was awake! I was alive! I gloried in every sensation, the small wet pop as the eyeball yielded, the raw sewer stink as Drummond's sphincter surrendered a losing battle, the panicky keen I supposed was issuing from the throat of young Waring.

The eye socket sucked sensually at the scalpel as I pulled it out. I would have left it there—such expedient instruments of cutting deserve their satisfaction—but I required a weapon. I wondered if I could push myself upright on the table, then realized I had already done it. Waring was backing away from me, toward the door. His escape now was unthinkable.

My hands were slick with Drummond's blood and vitreous humour. I pressed the left one to my heart and it came away bloodier still. I risked a glance down at the wound. The skin around it was puckered, lipped; the blood poured down my naked chest and belly, soaking my pubic hair, spattering the floor. I thrust my hand at Waring, cupped and brimming with my own pestilence. He threw himself away from it—and away from the door.

I advanced on him, scalpel in one hand, disease in the other, and I watched his eyes. They were a crystalline English blue behind little gold-rimmed spectacles with thin square lenses. His hair was the colour of cornsilk, cut blunt like a young boy's; his face was bland as butter. He might have stepped whole out of James Herriot's Yorkshire; but for the thread of drool on his chin he might have been the country vet's perpetually astonished young apprentice, stethoscope around his neck, a flush of sunburn staining his fresh-cream skin pale pink. Sweet simple lad!

"Please, Mr. Compton," he whimpered, "please—I'm a bit of a serial killer buff, you see, and I'd never tell on you—"

I backed him into a cart full of gleaming clamps and bone spreaders. It went over with a deafening clatter. Waring stumbled backward, then sprawled in the mess. He kicked uselessly at me as I bore down on him and raked his glasses off his face, wiped my left hand across his eyes, blinding him with my blood. He tried to bite my hand, managed only to get a mouthful of wet gore. I drove the scalpel into his throat and ripped it open to the collarbone. His sturdy farmboy body spasmed beneath me.

I twisted the blade in his throat. His hands came up and clawed feebly at mine. I grabbed him by that beautiful cornsilk hair, now black with blood, and smashed his head down on a bone spreader. The skull gave way with a satisfying crunch. Waring bucked once more and was still.

The almost-forgotten but instantly familiar thrill of the sagging weight in my arms . . . the rapturous glaze slicking the half-closed eyes . . . the little way the fingers would stiffen, tremble with some dying palsy, then curl into the palms . . . the sweet face lost in its endless empty dream. I always liked blonds. Their complexions are naturally milky, so that the tender veins show blue at the temples, and their blood-soaked hair is like pale silk seen through ruby glass.

I leaned over Waring and kissed him, reacquainting myself with the textures of lips and teeth, the rich metallic flavour of a mouth full of blood. He felt so good, I wanted to lie down next to him on the cold tiled floor of the morgue and play with him awhile. But I didn't dare. For all my studies of autopsy procedure, I had no idea how long a real autopsy should take. The door was locked, but sooner or later someone would turn up with a key, and I had to assume it would be sooner rather than later.

For the first time in five years I had a beautiful dead boy at my disposal, and there wasn't a damned thing I could do about it.

I let my gaze leave him for a quick look round. We were in a small rectangular room, apparently some antechamber of the morgue. Low concrete ceiling, tile walls, no windows. Drummond's greasy leavings were crumpled at the foot of a metal dissecting table, while young Waring and I lay entwined in a corner among a tangle of dark-stained rubber hoses that disappeared into the underside of a sink. There seemed to be no way out but the door.

I was stark naked and bleeding profusely. If employees of
the hospital knew I had been brought in for autopsy, my face
would be freshly imprinted on their brains. Still, I would have
to brazen my way through. I thought I could do it; in fact, I
knew I could do it. Of course it wasn't as if I had much choice.

I put on a pair of rubber gloves and raked through cabinets
and drawers, found a first-aid kit and packed my wound with
cotton, then taped gauze over it. Blood began to star the gauze
almost at once, but there was nothing I could do except be
thankful it was flowing again. As I wiped myself down with
paper towels at the sink, I was still uncomfortably sure I had
trespassed on the edge of irrevocable death.

Drummond's lab coat was soaked with every sort of foul
fluid in his suppurating sac of a body. But Waring had hung his
on a peg near the door, and died in his hospital greens. Silently
I blessed the boy. Then I slipped off his shoes and socks, tried
on one of the ugly rubber-soled loafers. It fit like a boat, but I
thought if I laced the shoes tightly and stuffed them with paper towels, I could keep them on my feet.

With much tugging and heaving, I managed to remove his
greens. In the pants pocket I found a small purse containing
two twenty-pound notes and a few coins, which I kept. Waring's body in its clean cotton briefs was smooth, pink, hairless
but for a fine golden floss on his legs and lower belly. I no
longer felt any attraction toward him; he reminded me of
nothing so much as a newborn rat.

It had been the same with my boys now and then. I'd have
one freshly laid out and ready for the night, but instead of div-
ing into his passive body, I would abruptly lose interest in him.
This happened most often with boys who had died without
any struggle at all.

Waring's greens were much too large, of course, and quite
bloody. But beneath the clean lab coat I thought this might go
unnoticed. I was in a hospital, after all. I saw his gold-rimmed
spectacles on the floor, smeared with bloody fingerprints but

undamaged. I wiped them and put them on, expecting the room to become a watery migraine blur. But at once my vision seemed sharper, the edges of things more clear. Imagine: this strapping lad's astonished china-blue orbs were defective in just the same way as mine!

Unsurprisingly, there was no proper mirror in the room. Who wants to examine his own face after slicing open chests and skulls all day? But some vain junior doctor (I suspected) had hung a small round glass on a nail above the sink. I studied my reflection, decided that the spectacles changed the look of my face a great deal, but I could still do better. Though prisoners' hair is supposed to be kept quite short, I hadn't seen a barber in weeks. My dark mane grew halfway down the back of my neck and hung messily over my forehead.

I found a pair of surgical shears in the mess and began hacking away. I left the back long, but chopped several inches off the front and sides until my coarse hair stood up spikily. This seemed a plausibly trendy hairdo for an aging pathologist. I'd seen a character on TV sporting the very same style last time I'd been allowed into the lounge.

I pulled the scalpel out of Waring's throat and used surgical tape to bind it to the inside of my calf, where it would be easy to get at later. I was humming, pleased with my new look. With the spectacles and the haircut I thought I looked five years younger, and very much unlike England's most notorious killer since Jack stalked whores in Whitechapel.

Murderers are blessed with adaptive faces. We often appear bland and dull; no one ever passed the Ripper in the street and thought, *That chap looks as if he ate a girl's kidney last night.* Years before my arrest I had seen several newspaper photos of an American killer of young women, all taken within a few months of one another. Without his name beneath them, you would not have recognized any two photos as the same man. He seemed able to alter the lines in his face, the shape of his eyes, his very bone structure. I could do none of this—at least I didn't think so–but I'd done all right with what I had.

When I pulled Waring's lab coat off its peg, two things fell out of the pocket. One was a well-thumbed paperback called *America's Favourite Cannibal: The Ed Gein Story*. The other was a set of car keys.

I picked up the keys and ran my thumb over the buttery leather tab stamped *Jaguar*. Keys had been forbidden objects for so long that they felt dangerous in my hand now. I had scarcely seen car keys at all. I knew how to drive, but had never owned a car. Driving in London is nerve-racking and, with the extensive tube system, unnecessary.

All I had to do now was find the doctors' car park and the right Jaguar. I went to the door, tried the handle. It was locked, and I felt a bright thread of panic. *They know I'm in here, the only one left alive, trapped.* But then I remembered that Drummond had told Waring to lock it from the inside.

I turned the deadbolt lock, and the heavy door clicked open, the first door I had opened for myself in five years.

The little room stank of formaldehyde, excrement, and terror, a musky sickish scent. I was glad to take my leave of it, this dank cubicle where an appalling man had thought to remove and pickle my innards, assisted by a boy scarcely old enough to be worth killing.

The door had nearly closed when I remembered that Drummond had been talking into a cassette recorder. Presumably it had recorded everything that had happened since my resurrection. I dashed back in, retrieved the cassette, exited again, and locked the door behind me. The deserted corridor seemed to stretch away forever. I wondered where all the other, real corpses were. But I hadn't time to think of that.

Doors loomed in shadowy recesses on either side of me. The few rooms not closed off were dark and empty. One turned out to be a lift. I pressed the button and stood waiting for the car. There was still no one in the corridor, no one anywhere in sight, though I heard faint echoing voices.

It seemed a rather sleepy country hospital Painswick had shipped me off to, perhaps trying to avoid publicity as long as possible. I supposed they wanted to know what killed me before the vultures of the press swooped down to rip the flesh from my bones. How those same vultures would feast now! But not on the tainted meat of Andrew Compton!

The lift door slid back like a thick metallic tongue, and the maw of the car disgorged two long pale figures, one vertical and one horizontal. I very nearly stumbled backward in surprise. But it was only a sullen spotty-faced theatre porter pushing a gurney covered with a white sheet. There was a twisted shape beneath the sheet, a shape that seemed not to have all its parts, to be caving in and crumbling even as I looked. But I did not let my eye linger on it, and if the porter was anxious to snub me, I was anxious to be snubbed.

I pushed the button marked *G*. A burnt smell lingered in the air. The lift rose, and my stomach felt the tiniest bit queasy. Then the door slid open on a scene of chaos: people running and shouting, trolleys rocketing past, blood fountaining from a table surrounded by white and green backs, and from their midst a writhing hand that shot into the air, trembled at the end of its arm as if straining to touch God, then disappeared again. And everywhere, much stronger now, that same smell of burning. I had taken the lift to the emergency ward.

I saw some white masks on a cart, took one and tied it over my nose and mouth. I took a pair of rubber gloves as well, thinking they were bound to help me sooner or later. Then I edged through the Danteësque milieu toward a set of double doors I could dimly make out on the other side of the room.

The doors only led to another wing of the hospital, but beyond them was a nurse at a desk, fingers flying over the keyboard of a computer. Her face was calmer and kinder than any I had seen so far. "Sorry," I said through the mask, "but I'm new and I've got a bit turned around. Which way is the doctors' car park?"

"It's just along this hallway and to your left, up two flights of stairs. Level Three. But can't you stay, Doctor? We've just had this horrid crash come in and we need the help."

"I've been on for twenty hours," I improvised. "My supervisor ordered me to go home and rest—said I was bound to snip the wrong tube if I didn't."

The sister blinked, then gave me an understanding (if slightly frozen) smile. I turned away and walked quickly down the hall. A few doctors were hurrying in the opposite direction, but none of them paid the slightest attention to me. I heard one of them saying, ". . . have a look at Compton . . . ," and another replying, with a certain smugness, "Drummond'll never let you in."

Minutes later I let myself into a multilevel car park, as deserted as the morgue and seemingly full of nothing but Jaguars. There were Jaguars of every colour and vintage, convertibles, coupes, roadsters, and sedans, some lovingly maintained, some utterly decrepit. Here and there I saw a Ferrari or MG, as if to ease the repetition, and off in an obscure corner I thought I could make out one pathetic Mini. But for every other sort of automobile, there were at least three or four Jaguars.

I tried the key in thirty-seven car doors before one finally clicked open. As I slid into the driver's seat, I saw a stack of books on the seat. Well-thumbed paperbacks, with lurid covers of pain red and void black. *The Acid Bath Murders. The Butcher of Hanover. Zodiac. Killing for Company. The New York Vampire. Buried Dreams.*

I fitted the key into the ignition, and the engine came on with a smooth low roar. A glowing gauge assured me that the tank was full of petrol.

London was less than two hours away. I would be there before the hospital knew I was gone, with a little luck.

And on this day it looked as if I had more than a little luck.

2

Jay Byrne left the cold stone comfort of Charity Hospital late in the afternoon and hurried down traffic-choked Tulane Avenue in the direction of the French Quarter. At Carondelet he turned left, crossed the gaudy thoroughfare of Canal, ducked down Bourbon Street, and was soon in the heart of the Quarter.

Even in November there were days when New Orleans was balmy, almost tropical. This was one of those days. Over his gray T-shirt Jay wore a jacket made of some matte-dull black fabric that seemed to absorb and consume all light. It was an expensive piece of clothing, but it hung on him awkwardly, his thin wrists jutting from the sleeves like chicken bones. Clothes had fit him badly for most of his twenty-seven years; his limbs never quite seemed to match up, and no fabric or cut was comfortable to him. He preferred being naked whenever possible.

Jay's fine-textured, longish blond hair blew about in the breeze coming off the river. As he walked, he trailed one hand along the ornate spikes of a wrought-iron railing, then along the timeworn texture of old brick. The afternoon light had taken on a golden cast by the time he reached Jackson Square.

A small figure was waiting for him on the steps of St. Louis Cathedral, faded red shirt with a trippy-looking flower on it, baggy black shorts, glossy black hair. A Vietnamese kid perhaps seventeen or eighteen; Jay thought his name was Tran. He'd seen him around the Quarter a lot. The boy's face put Jay in mind of a delicate scrimshaw mask in a museum, exotic-boned, not so much androgynous as beyond gender entirely.

But this mask was topped with a trendy haircut, a shiny shoulder-length sheaf tumbling into his eyes. He palmed the two crisp hundred-dollar bills Jay offered with no flicker of surprise, then slipped Jay a sealed, unmarked manila envelope.

"It's real clean," the boy said cheerfully. "Something called 'Nuke,' out of Santa Cruz. You won't need to take more than one at a time." His accent was like some strange gumbo, part Vietnam, part New Orleans, part the wisecracking American Generic young foreigners often picked up—from television, Jay guessed, though he had never watched it enough to be sure.

"Then I'm stocked up." Jay tucked the envelope into the silk lining of his jacket. He took a deep breath, then made the plunge. "I'm a photographer. I do nudes, you know, males, art studies. Would you want to pose for me tonight?"

The boy looked surprised, then something else—alarmed? Amused? His eyes were too dark for Jay to read.

"I can't do it tonight," he said. "There's a big rave in the Warehouse District, and I have a great dress. But maybe some other time?"

"Uh . . . sure. Fine." Jay knew he should suggest a date, but he had expended all his nerve on the first proposition. Without some sort of drink or drug in him, he could not make another.

"OK, see you 'round." Tran blessed Jay with a sunny grin, then turned and walked away down one of the cobblestone alleys that led away from the square. The spires of the cathedral loomed oppressively overhead.

That smile . . . it was as sweet as sex, as succulent as meat. But the boy's refusal had been too quick, and Jay thought he'd seen a glimmer of something distasteful—pity, revulsion?—in the elegantly tilted recesses of his eyes.

It was humiliating to be brushed off by a Quarter brat nearly ten years his junior. But through his shame Jay still felt a flicker of desire. He wished he could have brought the Vietnamese boy back to his house on Royal Street, his house set behind a locked iron gate, nestled like a dark jewel in a courtyard fringed with leaves and shadows. There he could have borne those insouciant lips, those slyly condescending eyes. He could have photographed and catalogued them, examined them, discovered exactly how they broke down, how they came apart.

The boy-children of the French Quarter didn't trust Jay, though they allowed him into their circle occasionally because he bought them vast quantities of drinks and drugs without batting an eye. Sometimes they posed for his Polaroids too, but with the locals that was as far as it went. He never touched them in any of his more arcane pursuits. If he couldn't find a tourist, there were always stragglers from the housing projects. He'd offer a kid money to pose, make sure little homey wasn't carrying a gun, then get him fucked up . . .

Jay often wondered why the local boys tolerated him at all. Certainly there were plenty of well-heeled men around the Quarter, ready with the price of a drink or a meal for a smooth-skinned, long-limbed boy. Probably there were women too, a little older, uncertain of their own allure, wanting the ego boost of a younger lover. The boys didn't need Jay; in fact, he knew he gave them the creeps. He had heard them saying so when they thought he wasn't around. He had a knack for not being noticed, for hearing things he wasn't meant to hear, for blending in and observing.

He supposed he was something of a curiosity to the boys. Probably they would ignore him altogether if they didn't know his last name. Even his notoriety wasn't his own; he stood exposed and shivering in the few scraps of notoriety tossed to him by his lusciously clothed family.

Lysander Devore Byrne, he'd signed in a small crabbed hand at the hospital desk before going up to see his mother, with her shriveling, collapsing face and her rotting brain behind it. He'd never answered to Lysander, which was his father's name. He had been Junior to his family as long as he would tolerate it, then just Jay.

The pain-besotted skeleton in the hospital bed had once been Mignon Devore, daughter of an old uptown family, former Queen of Comus, ostensible beauty. She had married a rich boy from Texas and brought him home to get richer. Ensconced in a Gothic mansion on St. Charles, she had put up with Lysander's mistresses as long as he didn't open bank accounts in their names. She had consumed quantities of Pernod, an ersatz form of absinthe that was equally loathsome but legal. She had paid little attention to her only child. She had entombed her husband in style, and she would fill an equally handsome place in the family crypt.

When the cancer was discovered marbling his mother's temporal lobes like the fat on a particularly tender cut of beef, Jay had installed her in Charity Hospital rather than the posh private place where Lysander had died of the same cancer five years earlier. Mignon didn't want to go; she was terrified of the place and scandalized by the thought of dying there, so Jay figured she would go faster. It was an act of mercy, a small evil for the greater good.

He was halfway across Jackson Square, heading toward Café du Monde for a cup of au lait, when he heard sneakered feet running up behind him. Jay turned so quickly he surprised himself. Tran stopped, uneasy surprise flickering across the fine planes and hollows of his face.

"I was just wondering," he said, and stopped. Smiled. Toyed with the hem of his shorts, exposing the smooth skin of one knee. "I was just wondering if you'd like to go to that rave with me. I mean, to take pictures or something," he added as the surprise registered on Jay's face.

"To take . . . ?" Jay felt his heart racing, apparently trying to batter its way out of his chest. He imagined it bursting through bone, smacking wetly into Tran's face, leaving a streak of lurid maroon across those perfect rose-almond lips. "Uh . . . what exactly happens at a rave?"

Tran grinned and rolled his eyes. "Better ask what *doesn't* happen. It's strictly bring-your-own-drugs, but you can get smart drinks, energy shakes, all kinds of legal mind candy. Almost everyone is on 'shrooms or X, so it gets pretty touchy-feely."

"Well . . ." Jay hated the very sound of the word *rave,* the picture it painted in his mind of a fleshy festival edging out of control toward delirium. He saw a clubful of adorable kids babbling in tongues, perhaps foaming at the mouth. "It doesn't really sound like my kind of thing. I don't enjoy hallucinating in public."

"Yeah, I know people like that." The boy nodded sagely, as if he had tallied countless opinions on public use of psychedelic drugs—and maybe he had. Many of the Vietnamese families in New Orleans were Catholic, and after a childhood spent memorizing taboos, Catholic teenagers were often the wildest of all.

"But I *would* like to take your picture," Jay said. "Come by sometime. Here . . ." He took out a pen and a small notebook, jotted the address.

"Thanks." Tran pocketed the paper, favored him with a last sweet smile, and disappeared into the swirl of tourists, Tarot readers, street musicians, and assorted Quarter rats. God, he was pretty. But he was also a local kid, Jay reminded himself. He could take local kids' pictures, maybe, but nothing more.

Jay decided to walk along the river before having his coffee and heading home. The air was cooler up here on the levee, suffused with a clear near-sunset light. Jay stared down at the surging, glowing river as he walked. It was so mighty and so polluted; doubtless it had been the carrier and deliverer of more poisons than one factory could ever be. But no one called the Mississippi a murderer.

It was forty years now since Byrne Metals and Chemicals opened in Terrebonne Parish, spanking new, marvelous as plastic, ready to help usher south Louisiana into the atomic age. At first his father's factory had been a boon to the impoverished area, creating jobs for people who were too old or weak to make their living off the bounty of the swamp. It didn't seem to matter that the factory was pumping waste water into the same waters that nourished that bounty. The swamp was immense, boundless; surely it could absorb whatever went into it. It had the bayous to drain into, and beyond that the whole Gulf of Mexico.

But as the years went by, more able-bodied men and women began turning up asking for factory jobs. It seemed there weren't as many fish, fur animals, or gators in the area as there had once been. The crawfish were as plentiful as ever, perhaps more so, but they throve on any kind of sludge. Many of the remaining animals were sick or small. To an untrained eye, the swamp still teemed with rich life. But the people who lived there could see it dying.

Then they began dying too. A citizens' group alleged that people within a fifty-mile radius of Byrne Metals and Chemicals got cancer at fifty times the usual rate. There was a rash of babies born with gaping craniums, half-formed faces, stunted brains or no brains. There was a nasty incident involving a Cajun who'd been laid off from his job in the solvents division after eighteen years' service. Diagnosed with intestinal cancer a month later, the man had rammed the factory gate with his pickup truck, then parked in the yard, pulled out an ancient double-barreled shotgun, and started blasting away. A security guard had most of his left leg blown off before he was able to put a slug in the Cajun's brain.

Mignon's older brother Daniel Devore had stepped in to help. He had a gifted tongue with the politicians and reporters, and a talent for juggling facts. He also had a proclivity for the young male hustlers who haunted Burgundy Street past midnight in the lower Quarter. Eventually he set up his favorite in a slave quarters apartment and spent three or four nights a week down there. When Jay moved to the Quarter years later, the ex-hustler was still around, having been generously remembered in Daniel's will. A faded pastel blond, schooled in the ways of the Quarter but no longer able to make the grade, he managed to lure an occasional boy back to his apartment by flashing a bankroll. Jay observed him from afar, fascinated by the knowledge that that bankroll was steeped in the blood of the swamp his father had poisoned.

A calliope was shrieking "Dixie," insanely loud, very near. He realized he had walked all the way up the wooden riverwalk to the steamboat landing. The brightly colored boats towered over the dock, all wooden scrollwork and glittering brass, the *Natchez,* the *Cajun Queen,* the *Robert E. Lee,* big gaudy wedding-cake boats. He imagined one of them tipping over, spilling its human cargo into the toxic soup of the river.

He reached inside his jacket and touched the manila envelope. The feel of it against his heart was reassuring. *Nuke,* Tran had told him. One hundred doses of top-grade LSD. He'd take four or five, put the rest in the freezer. He had all sorts of treats in there.

Jay walked back to Café du Monde for the cup of au lait he'd been wanting. The very air beneath the old green awnings was luscious with fried dough and powdered sugar, a sweet miasma that always lingered here. The aromas of the café intertwined with engine exhaust from Decatur Street and the grassy smell of dung from the mule-drawn carriages that parked in front of the square collecting cartloads of tourists.

The afternoon was beginning to shade into evening. Thousands of birds circled over Jackson Square in the clear twilight, preparing to roost. Their erratic song, the saxophone player on the sidewalk, the crowd's chatter, the rumble and blare of passing traffic on Decatur Street: all were part of the French Quarter's festive eventide. Jay chose a table by the iron railing, where he could watch the circus. The chicory coffee tasted rich and strong, the milk frothy and sweet.

He became aware of a presence near his elbow. A boy stood on the other side of the railing, puppy-dog gaze melting over Jay like warm butter. He wore the costume of young drifters everywhere: bandanna wrapped around a close-cropped head, ears and nose studded with metal, army jacket a work of art done in safety pins and black marker, Doc Martens that had seen serious street time. His face was strong-boned, unwittingly angelic. He was perhaps eighteen. Perhaps.

"Will you take me home?" he asked Jay. "I wanna be your pet. I don't eat much and I'm very affectionate."

Jay sipped his coffee, cocked an eyebrow. "What if you urinate or defecate on the floor? I might have to put you to sleep."

"I'm housebroken," the boy assured him earnestly.

There was hunger in his face, plain and sharp; but it was unaccustomed hunger, the hunger of a kid spending his first weeks on the street, missing his parents' well-stocked kitchen. That was the kind of hunger Jay liked; strong enough to make them incautious, but not so strong that their muscles were wasted. He ordered the boy a café au lait and a plate of beignets.

"Now seriously," said Jay, watching the boy pour an endless stream of sugar into his coffee. "What about this pet business? Are you going to let me put a leash and collar on you? Do I get to chain you up?"

"Sure." The boy grinned through a mouthful of beignet. Powdered sugar spangled his lips, his chin, the front of his black T-shirt. "Anything you want. Just let me curl up at the foot of your bed."

Jay wondered why such an exotic pup was begging for scraps at his back door. He looked rich, he supposed, but not *that* rich. Nowhere near as rich as he really was. In New Orleans, where robbery and murder were as common as afternoon rainstorms, only the tourists wore wealth like a sign plastered across their foreheads.

"You might even get your own pillow," he said. "Been traveling long?"

"Just a couple of months."

"Where you from?"

"Maryland."

"What's it like there?"

A diffident shrug; might as well ask what it's like on the moon. "Sucks. You know—boring." The last of the beignets disappeared down that hungry pink gullet. "So, uh, you wanna take me home?"

Jay leaned forward and put his face close to the boy's. "Let's get a few things straight. If you want to be my pet, then *be* my pet. Sit until I'm ready to go. Heel when I walk. Roll over when I say so. And when I pet you, *lick my hand.*"

He reached out and smoothed the boy's hair, slid his fingers down the side of the boy's face, over the soft hairs at the ridge of the jawbone. Just as he was about to pull away, the boy turned his head and took Jay's first two fingers into his mouth, lipped them softly, rolled them over his tongue. The inside of his mouth was as soft as velvet, as warm as fresh blood.

From the corner of his eye, Jay saw an elderly tourist couple at the next table staring as if hypnotized. He could not make himself care, could scarcely move or breathe while that wet heat caressed him.

"Just call me Fido," said the boy.

3

The sky over Chef Menteur Highway was tinged lavender with the first traces of dawn. Tran drove past the crumbling architecture of half-vacant strip malls and bottom-end motels, past the awesome neon planet that was the beacon of the Orbit Bowling Alley, past a sleazy rainbow of cocktail lounges and dirty bookstores still gamely angling for the night's last human dregs. Soon Tran's little Escort was speeding through green country, lush expanses of water, reeds, and grass dotted with occasional small houses. East New Orleans was an odd mix of the tranquil, the trashy, and the wholly exotic.

Tran was twenty-one, born in Hanoi to parents who escaped the country three years later, during the mass exodus of 1975. Somewhere in his ancestry was a dash of French blood that lent his shoulder-length black hair a crisp wave, underlaid his smooth complexion like almondflesh tinged with peach, and lent a faint golden cast to his dark eyes. His only memories of Vietnam were of hushed voices late at night, someone hurrying him down a street illuminated with tiny colored lights that shimmered and blurred in the humid air, the raw

sap smell of machete-cut greenery. Sometimes he thought he
recalled other things—shells exploding in the distance, the sil-
very hulk of a jetliner—but he could never be sure whether
these fragments were memory or dream.

Because of a man his father had known in the American
army, the family was able to settle in New Orleans without
passing through the mud and concrete horror of the refugee
camps. His birth name was Tran Vinh. When his parents en-
rolled him in American kindergarten, they reversed the order
of his names so that the family name would come last, like an
American child's. And they elongated his first name to Vincent, which he hated and had never answered to, even at five.
His family still called him Vinh. To everyone else he was Tran.
In English, the short sharp syllable suggested movement
(transmission, transpose) and the crossing of boundaries
(transcontinental, tranquilize, transvestite), both of which he
liked.

Tonight Tran had swallowed acid and ecstasy until the
lights and the video and the barrage of sound ran together in
a gaudy candy-colored blur. At the rave there had been a
smart bar where girls in green lamé whipped strange powders
into allegedly IQ-raising concoctions that tasted better than
Tang. There had been kids in full riot gear and flowered hel-
mets, kids armed only with water bottles and baby pacifiers,
kids who looked like Dr. Seuss characters on mushrooms.
Which was no big surprise: they had all grown up with Dr.
Seuss, and many of them *were* on mushrooms.

Tran wore a loose knee-length dress covered with giddy
loops of purple and red. He'd kept his shorts on underneath,
so that when he got home he could tuck the dress into their
waistband and it would look like a shirt, sort of. His eyes were
smudged with greasy black liner, badly applied, which made
him look even younger and slightly insane. He'd gone to the
rave alone and had a wonderful time. These days, that was
something to be proud of. He hadn't been getting out much in

the past few months. When you knew you might run into someone you didn't want to see, it was so easy to stay in your room reading, writing in your journal, listening to music, brooding over old love letters.

He recalled an interesting bit of trivia he'd picked up somewhere: an old film star named Jayne Mansfield had died out here on Chef Menteur Highway. Her car had slammed into the back of one of the mosquito trucks that went steaming through the byways of the city, spraying enough poison to kill tens of thousands of insects. Tran imagined the famous decapitated head sailing through the cloud of insecticide and gasoline fumes, comet tail of blood describing a graceful arc.

The image of the movie star's death had haunted him since he'd first heard of it. He'd described it in one of his notebooks, in the purplest and most gleeful prose he could conjure. But if he tried to tell it to any of his friends—Vietnamese or Anglo—he knew exactly what they'd say. *You're sick, Tran, you know that? You're really fucked up.*

Now he was almost home. A tangle of factory smokestacks and towers loomed ahead on one side of the highway. A dimly lit cluster of buildings on the other side was the heart of the community where Tran had lived most of his life. The swampy green land surrounding these buildings, the ragged blue-gray shroud of mist, the slightly ramshackle aspect, and the Vietnamese characters on the signs suggested a tiny foreign village, but the whole thing was only about twenty minutes away from downtown New Orleans. Known as Versailles or Little Vietnam, the neighborhood had been established by North Vietnamese refugees, perpetuated by the family they brought over and the children they raised.

He turned off Chef Menteur, navigated streets of little brick houses with poultry coops, fishing docks, vegetable gardens, and rice paddies in back. Eventually he pulled up in front of a house that had none of these exciting features. As a kid, Tran had envied his friends whose families fished and farmed. He used to beg to help feed the ducks or go netting for shrimp. Only later did he realize his manicured yard seemed so boring because his family was a bit richer than most of the others in the community. Not wealthy by any means, but they didn't have to raise their own food. A lot of people out here did.

He wondered what the slackers, technoheads, and baby peaceniks at the rave tonight would think of that. Probably they would think it was cool, that such people were in touch with the earth, which they all wanted to save as long as they didn't have to stop dancing to do it. But Tran was willing to bet none of those ravers had ever wrung a duck's neck and plunged the carcass into boiling water to remove the feathers. Nor, he wagered, had any of them picked leeches off their ankles after wading in a stagnant pool of canal water to catch crawfish.

Like most Asian-American kids he'd met, Tran lived in two worlds. Since his twin brothers were still too young, he often helped in his parents' café. His table service was barely adequate, but he ran the cash register like nobody's business and knew how to make perhaps a third of the eighty-seven traditional dishes on the menu.

That was one world, the existence spanning the restaurant, his home, his family. The other world was the French Quarter, his tidy little acid business, clubs and raves, people like Jay Byrne. Glamorous, dangerous men . . . like the one who had introduced him to this other world. But that was over, and something he didn't want to think about after such a fine night.

He got out of the car, crossed the damp lawn, and let himself into the house. The living room was a mass of overlapping blue and gray shadows, swathed in dawn. He made his way down the hall, past the closed door of the twins' room, and let himself into his own room.

His father was sitting on the bed.

This in itself was a shock. Tran wasn't sure his father had ever been in his room before. He and his father were seldom even home and awake at the same time. But the real shock was the look on his father's face. Truong Van Tran had a couple of expressions that seemed to serve him well in almost every situation: an acquiescing but faintly impatient smile, a tight-lipped glare, a steady gaze that was almost neutral if you failed to notice the slight disdainful crook of an eyebrow. T.V. did not approve of wasted time, and he did not suffer fools gladly. He did not suffer them at all when he had a choice.

So the look on his face was new to his oldest son. It had elements of sorrow, anger, fatigue, and, most frightening of all, bewilderment. Bewilderment in a man who had always seemed sure of everything, who ran his small café like a barracks. His father's gaze made Tran feel like a stranger, like an intruder in his own home, in his own room. There was a dark smudge on T.V.'s forehead, as if he had handled something grimy and then wiped his hand across his brow. Tran could not remember ever having seen his father anything but immaculate.

Awful scenarios ran through his head. Something had happened to his mother, or the twins. But if so, why was T.V. waiting for him in here, alone? Vietnamese families congregated in times of catastrophe. If anything bad had happened to a family member, the living room and kitchen would be full of milling relatives, and the house would reek of strong coffee sweetened with condensed milk.

This was something for him, then; for him alone. Tran began ticking off the possibilities in his mind. All of them were very bad.

"Dad?" he said uncertainly. "What's wrong?"

His father stood up and reached into the pocket of his trousers. At that moment Tran realized he was still wearing the sweat-soaked, gaudy rave dress; he hadn't even bothered to tuck it into his shorts. It seemed the least of his worries. T.V. was going to pull one of two things out of his pocket: Tran's stash of acid or the letters. The letters would be infinitely worse.

T.V.'s hand emerged clutching a sheaf of half-crumpled paper, a few ripped-open envelopes.

Tran felt his stomach trying to cave in. All at once the acid and ecstasy he'd taken came rushing back tenfold. He did not even feel angry about the invasion of his privacy: there would be no point to such anger. His father wouldn't understand it. He owned the house; therefore all its rooms and all its contents were his to peruse as he saw fit. Tran thought he might vomit as T.V. glanced at the first sheet of paper and began to read.

"I want you underneath me *right now,* dear boy, my heart, my intestinal maze. I want to slide two fingers into the crook of your arm, there where the skin is as smooth as the crushed-velvet head of your cock. I have a fresh needle just for you, just for the arterial hard-on that throbs there. I slide stainless steel into your flesh, and the bead of blood that wells when I take the needle out is as tender as your . . ."

T.V. stopped reading. Tran knew the next three words, could even visualize them scrawled in psychotic purple on the sheet of notebook paper his father held crumpled in his hand. They were "sugar candy asshole."

Tran attempted a smile. It came out nearly stillborn, a sickly mewling thing. "Yeah, um, Luke has quite a crazy style. He wants to be the next William S. Burroughs. He . . . uh . . . sends me all his fiction."

"Vinh, please don't insult me." His father was speaking Vietnamese, which was a bad sign at such a time: it signified a complexity or depth of emotion he did not trust himself to express in English. The tonal qualities of the language alone comprised thousands of nuances and shadings. "This is not fiction. These are letters written to you about things you've done. Are these things the truth?"

Not *Are these things true?* but *Are these things* THE TRUTH?, the one truth, as if there might be no other.

Tran shrugged. His father's gaze drove through him like long nails. "Yeah, at one time or another I did all that stuff. It wasn't like I injected drugs every day or anything."

"Who is this man? This Luke?"

"He's a writer. Seriously, Dad. He's had four books published and he's a brilliant writer. But he's . . ." *Sick, vicious, as
crazy with pain as a run-over dying dog.* "Kind of unstable. I
quit seeing him months ago."

"He lives in New Orleans?" There was no return address
on the letters—Luke was no fool—but all the envelopes bore
local postmarks.

"Not anymore," Tran lied. Well, it could be true. He didn't
know if Luke was still terrorizing the airwaves, hadn't tried to
tune in the show in months. Only shreds and tag ends of gossip told him that Luke was even still alive.

The best defense was a good offense. "Look, Dad, I don't
know what you want from me. You came in my room, you
went through my stuff—you must not have trusted me in the
first place. Are you really surprised?"

"No, Vinh . . . no." His father stood before him with bowed
shoulders. He couldn't recall ever having seen his father's
shoulders bowed before. T.V.'s usual posture was straight, almost stiff. But not now. "I wish I could be surprised, but I'm
not. That is precisely why I looked. And I'm sorry."

"Sorry for what?" Tran heard his voice crack, cursed it. But
he sensed that the end of the talk was drawing near, and he
knew nothing good could lie at the end of this talk.

"For my own part in this. Your mother and I must have
done something terribly wrong. And what if the twins turn out
like you?" A new shadow crossed his father's face, a depth of
darkness previously unplumbed. "You would never . . . you
have never *done* anything to them?"

If the possibility of violence had been anywhere in him,
Tran would have hit his father then. He was taller than T.V.,
and broader in the shoulders. He would have grabbed his father by the front of his expensive, tacky polyester shirt and
smacked him twice across the face, hard.

But Vietnamese children did not strike their parents. The
tradition of ancestor worship had died only two generations

back, and it lay uneasy in its grave. The parents of Versailles complained about the terrible rudeness their children learned at school, the lack of respect they seemed to revel in. But the thought of physically harming a parent was as foreign to these children as the idea of burning incense before a photo of a dead great-grandfather.

And Tran had no violence in him; he was only drawn to it in others. That was one of the first reasons why he had loved Luke.

But the notion that he would hurt his brothers . . . the idea that an integral facet of his character was the fault of some dreadful mistake his parents had made . . . it was all too much to bear. The talk was over, Tran realized, and he was the one ending it. "Fine," he said. "Get out of my room. Go to work. Tell Mom to give me two hours after she takes the twins to school—go shopping or something. I'll be gone by the time she gets back."

"Vinh—"

"I want my car. It's in my name. I won't take anything else from the rest of the house, just the stuff in here."

"Where will you go?" T.V. asked. He didn't really sound as if he expected an answer.

"Where else? The French Quarter."

Tran might as well have said *Angola* or *the lower pits of Hell.* T.V. shook his head hopelessly. "To spend so much time there is bad enough. How can you live in the Quarter? We'll never hear from you again."

"What do you mean?"

"It's dangerous."

"East New Orleans is dangerous. People get shot out here all the time. The Quarter's a safe place." Relatively speaking, this was true. The Quarter had its share of robberies and oc- casional killings, but most of them happened to tourists who didn't know any better than to stray into pockets of desertion late at night: Rampart, upper Barracks, the ghostly area near

Canal where the burned-out facade of the old D. H. Holmes building loomed over the narrow street. If you knew where you were and who was around, you were usually fine.

"We thought we could take you to a doctor."

Tran closed his eyes. A slow burn was spreading behind his lids. "I'm not going to any goddamn doctor," he said. "There's nothing wrong with me."

"You don't realize how sick you are. Sick in the brain. So intelligent, such potential—and yet you are doing everything wrong."

Tran turned away from his father, started pulling books off the shelves and piling them on the floor.

"We only want to help you."

That's what Luke said to me once, Tran thought, *and he meant he wanted me to die with him.* But he stayed silent.

"Have you been tested for AIDS?"

Ask me anything. Ask me how I felt puking my guts out the first time I let him shoot me up. Ask me about the time he accidentally came in my mouth, and all I could taste was death spilling over my tongue, down my throat, seeping through my tissues. Ask me about the phone calls that lasted till dawn, the receiver slick with sweat and tears, sealed to my ear like a barnacle. Ask me any of those things. Please, Dad, ask me anything but that.

"Yes," Tran said as calmly as he could. "I got a test. It was negative."

It was true; he had gotten one negative result. But that was only three weeks after the last time he'd slept with Luke. And they had told him to come back in six months, and six months after that, and six months after *that* . . .

Tran saw his life stretching away before him, measured out in half-year increments, discrete pockets of time. Each pocket became a glass vial capped with a circle of red plastic. On each cap was a tiny label, and Tran's initials neatly lettered there. Each vial was three-quarters full of dark blood. He could shatter them one by one, waste them all in a blind search for the poisoned vial. But when he found it, it would contain nothing but his death.

So what do I do with the rest of my time? he thought. *Live rent-free with my parents, write in my notebooks, go out dancing, catch a buzz, get laid? It doesn't sound so bad. But what if I only have, say, five more years to live?*

The life he had known up to now would not be enough. This unfortunate scene with his father had only hastened a decision Tran knew he had to make. It was the next step of his adventure, the step that would keep him alive. How could he die in the middle of his great adventure?

He wondered if Luke had ever thought the same thing. Then he reminded himself that he did not care, could not care what Luke thought.

"I'm negative," he said again. "I don't have AIDS, and I haven't been screwing the twins. Now get out."

"Vinh, if you—"

"Dad." Tran went to his father, took the letters from his hand. "You don't know me. This is who I am. Here. In these letters." He waved the ragged sheaf of paper in T.V.'s face. "Now leave me alone."

His father looked at him a moment longer. His dark eyes had a regretful but faintly impassive cast, as if he were looking at his son's corpse already in its coffin. Tran could almost see a miniature of himself reflected there, a wan and wasted image in a mahogany box, propped on a trestle in the Catholic church, surrounded by white flowers and grieving relatives. If he died in five years, if he died tomorrow, that was how it would be.

For several seconds Tran felt himself falling into his father's eyes, into that future. Then T.V. turned and left the room, and Tran was free.

Luke's letters were still crumpled in his hand. He stared at them for a moment, then put them on the nightstand atop a pile of books. For a long time the very sight of Luke's handwriting had made his flesh crawl with loathing. That purple scrawl looked exactly like Luke's voice sounded, thick with whiskey and self-pity, on the phone at three in the morning. Ziggy Stardust after the band broke up, rubbing his face in broken shards of gutter glass, swearing he could see the stars. Cockteasing death, courting and seducing it at every turn, but never going all the way as long as he had a choice in the matter.

Tran looked around his bedroom, wondering what to take first, and felt a fresh wave of helplessness sweep over him. There were clothes everywhere, clean and dirty; there were notebooks, sketches, random books and papers.

Prioritize, he told himself. *Start with the important stuff.* He went to his bookshelf, took down a large glossy volume on death and dying. He knew his parents had seen plenty of mangled corpses up close in Vietnam—neighbors, teachers, family. They'd never take such a book off the shelf. Tran flipped through full-page color shots of humans in various stages of mutilation, decay, and general disrepair until he found the Baggie he'd stashed there, which contained fifty hits of LSD and five crisp green portraits of Ben Franklin.

He sat on the edge of his bed holding his ready assets, silently cursing the name of Lucas Ransom and every word the man had ever committed to paper. When he was done with that, he cursed himself for a while, until he was sick of it. Then he got up and started packing.

4

Remember, remember, the fifth of November,
Gunpowder, treason, and plot!

In 1605, the celebrated traitor Guy Fawkes and assorted ruffians in his sway conspired to blow up London's Houses of Parliament. Fawkes himself was only a scruffy soldier of fortune, a well-paid dupe of some rich Catholics with a grudge against the king, but history has remembered his name and preserved his effigy. After planting explosives beneath the House of Commons, the conspirators fled to a hill at the southeastern tip of Hampstead Heath, hoping for a good view of the fireworks. This hill, incidentally, owes its magnificence to plague victims buried in mass graves on the heath.

From terrain shaped by millions of pestilent bones, the ruffians watched their dream expire. Fawkes himself was caught in the basement with a blazing torch and a great lot of gunpowder. He was tortured in the Tower of London, tried in Westminster Hall, then drawn, quartered, and hanged in the Old Palace Yard outside the Houses. The foundations he had hoped to see crumble and burn were soaked with the blood from his living intestines, and generations of yet-unborn English children were given an excuse for extortion and pyromania.

Pity. All those needly spires and pinnacles, all those soaring walls with their windows like little rotten pits in a great gray cheese, and the damned clock, all sliding majestically into the Thames! Of course the Houses looked quite different in 1605. But they are stamped in the memory of any lifelong Londoner just as they are now, eight acres of powdered wigs, musty scrolls, stone spindles shrouded in gray and purple fog. One cannot help but picture a brilliant flower of fire rupturing from the dark innards of the complex, and wonder whether Westminster Bridge would have gone too.

Without so much as a nod to the actual instigators of the plot, English sentiment required that a holiday be set up in honour of Guy Fawkes, and his effigy tortured and burned each year. And the C of E claims to have stamped out paganism!

Guy Fawkes' Day plagues certain sensitive souls, haunts their eyes, keeps them looking uneasily over their shoulders and staying in well-lighted streets. The staccato of fireworks sets their nerves on edge, and the rich smoky smell of a bonfire is as charnel to them. They deplore the clamour of ragged schoolboy mobs; they say they cannot abide the taunts of "Penny for the guy, mister? Penny for the guy?"

But watch any of these sensitive souls when they are accosted, and you'll notice it is the guy they cannot look at—or cannot stop looking at. The straw guy in old coat and trousers and shapeless hat, sprawled on his bed of copper pennies in his rough wagon . . . the helpless, harmless effigy seems to frighten them. He was born from the rag pile yesterday; he will die on the bonfire tonight. But they do not like looking into his ashen smudge of a face.

I think they can feel the anger given shape and form in these creatures, the incredulity of a soul made to burn perhaps a billion times for a crime that never happened. I hope for what the nervous souls fear: that one year the guys will rise up and finish off those Houses.

It was Guy Fawkes' Day when I returned to life. Like a guy, I had been on the wagon too long; but I suspected I would be blazing merrily before the night was done, and by morning I would be but a memory to those who had once jeered at me, a bit of ash spirited away into the sky.

I came into London on the M1 and left the Jaguar in a quiet residential street near the Queensbury tube station. Then I descended into the creaky, dusty bowels of the Underground. This was an old station with no automatic ticket vendors. Using the window meant speaking to a person who might remember me. I was still dressed in Waring's blood-spotted hospital greens and white lab coat, though I'd put away my mask. In the end I pulled the coat up under my chin, went to the window, and bought a ticket for Piccadilly. Anyone could be going to Piccadilly, absolutely anyone. The ticket seller never even looked at me.

The empty echo of the platform, the bland colourful exhortations of the posters and automatic sweet vendors, the lulling motion of the train, the murmur of the sparse midday crowds, the tunnels and stations flashing by nearly put me to sleep. But I resisted Morpheus, who had been such a faithful lover these past five years.

The next time I emerged from the tube, I was in Piccadilly Circus and all the world seemed to explode around me, written in neon swirls and punctuated with shiny red double-decker buses. Piccadilly is a giddy hub of London, a cross between a traffic hazard and a funfair ride. Faded wax rock stars leer down from the wedding-cake balconies of Victorian music halls; behind the ornate facades, glittering modern shopping centres are cleverly concealed.

The traffic was deafening, the smells stunning: petrol, exhaust, a spicy blend of restaurants. I bought a souvlaki from a takeaway and ate it in three bites. It was the most delicious thing I had ever tasted, the soft fragrant bread, the tender meat sauced and seasoned as if someone cared whether it was good, the subtle salty oils, the juices trickling over my tongue, staining the corners of my mouth. And the smells of the *people:* their clean skins, their perfumes, their scented soaps and shampoos, their sweat that did not stink of desperation!

On impulse I stopped at a news vendor's to scan the advertisements in the *London Gay Times.* I remembered when this paper had been tucked away at the backs of shops, half-hidden behind magazines featuring glossy colour photos of greased arses and tumescent circumcised cocks. And that was when the shops carried it at all. Now it was up front with all the other city papers.

In addition to the AIDS information lines and HIV counselling centres that had sprung up like mushrooms on a wet lawn, a great many new pubs and dance clubs seemed to have opened, each promising more decadence than the last. None of these chatty pubs or glittering flesh palaces seemed quite what I wanted. Too many people noticing you, talking to you, their brains as likely to be hypertuned on stimulants as dulled with drink. I put the paper back on the shelf and headed up Coventry Street toward Leicester Square, Chinatown, the shimmer of Soho. My old hunting grounds.

I knew a secondhand clothing store where one could buy a coat, a jumper, and an old pair of trousers for three quid in 1988. Now these same musty-smelling items cost the better part of a tenner. "Count yourself lucky to find trousers that fit," the proprietor said when I raised an eyebrow at the price. "We've nearly sold out. Guy Fawkes, you know; the kids want them."

I traded Waring's ugly rubber-soled loafers for shiny wingtips that fit me perfectly, and the old man threw in a fresh pair of socks. (Waring's socks, I am sorry to say, were so ripe they had to be disposed of.) The scalpel was still taped securely to the side of my leg, and I left it there for now.

I outfitted myself in basic black, good for hiding blood-stains and blending into crowds. Not flash enough to be no-ticed in the trendy bars of Soho, but nothing to sneer at, either. With the little gold-rimmed spectacles and new haircut, I thought I looked rather smart.

No one would guess I had already killed two men today, and meant to do a third. But that was the whole point, wasn't it?

Outside the shop, a pack of boys accosted me, wagon trundling along behind, misshapen form sprawled on a heap of lucre. "Penny for the guy? Penny for the guy?" I surren-dered all my coins to their grubby fragile-boned hands. I couldn't help it. There was a crisp November bite to the air, seasoned with the smoke of firecrackers and bonfires, and the boys' eyes were bright and wild, and their cheeks were ruddy as autumn apples, dusted with fine golden hairs, smudged with ash.

In Leicester Square, children of a different sort sat smok-ing in the park, painted children who of a Saturday might pa-rade up and down the King's Road staring in the shop windows at zebra-striped vinyl raincoats, at Dr. Marten boots done up in purple glitter, at lace body stockings for all sexes—and at the gaudiest, prettiest things of all, their own reflections in the glass.

Below the neck these children wore black, gray, and white garments of various materials and textures, held together with bits of metal. Above the neck they were like abstract paintings done in furious rainbow hues. A technicolour scribble of tor-tured hair, great panda-smudges of azure or chartreuse round the eyes, a slash of vermilion across the soft young mouth, and off they went.

I used to envy these kids their freedom, even if all it meant was living off Mum and Dad or on the dole. They could look like strange crosses between birds of paradise and walking corpses if they so desired. They could spit on the sidewalk, lounge insolently where they were not wanted, make rude remarks to the tourists who gawped at them. They could be as conspicuous as they liked. They never had to blend in anywhere, and never cared to try.

It was these children, indirectly, who caused me to quit my last civil service job three months before I was arrested. I had a position behind a desk at the Metropolitan Water Board. The English civil service allows a man to rise to his highest level of incompetence; I had already been dismissed from three or four such positions, but they were perfectly willing to hire me on again and see how long I might last at this one. They knew vaguely that I was intelligent and could type, and my work history showed that I would perform the job flawlessly right up until the moment I told some petty supervisor or other to stuff it as far as it would go.

But one day very much like this, when autumn nipped the city and the sky was a rare, clear blue, I looked at the stack of meaningless papers on my desk and the balled-up wrapper of the greasy takeaway chicken I'd eaten an hour ago, when they said I could, even though I was always hungry well before that. I listened to the conversations unspooling around me, and I heard dialogue straight out of a Joe Orton play ("How dare you involve me in a situation for which no memo has been issued"). I thought of a boy I'd seen in the King's Road the night before, his black hair teased wild, his smile open and easy and free. Quite possibly he didn't have the price of a meal in his pocket, but nobody could tell him when he might or mightn't eat one. Very quietly but very firmly, something in me rebelled.

I stood. I dropped the greasy wrapper in the rubbish can; I never thought anyone else should have to clean up after me. And I left that office forever. No one spoke to me, no one saw me go. I spent the rest of the day in Chelsea, drinking in the pubs. I watched the kids prance up and down eyeing one another (and, most often, finding one another sadly deficient). I spoke to no one. I brought no one with me when I staggered home. There were already two I had to get rid of, one crumpled in the wardrobe beginning to bloat, the other still fresh enough to share my bed.

I had no prospects at the time, only a small savings account and an insatiable appetite for killing boys. As it turned out, this was all I would require to get me through those last few months. But the wild children of Leicester Square would not serve my purposes today. I needed someone less conspicuous, more anonymous; in short, someone more closely resembling myself.

Most of all, though, I needed a drink.

I slipped into the stream of humanity on Charing Cross Road, succumbed to an irresistible impulse and ducked into a bookshop to scan the true crime section. I was the subject of three garish paperbacks: jackets the colour of fresh blood and fleeting love, well-thumbed central photo inserts documenting my bath, my bedroom closet, my kitchen knives, the stairs leading up to my flat, all with breathless captions ("Twenty-three men climbed these stairs, never expecting it would be their last trip!"). I left the store feeling obscurely pleased, turned at Lisle Street, and walked through Chinatown, marvelling at the strange stew of smells, the exotic spell of the fairy lights draping the storefronts, the vivid Asian faces of the boys. Then I crossed wide, chaotic Shaftesbury Avenue and was in the part of Soho I remembered best.

Gay London has a strenuously sanitary feel to it, a kind of hygienic glitter. Even the sex shops and video stores are staffed by clean-cut young men who answer every inquiry with cheerful courtesy, whether it is about the best coffeeshop nearby or the proper way to insert an anal plug. I went into a gloomy little pub I hadn't frequented much before. Its expanses of dark wood and fixtures of tarnished brass gave it that famous British-pub atmosphere, so of course it was always full of American tourists.

I laid a five-pound note on the bar, got back half the change I'd expected and a pint glass filled with one of my earliest and truest loves: cold lager. I never went in for the English tradition of warm, murky beer that tastes like something more properly used to feed livestock.

I carried my pint to a corner table and sat just looking at it for a moment: the creamy head of foam, the tiny bubbles ascending through clear gold, the droplets condensing on the sides of the glass, then running down to form a wet circle on the beer mat. Reputations are ruined, marriages destroyed, life's works forsaken for the beauty of such a sight. There are seven thousand pubs in London.

At last I picked up the glass and, very slowly, drank off half my pint without stopping. My throat felt like a cactus in a drenching desert rain. My tongue had its own sort of orgasm. The taste was liquid silk, slow-brewed joy.

Capital punishment was never any deterrent to murder. The worst of us would welcome death. But to tell a man he can never again taste cold lager! I vowed I would die, and remain dead, before I would return to captivity.

Tonight I must pace myself. There would soon be plenty of opportunities to drink until the room spun, when I had finished slipping between Her Majesty's iron fingers. Now I had to keep an eye on the tourists who were starting to pour in. The next part of my plan depended upon them, or upon one of them at any rate. Still, after five years one cannot help getting a bit light-headed. I had just started on my third pint and was marvelling at the pleasantly watery feeling in my limbs when Sam came into the pub.

Of course, I didn't know he was called Sam then. I only knew he was a male of my approximate height, build, age, and colouring, and that he was looking at the men in the place much more keenly than the scattering of women. Our facial resemblance was sketchy, but it would do. If he was a local chap or a European tourist, I could forget him without ever learning his name. But if he was American, I intended to make him my companion for the evening.

I let him order his first round (a Guinness, which told me nothing except where our similarities diverged), saw him pay for it from a brown leather wallet he kept inside his coat, and watched as he stood drinking alone at the bar. He kept scanning the room, and our eyes met more than once, but I broke the gaze each time.

When only a swallow of vile black brew remained in his glass, I carried my lager to the bar. He polished off the Guinness, flagged the bartender with an expansive gesture no Brit would own, and said in a perfectly atrocious twang that could have originated nowhere but the American South, "Gimmee another stout, please."

Inwardly I rejoiced. But to him I only said, "You can stand a match on end in that head, you know."

His dark eyes lit with pleasure when he realized I was talking to him. I wondered whether anyone had been friendly to him on his holiday, or if he had encountered a lot of prats who immediately wrote him off as a stupid Yank. Of course, he would have been better off with one of those silly bastards than with me. But he needn't know that yet. He needn't know it ever, if I did this thing right.

"Huh?" he said, and grinned. I supposed I could understand the perception behind the dumb-Yank stereotype. But I'd met a number of Americans in a job I had with the tourist board, and I hadn't found them stupid at all. They simply weren't taught to be articulate. Either they were so intimidated by our accents (which all sounded posh to them) that they couldn't think of anything to say, or else they fell all over themselves saying the same thing five or six different ways. Overeager, yes. Frustrating to talk to, yes. But not necessarily stupid.

I leaned against the bar. My left arm was pressed to my side, near the small constant pain of my wound. Beneath my new black jumper I could feel my heart jumping like a frantic animal in a heated cage. Fluttery, nasty feeling.

"You can stand a match in the head of your stout," I said. "It's quite thick enough." I picked up a box of wooden matches lying on the bar, shook one out, and stood it on end in the silky white foam. It did not waver, but stood straight and erect like a little redheaded sentinel.

"I'll be damned," said the American. "What makes it do that?"

"I suppose it would be the air bubbles."

"Yeah, but the surface tension of each bubble must be pretty strong to produce a cohesive effect like that . . ." He laughed. "Sorry. I left my physics manuals at home, but I guess I brought the mind-set with me."

"You're a student?"

"Doctoral candidate. Particle theory. I'm trying for a research grant to study quarks."

"Quarks?"

"Elementary particles that feel the strong force—the strongest of the four fundamental forces. They come in six flavours, up, down, strange, charmed, top, and bottom. And each flavour comes in three colors, red, green, or blue."

"Like an ice lolly," I mused.

"Huh? Oh, a Popsicle! Yeah, sort of! I bet I can use that in one of my classes. Anyway, you know atoms? Well, see, atoms are made of protons, neutrons, and electrons, and those are made of quarks."

"What are quarks made of, then?"

"Waves."

"*Waves?*" I had now finished my third pint, and was beginning to be outraged. "But waves aren't *tangible.* They're just *disturbances.*"

"Vibrations, right! The whole universe is made of vibrations." He beamed, oblivious to my dismay. "Neat, huh? Anyway, we haven't been introduced yet. I'm Sam." He held out a long-fingered, smooth-palmed hand that looked very much like my own. I grasped it, half-expecting my flesh to pass

ghostlike through his. After all, we were nothing but vibrations. All the stone and iron of Painswick Prison was nothing
but vibrations. Had I known, I could have begun vibrating at
a different frequency and gone right between the bars.

I said my name was Arthur. The wraiths of my eighty-seven
prison journals rose before me, and in a flash of inspiration I
told him I was a writer.

"Oh, neat! What do you write?"

"Tragic fiction."

"You know," and his dark eyes took on a wistful glaze, "I
always wanted to write. I've got a bunch of great ideas. Maybe
I could tell you some of 'em and you could use them." I waited
for him to say, "And we could split the money," but he didn't.
Poor Sam; he was a good and generous soul who meant no
one any harm. I felt the scalpel blade pricking the inside of my
leg as if anxious to get on with it. We finished our beers and
ordered another round.

Half an hour later we were leaning against a brick wall in a
narrow alley just off Dean Street, our hands burrowing beneath each other's clothes, our bodies pressed together, our
tongues intertwined. My face was wet with his kisses. A chill
November wind sang through the alley, carrying the smell of
bonfires and burning straw, cutting me straight to the bone. I
could hear fireworks exploding in the distance, and faint
cheers.

Sam's hands fumbled with the button of my trousers. "I'll
bring you off right here in the alley," he slurred.

That would never do. "Don't you have a room somewhere?"

"Course I have a room." His mouth was a damp soft flower
against my ear. "But it's in Muswell Hill . . . and I don' wanna
wait . . ."

"Do all American physics students make a habit of sex in
alleyways?"

"No!" he assured me. "Hardly any do. But you're the

hottest guy I ever met . . ." He attacked me with his tongue again, leaving me to ponder the subtle mechanics of narcissism. I didn't fancy Sam quite as much as he fancied me, but I knew I would find him more appealing after he was dead.

But his room was in north London, the wrong direction from Heathrow Airport. And though a public spectacle was the last thing I wanted, the idea appeared to excite him. Sex in alleyways, in parks—it seemed a throwback to the London of the late sixties and early seventies, the furtive, sordid underside of a London I had barely known. It also gave me an idea.

I gently disengaged from Sam, pulled him out of the alley and up the street. He followed, unresisting. "There's a park a few blocks up," I told him. "The street isn't safe. But the cottages are."

"Cottages?"

"Public loos."

"Bathrooms?"

"Men without rooms sometimes fuck in the public loos," I explained. "And men who *do* have rooms, but like a bit of rough trade now and then. You can be put in jail for doing what we're about to do, you know. So a bit of privacy is essential."

I was always well aware of my victims' social disenfranchisement. But I used it against them only when I had to, as I did now.

The cottage was at the edge of a tree-lined square the other side of Tottenham Court Road, hidden in foliage, shrouded in fog, set partly underground at the bottom of some cement stairs. I went down first to make certain no one else was using the place, then pulled the door open a crack and motioned Sam in.

Our footsteps rang on the dirty stone floor and echoed off the tile walls. The urinals were like a row of vacuous mouths with pale jutting lower lips. The porcelain had a faint ghostly sheen beneath its patina of dried urine and grime. Sam looked around, gave me a smile as full of wonder and gratitude as a small boy's on Christmas morning, and pulled me into one of the stalls.

I shoved him back against the cold wall and covered his mouth with mine. He tasted bitter as the Guinness he had drunk, but with a spicy undertone of lust. I put my foot up on the toilet seat. With my left hand I cupped the back of his neck, where the hair was clipped short and soft. With the right I reached down and—slowly, slowly—pulled up my trouser leg.

The scalpel was stuck fast to the tape. I tried to twist it without moving my arm, to work it free a bit at a time. This deliberate action made me realize I was drunker than I'd thought. For a man who hasn't had a drink in half a decade and needs his wits about him, four lagers are too many.

Sam moaned and pushed his hips against mine. The stall smelled of disinfectant, human filth, a faint rancid trace of semen, a whiff of cheap cologne. The scalpel would not budge. Sam was biting at my lips, sliding his hands down my body. He touched my right arm and pulled back a little. "Arthur?" he whispered into my mouth. "What are you doing?"

I gave a great tug and the scalpel came free. It sliced through the tape, slashed the heavy cloth of Sam's trousers, and plunged deep into his leg before I could stop it.

His body went rigid. He grabbed my jumper with both hands, shouting inarticulately. Hot bright pain shot through my chest as Dr. Drummond's incision came open again. I sliced at Sam's fingers, felt the blade scrape across bone. He made an awful sound halfway between a sob and a scream. I imagined him trying to comprehend what was happening through his alcoholic haze, and I cursed myself for drinking enough to make me clumsy. I'd meant to send him off quick and clean. This was no better than butchery.

I grabbed the collar of Sam's coat, pulled him toward me as if I meant to kiss him again, and drove his head back against the wall as hard as I could. It sounded like a ripe melon landing on marble and left a dark smear on the tiles. A thin, beery stream of vomit bubbled out of his mouth.

I met his gaze steadily as I slammed his head into the wall again, trying not to let my face contort, trying not to look angry or cruel. Most likely he was past knowing anything. But if he could still see me, I wanted him to know I wasn't doing this because I hated him. Quite the contrary. Before, I had only seen him as a means to an end. But in these final moments of his life, I loved him.

I told him so as I pushed the scalpel into the soft spot just below his left ear. His eyes were alight with pain and dread— two emotions I always regretted seeing under such intimate circumstances—but they had already begun to fog. Warmth soaked my fingers, trickled over my wrist, pooled in the crook of my arm.

Sam's head fell back. A great wet red mouth yawned in his neck. For an instant its edges were a pristine delineation of tissues, a perfect cross section of his throat's various layers. Then it disgorged a solid torrent of blood, painting the stall, raining into the toilet, drenching Sam's face and the front of his coat. I thrust him to one side and barely got out of the way.

His dying body crumpled into a corner of the stall, wedged in between the wall and the toilet. His face was a red slick, featureless, blind. He was nothing but particles now, if he had ever been anything more. I had only altered the speed at which his particles were vibrating. Nothing in the universe had been disturbed.

I unzipped his trousers and tugged them down, telling myself this was not a foolish waste of time; I was only trying to make it look more like a random sex killing. Such things happened every day. The authorities will be diverted entirely, I thought as I took Sam's penis in my hand and felt a fresh stickiness. I looked down at the glistening white streak on my palm, like a snail trail in the garden. Sam had liked rough trade more than I'd suspected.

I brought my hand to my mouth and licked the salt stickiness away. It was bitter, faintly caustic. I thought I detected a
coppery trace of Guinness, but that could have been the blood
already on my hand. I licked off some of that as well. When I
stood, my legs were trembling and my head felt too heavy on
my neck, but I was careful not to support myself against the
wall. I couldn't touch anything yet.

I'd drunk too much. I had given Sam a bad death. But none
of that could be helped now. I had to clean up and get out of
this place. If anyone else came in, I would have to kill him too.
Today had been the first time I'd killed two men within minutes of each other. I didn't fancy trying it again so soon.

I went to the sinks, ran a thin stream of cold rusty-smelling
water over my hands, used paper towels to scrub away the rest
of the blood. When my hands were dry, I wiped the faucet
handle, then put on the rubber gloves I'd taken from the emergency room. I went back to Sam, found the scalpel on the
floor under his leg, cleaned it on the hem of his coat, and put
it in my pocket. I'd have to get rid of it as well as the gloves before I reached the airport, but I couldn't leave it here. For all I
knew, the hospitals marked them.

I felt inside Sam's coat and pulled out the brown leather
wallet I'd seen earlier. It held a driver's license issued by the
Commonwealth of Virginia, a student ID, three credit cards, a
condom, and a sheaf of crisp fifty-pound notes with some
smaller bills folded around them. In the same pocket of his
coat was a passport folder. The passport had been issued in
1989, and the smiling face in the photo was thinner, the hair
shorter, the aspect generally scruffier than that of the well-
groomed American tourist I had met tonight.

I thought I could easily pass for the man in the photo. My
name was Samuel Edward Toole, and I hailed from a place
called Charlottesville. I kept the entire wallet. The less identi-
fication was found on Sam, the more it would look as though
he'd been murdered and robbed. Which of course he had.
Upon reflection, I took the black plastic Swatch from his wrist

and fastened it around my own. Sam may have considered time a relative concept, but I had to catch the tube to Heathrow Airport before midnight, and it was already half past nine.

I backed out of the stall, glanced at my pale bespectacled image in the filthy mirror over the sinks, wiped a smudge of blood off my chin and pushed back a sweaty lick of hair that had fallen into my face. *What am I forgetting?* I wondered. *How have I left my stamp on this scene, my signature on Sam's poor outraged body?* I could think of nothing.

Something was seeping into one of my socks, oozing warmly between my toes. I glanced down at my feet and swore. A small lake of blood was already spreading out from the stall, shiny as black lacquer in the dismal light. The bottoms of my shoes were foul with it. I'd tracked his blood all over the floor, and the prison knew my shoe size. But I couldn't risk taking the time to wipe up the footprints.

The sink farthest from the door already sagged loose from the wall, probably as a result of men leaning against it with their flies unzipped. I threw all my weight onto it, sat on its edge and bounced up and down, felt it loosen further, then give. The metal shrieked as it ripped away from its moorings. The ancient plumbing gave a great rattling groan. The sink toppled to the floor and broke in half. The orphaned pipe began to spew water in great whirling arcs.

Within seconds the floor was covered with a thin film of dirty pink-tinged water, which I trod in to clean my soles. I had a last look at Sam, offered him a silent apology for not being able to linger, for leaving him alone here. *Your life collided with mine,* I explained, *and you simply failed to survive the wreckage.*

Then I hurried up the cement stairs and left that dreary place forever. Suddenly I was a great one for leaving dreary places, it seemed.

I only hoped I would find somewhere I wanted to stay.

. . .

At Painswick there had been (and likely still was) a petty thief and occasional rapist called Mason. I met him on Christmas Day, one of the few times I was allowed out of my cell to visit the television lounge. One of the holiday programmes announced a string quartet playing a piece by Mozart. Before anyone could change the channel, Mason hurled himself in front of the telly and turned the sound as far up as it would go.

He was an unimpressive, weaselly little fellow, and a great grunting murderous yob soon tossed him aside and switched over to repeats of rugby playoffs. Mason spent the rest of the day in my corner, explaining to me the kinship he felt with Mozart. He'd seen the film *Amadeus* seven times. He considered himself a blazing talent unrecognized in youth, left to rot on the vine.

"What kept you from fame and fortune, then?" I asked him once.

His answer astounded me. "My mum 'n' dad wouldn't let me have piano lessons."

So it was with murderers, I often thought. There were would-bes and would-nevers, and those who killed accidentally or thoughtlessly. But how many people had experienced an actual *need to murder,* a need to *appreciate* someone else's death?

Some may think killing is easy for men like me, that it is a thing we murderers do as casually and callously as brushing our teeth. Hedonists see us as grotesque cult heroes performing mutilations for kicks. Moralists will not even grant us a position in the human race, can only rationalize our existence by calling us monsters. But *monster* is a medical term, describing a freak too grossly deformed to belong anywhere but the grave. Murderers, skilled at belonging everywhere, seed the world.

Thumbing through Sam's wallet on the train, I had a nasty flash of alarm. My plan had been to visit the automatic bank machines at the airport, withdraw the largest cash advances

Sam's three credit cards would allow, and use the cash to buy a ticket on the first flight that caught my fancy. But as I handled the stiff plastic rectangles, I remembered the Barclaycard I'd had in my other life. A machine would give you all the cash you liked—as long as you'd memorized your four-digit access number. That was what kept people like me from knocking you over the head, taking your card, and withdrawing all your money.

I could hardly go back and ask Sam what his PINs were. I supposed I would have to buy a ticket with one of the cards, but if Sam's body were identified and his death connected with me, there would be a perfect record of where I'd gone. Of course, I wouldn't stay where I landed. But it would give them a place to start looking for me. I didn't want them to have even that much.

I tipped the card marked *Visa* back and forth in my hand, making the hologram of an eagle flutter and take wing. I rubbed my finger across the nubbly raised letters of Sam's name, trying to absorb his identity, his memories. I thought of his brain dying back in the loo, the cells turning to rancid slush, the cells that held the knowledge I needed. Just this morning I'd been dead too. I wished there were some sort of information interchange beyond the grave, some ghostly data bank listing the vital statistics of no-longer-vital souls. But if there was, I hadn't stayed long enough to tap into it.

I would buy a different ticket with each card, I decided, and use some of Sam's cash if necessary. At least that way they would have to start looking for me in four places instead of one.

Heathrow Airport just before midnight is a cacophony of shoving, hurrying travellers, disembodied voices, stroboscopic lights. There are breakfast bars and snack stands, rocklike sticky buns collaborating with tea of inferior vintage to mount an assault on the taste buds and the stomach lining. There are bookstores and caviar kiosks and luggage carts and escalators

and duty-free zones. And everywhere there are boards an-
nouncing imminent departures, exhorting you to go any of a
thousand other places, anywhere but here. Heathrow is the
busiest international airport in the world. A flight leaves every
forty-seven seconds. No one can watch them all.

Bangkok. Zaire. Tokyo. Salt Lake City. The names whirled
and clicked about my head, tempting, confusing, seducing me.
Tangier, I knew, was full of adorable young boys lounging on
soporific sands, begging to be interfered with. Singapore was
the gourmet capital of the world, but had a brutal police system. Anyone could get lost in the backstreet mazes of stinking
Calcutta. And this was only one terminal.

In the end I bought tickets to Amsterdam, Hong Kong, Can-
cún, and Atlanta. All four flights left within the hour.
Whichever gate I arrived at first, that was where I would go.
Once I had the tickets, I went into a men's loo and shoved
Sam's credit cards deep into a rubbish bin. They were of no
more use to me. Then I took the cassette from Drummond's
tape recorder, pissed on it, and flushed it.

I walked past a news vendor and glanced at the front page
of the *Evening Standard,* and the core of my heart went cold.

GAY HORROR KILLER MISSING!

Below that, in type almost as large, my name. Better, my
names: the one I had been given, the one I had earned.

ANDREW COMPTON—LONDON'S ETERNAL HOST

And that same blurry photograph, more than six years old
now, my hair tumbling over my brow, my lips so white they all
but disappeared into the surrounding paleness of my skin.
Nothing like how I looked now, but making people think of
me nonetheless. Making them wonder where I would turn up.

Every policeman in England would be looking for me, I realized, and any curious sod who happened to read the papers as well. Heathrow Airport must be crawling with such people.

I had to know everything they knew. I bought a paper, trying to examine the Pakistani vendor's reaction without looking him in the eye. He was cleaning his fingernails with a wooden toothpick and didn't appear to take any notice of me. I scanned the article.

Andrew Compton, convicted in 1989 of 23 London murders . . .

". . . signed his death certificate," said Dr. Selwyn Masters, "There couldn't be any mistake, I'm sure." (I felt a twinge of affection for the incompetent old man.)

Police declined to say whether the morgue showed evidence of a break-in . . .

. . . doctors savagely murdered . . .

"What sick purpose could be served by stealing the corpse of a notorious . . ."

THEY STILL THOUGHT I WAS DEAD!

I felt like doing a triumphant dance in the middle of the thronged corridor. Instead I surged along with the crowd, reading a sidebar about famous grave robberies but making no sense of it, marvelling at my insane luck, feeling very proud of my convincing imitation of death. Did I say *imitation?* I should call it my *intimate acquaintance with death,* for surely no imitation could have fooled everyone so well.

But of course collaboration requires an intimate acquaintance, if not necessarily a comfortable one. And what was I if not death's ghostwriter?

The departure lounge loomed ahead, a long bright hall receding to a chaotic point, latticework of escalators crossing high overhead. Passing through the metal detector at the security check, I had a sudden horror of these kindly, efficient ladies finding the bloody scalpel still taped to my leg—but the scalpel was resisting rust at the bottom of the Thames, and the latex gloves were balled up in a vomitous-smelling rubbish bin somewhere in Soho. I had no metal on me, not even a key or a pen nib.

I looked at my four tickets, looked at the gate numbers. The plane to Atlanta was taking off in five minutes not ten feet away from where I stood. "Final boarding call," a whore-eyed Greek steward was saying into a microphone, "final call please for Atlanta, Georgia."

I imagined myself lounging on the porch of an old Southern mansion turned country inn, gnarled oaks arching over the carriageway, a mint julep in my hand. The day was clear and warm, with just a crackling hint of autumn. I didn't have the foggiest idea what went in a mint julep except bourbon, which I didn't like, and I suspected even Georgia might be cold in November. But none of this mattered. I would decline to give a damn.

I gave the Greek boy my ticket. He let his fingers touch mine as he handed it back, and for an instant I ached to slit his throat, let him cool, press my steaming stinking flesh into the lovely calmness of him. The feeling never quite passed, only ebbed to a low-grade discomfort. I'd created three corpses today, and hadn't had a quiet moment with any of them.

I walked down a telescoping tunnel to the plane. A flight attendant directed me to my seat, the lovely window seat my ticket had promised, the seat Sam would never have to pay for, saved for me just as if I deserved it. Then the heavy doors were sealed shut, the plane was pulling away from the terminal, taxiing down the runway, lifting into the air. London unfurled below me, a shimmering net of lights cast adrift on a sea of darkness. In less than a minute we had risen above the gray matting of cloud that always hangs over London, and I left the city behind me forever.

Soon we were over the Irish Sea heading out across the Atlantic Ocean. From my window it looked as if there were nothing below us at all, or above us either. The killer with a thin scrim of blood still greasing his nail beds, the unsuspecting fellow travellers clutching their briefcases and infants and fat paperbacks like talismans guaranteed to bring them safely back to earth, the fragile metal tube that cradled us—all might have been suspended motionless in some viscid black pudding. I felt as vulnerable yet protected, as edible yet impervious as an oyster in its shell.

I liked the idea so well, I decided to have a plate of oysters when I landed in America. I'd heard they were eaten raw there, particularly in the South. I couldn't imagine a raw oyster in my mouth, oozing between my teeth, sliding slickly down my throat. But I resolved to try. I would learn to enjoy the feel of an undifferentiated mass of tissue on my tongue, the flavour of briny glue seeping into my taste buds. It would be a part of my rebirth.

As it turned out, oysters were the least of what I had to learn.

5

Jay was curled up in a voluminous black leather chair in his library, the angles of his naked body swathed in a soft angora blanket. The first tinge of dawn turned the window glass purple and sent a watery shadow across the floor. He paged through the color plates of a surgical textbook his father had acquired at some point, for what reason Jay could not even begin to imagine.

He'd stolen the textbook last time he visited the ancestral manse on St. Charles, where his cousin, Daniel Devore's son, lived now with his family. Mignon had bequeathed the house to them in return for Daniel's help in business. She'd known her son Jay would never want to live uptown.

He stared at a colorful cross section of prostate surgery, a pair of hemostats inserted through an incision in the scrotum to clamp a small vein, a gloved finger sneaking up the rectal cavity, caressing the diseased gland, then puncturing it with a scalpel and letting its sweet juices escape through the muscle wall into the intestine. The prostate looked like a dark wrinkled walnut. The walls of the rectum undulated in slick pink waves around the stainless steel blade. Jay found himself thinking of Tran, the Vietnamese boy he'd scored the sheet of acid from yesterday. Tran's young prostate would be smooth and fine, no larger than an almond.

The spine of the heavy book pressed painfully against Jay's crotch. He realized he had a boner again, as if the night had not been enough to exhaust him. There was a hollow at the top of the rectal canal, just above the prostate, where any number of objects fit so beautifully . . .

He pushed himself out of the chair, slid the book back into its space on the crowded shelf, and left the library. The house was silent but for the occasional drunken laughter of revelers still roaming the Quarter. On an ordinary night, Jay would have been reading, watching a video, or doing his accounts; he loved math for its exquisite symmetry. But this was no ordinary night. He had a guest.

No, he reminded himself, not a guest this time. A *pet.*

The luminous dial of the grandfather clock in the hall read ten to five. Strange shadows moved like ghosts trapped behind the barbed design of the gold-flocked scarlet wallpaper. Jay entered the parlor, a baroque fantasy of draped velvet and satin tassels and dark carved teak, syrup-smooth hardwood floor covered with an enormous Chinese rug. The dominant colors of the room were purple, rose, and gold; in daylight it had the aspect of a gilded womb.

Taking up most of one wall was a fireplace of pink marble inlaid with art deco plumes of malachite, carnelian, and jet, an exquisite piece of stonework. Its beauty was obscured beneath a layer of greasy black ash that would not yield even to a wire scrub brush soaked in industrial-strength bleach.

Jay paused as if at loose ends, then lifted a delicate china teacup from a claw-footed table and drained its dregs. A slow shudder ran down his spine like notes on a xylophone. The tea was spiked with cognac and LSD. He had been sipping this potent brew all night, since he brought his new pet home.

The boy from Café du Monde had come docilely, keeping a few respectful paces behind, just close enough so all the tourists and Jackson Square hustlers could see that this beautiful creature was with him. Normally Jay was cautious about such things, but this time he felt just as if a prize greyhound or some other valuable sleek animal were voluntarily following him home.

Prize greyhound. That was a laugh. If Fido really was a dog, he'd be a street cur with an appealing face but a dirty coat. Luckily, his coat came off. As did his boots, his grubby T-shirt, his filthy jeans, his stinking socks, and his unspeakable underwear. Underneath it all, Fido could be made clean.

Wire brush and bleach hadn't worked on the marble fireplace. But boys were made of softer stuff.

As Jay glided through the parlor, he caught sight of his reflection in the enormous mirror that stood in one corner, heavy gilt frame succulent with carved fruit and vegetation. He was a silver-white specter awash in the waterlight of dawn, his naked flesh luminously pale. His chest and abdomen were crisscrossed with dark spray patterns of blood, delicate as sea foam. His hair was stiff with it. His eyes were wide and wild, glittering.

He entered the bathroom. The dazzle of light on black and white tile was relieved by glistening scrawls and blots of red, like handfuls of rubies thrown about. The boy was curled upon himself in the bathtub, trussed at the wrists and ankles and tightly round the skinny smooth thighs, his eyes bright with acid and hideous awareness. His body was scoured, scraped away to raw nerve. Over the sharpest points of his body, cheeks and knees and hips, Jay could see the blue-white gleam of bone. The bleach had raised angry chemical burns on what little skin he had left. His cock was as wet and shapeless as a spit-out mouthful of food. At some point his stomach had been partly slit open, the layers pulled apart and a shiny bubble of intestine exposed.

Jay smiled. The boy smiled back. He had to; most of the flesh around his mouth had been scraped or burned away, and his smile was a rictus of bleach-white teeth set in bleeding gums. Jay supposed he hadn't taken care of his pet very well. No doubt the ASPCA would be pounding on his door any minute now.

The revelers could howl in the streets all they liked, but the French Quarter did not belong to them. Tomorrow, next week, next year they would be gone, their passage as ephemeral as the wake that swirled behind a ship on the river. Jay would be here still. The Quarter was his, its gaslit nighttime streets, its sordid alleys and neon-starred byways, the secret courtyards swathed in leaflight and shadow, the huge purple moon that hung above it all like a bleary eye. It delivered offerings up to him, and he accepted them gratefully, voraciously. Jay did not mind the noise of the revelers. But in here, it was a night of revelry for him too.

The sun would be risen before the boy died.

6

At about the same time Tran was staring helplessly at a Baggie full of LSD and hundred-dollar bills, Lucas Ransom awoke to a blaring clock radio in a dirt-cheap motel room on the other side of New Orleans. He slapped at the snooze button, pulled night-stale covers up around his collarbone, felt nausea rising in his gut but quenched it, refused it, willed it away. He couldn't afford nausea this morning.

He slipped briefly back into dream. Something about Tran, as they always seemed to be these days. When the alarm went off again ten minutes later, he awoke with tears on his face. WBYU was playing "A Taste of Honey."

"A taste—more bitter—than wine," Luke sang along to wake himself up. His voice sounded as brittle as a saltine cracker. His lungs felt like sponges dipped in formaldehyde and left to dry in the sun. All this would have to change before showtime.

He stumbled into the shower. A cockroach squeezed its greasy-looking brown body down the drain hole as the rusty water drummed into the tub. Luke soaped himself apathetically, his hands sliding over ribs and hipbones sharper than they had been a month ago, two weeks ago even. Other than an attack of thrush, a vile white fungus that had invaded his mouth and throat for a fortnight, Luke hadn't had any opportunistic infections yet. But his lymph nodes had been swollen for over a year, the number of T-cells in his blood was a little lower at his free clinic checkup each month, he got the shits on a regular basis, and he was dropping weight fast.

Even when he was using heroin, he had worked out at the Lee Circle YMCA a couple of times a week. He had never been pumped up, but he liked the way his muscles felt when they were sleek and taut. He was living then in the Faubourg Marigny, a neighborhood of shabby little Creole cottages a stone's throw from the French Quarter, and because he loved lying in a bath of subtropical sunlight on the roof of his apartment, his skin stayed darker than Tran's and the dusting of hair on his chest, belly, and legs bleached to pale gold, lighter than the hair on his head. Even his pubic hair had lightened a shade; even his cock had acquired a healthy glow.

He'd kept all that up as long as he could. But it had been a long time since he could. The muscle had melted off his sturdy frame until he was all painful edges and awkward bone-ends. One of the medicines he was taking made him horribly sensitive to sunlight, and his tan had been replaced by a pale gray like the color of an uncooked shrimp. His entire body felt jagged and pallid and pasty.

These days it took all of his strength to walk to his car in the motel parking lot, get the engine started after two or three tries, and drive the thirty miles to the bayou. That meant the radio shows were coming from something that ran deeper in him than strength, and the only thing Luke knew of that ran deeper than strength was insanity.

He figured Lush Rimbaud was insane, probably had been for some time. But he was starting to wonder about Luke Ransom, too. He believed bad influences were inevitably stronger than good ones: just as he knew Tran had to have some sweet memories of him, he also knew those memories were likely soured in Tran's heart by the sheer awfulness of what had come later.

So Luke had always assumed the insane part of his mind would eventually overtake the sane part. It was the part that had wanted Tran to inject diseased blood, Luke's own blood, into his vein. It was the part that had wanted Tran to die, not even *with* him, but *instead of* him.

And what was there to stay sane for now? A trip to the clinic once a month, his pentamidine inhaler and his egg lipids, a long night spent tapping out useless words that paled next to his memories, a filthy cubicle on the Airline Highway among hookers and junkies?

The junkies didn't make it easy, either. Always knowing someone was snorting or shooting up somewhere in the motel court, maybe right next door; always knowing he could lay his hands on some junk if he only wanted to. And he wanted to almost all the time. He never stopped imagining how it would relieve the nausea, render the bone-grinding fatigue irrelevant, wipe away the imprint of Tran's body on his own.

But he knew it would also eventually stop him from giving a shit about anything, including staying alive. And he wasn't ready to give the world the satisfaction of watching him die just yet.

He'd started using heroin ten years ago, back in San Francisco, when he was Tran's age: snorted some at a party, loved the rush and the ensuing lull, the longest period of utter calm his mind had ever known. He went back for more, eventually started putting it in his arm instead of up his nose. The rush was purer that way, the lull longer and far sweeter. It turned out he had a heroin metabolism. A habit tended to sap a normal person's vitality, as if a tiny droplet of the life force were siphoned off by the needle each time. Steady use of heroin would kill most people eventually. But certain systems drew strength from it.

He had kicked for a while around the time he met Tran, three years ago. No methadone self-deception for Luke; just the frigid sweats, the crawling itch, the nausea that boiled like red worms in his gut. You can use one substance to cure your addiction to another, he told himself as he clutched his bottle of Jack Daniel's in the aftermath of junk sickness, but the new substance should be something different entirely. Something to take your mind off the desire that still pours through your veins. Methadone was a rubber sex doll; whiskey was a brand-new lover.

So what should he use now, Luke wondered, to cure his addiction? Tran was in his veins sure as the memory of the needle, in his tissues sure as the ghost of junk sickness. Nothing touched the deep, slow ache that came to him whenever he remembered being in bed with Tran, fucking or talking or just memorizing each other's face as obsessively as two lovers ever had. Tran's eyes were difficult to think about, too. Luke remembered how they would take on the golden cast of the afternoon light, and the liquid blackness of the pupils, and the feel of delicate skin against his lips when he kissed the subtle, perfect curve at their inner corners. Oh yes, he knew how to torture himself with memories.

He turned off the water, dried his scrawny body with a threadbare towel, dragged himself out of the bathroom and sank into the ugly vinyl armchair. An ancient burn hole from someone's cigarette nipped at the back of his leg. There were days when he had to rest after doing anything: showering, walking half a mile down the highway to the McDonald's or Popeye's, even reading the paper. Apparently this was going to be one of those days.

Since he'd gotten on the subject of memories, Luke decided to treat himself to a flashback. He was doing this more and more these days, reliving vivid moments from his past. Often they had to do with Tran, and since the good moments were exquisitely painful to recall, he usually chose the bad ones.

Luke leaned back in the chair and closed his eyes, and it was December of two years ago. A few days before Christmas, a holiday he'd always found wretchedly depressing anyway. Tran had escaped his family festivities, and they were curled like spoons on the mattress of Luke's loft. Luke lay with his face pressed into the hollow of Tran's shoulder, dreamily nuzzling the fine black hair at the his nape, which smelled of sweet gel and sex sweat. Tran was nineteen then, and his hair was much shorter, nearly buzz-cut. The style made his face look fiercely exotic, feral. It also showed off the three tiny silver hoops in his earlobes—two in the left, one in the right—each of which had reportedly driven his parents into new paroxysms of horror.

Suddenly Tran said without warning, "I'm sorry."

Luke knew by now that Tran was prone to disjointed inter-jections, often in belated response to a conversation he'd been having hours or days ago. But for some reason, this meek *I'm sorry* set off a warning bell in his head. "For what?" he asked.

Tran didn't answer, and a shrieking klaxon joined the bell. Luke propped himself on one elbow and used Tran's sharp hipbone as a handle to roll him over none too gently. "What?" he said again, more urgently. Tran looked away. Luke grabbed Tran's face, forced it toward him. A small tortured sound es-caped Tran's throat, not quite a word, not yet a sob.

"What have you *done?*"

Answer me, Luke thought, *answer me right now and save me the suspense.* Instead came Tran's usual long silence preceding the answer to a tough question. Then, "Nothing. Only . . ."

Tran twisted his face out of Luke's grasp, which had tight-ened involuntarily at the word *only.* Luke saw five white fin-ger-shaped marks on Tran's golden skin. As he watched, the marks deepened to rose, the color of Tran's blood just below the surface.

"Last week when you went to Baton Rouge . . . I was in the French Quarter one night and . . . there happened to be this party."

Luke shut his eyes tightly and willed his hands away from Tran's smooth throat. He knew what was coming. Couldn't

Tran be merciful and tell him straight out? Of course not.

"Everybody was really hammered," Tran said pleadingly.

Luke ground his teeth, counted to five, and opened his eyes. Tran was watching, but something in Luke's eyes made him look away. "So everybody was hammered," said Luke. "Imagine that, at a party in the French Quarter. SO FUCKING WHAT?"

"They played some kind of kissing game with this clove and this orange—"

"Tran. Just say it, goddamn you, please just say it." *Don't say it,* Luke's heart begged in agonizing counterpoint, *as long as you haven't said it out loud then it didn't happen, so just shut up, just don't say—*

"Well-I-ended-up-fooling-around-with-this-guy," Tran said all in a rush, then hitched in a deep shuddery breath as if the unspoken revelation had deprived him of air.

A strange burning sensation had begun to spread through the muscles of Luke's shoulders, as if corrosive acid were eating into the tissue. Luke wondered what the physiology of that particular phenomenon might be; why should the news of his lover's betrayal make his muscles corrode? But he only said, "I thought we weren't going to do shit like that."

"I did too! I didn't want to! It was just . . ."

"It was just that you were drunk and your dick was hard, right?"

"Well, yeah."

"At least you admit it."

"But he wouldn't leave me alone! He's already fucked most of my friends . . ."

"Great. I'm glad you're so selective about your sordid affairs."

Tran's eyes closed in defeat, and the dark smudge of his lashes on the butter-smooth skin beneath his eyes was enough to twist a barb through Luke's heart, even now. "I didn't mean to, Luke. I was basically seduced into it."

Luke's vision went red. He could see directly into the core

of his own rage, and that core was on the point of meltdown.
He grabbed a pillow off the bed and punched it, then throttled
it. He didn't know what else he was going to do until he saw
a cascade of tiny feathers swirling around the bed, drifting to
the floor. He had ripped the pillow open with his fingernails.
One of his expensive goose-down pillows, no less.

"GO AHEAD!!!" he heard himself screaming. *"Why don't
you just take this amazing thing we have and throw it away?
Why don't you just toss it in the gutter and piss on it because
you happened to GET DRUNK AT A PARTY??? What a
FUCKING BRILLIANT IDEA!!!"*

He forced himself to breathe several times, then resumed
speaking in a soft, precise voice. "I mean—could you be any
lamer if you *tried?* You did this—you ran home to *tell* me
about it, God knows why—and now you're saying you
weren't even *responsible?"*

Tran was staring wide eyed at the feathers on the floor. His
gaze flicked back up to Luke's, then away. "No. I'm not saying that."

"Sounds like it to me."

"Well . . . hmmm . . ."

"Don't *hmmm* me, you damned devil! I know how that de-
vious Oriental mind works. You can't save face on this one.
Just tell me . . ." Luke's steam ran out and he lay staring at
Tran. His face felt terribly naked. He was sure he looked
ghastly. "What happened."

"Okay. There's this guy I sometimes see out at the clubs."

"What do you mean, *see?"*

"I'd noticed him in the Quarter. I talk to people, and this
guy gets around. I'd talked to him a couple of times."

"Does this *guy"*—it was a word Luke never used, a word
that made no distinction between the myriad subspecies of the
male gender—"does this *person* have a name?"

"Zach."

"You mean that pallid little fuck who looks like Edward
Scissorhands, only more pleased with himself?"

Tran nearly laughed. He bit at the inside of his lip to stop himself, and seeing his white teeth against the dark pink wet flesh made Luke wish they were soul-kissing, ass-fucking, anything except having this wretched conversation.

"Yeah," said Tran, "that guy."

"What did you do?"

"He kept . . . um, *embracing* me. He said I was his long-lost twin brother."

"How original."

"Then we started kissing in the doorway."

"Oh, under the disgusting vegetable parasite?"

"The what?"

"The mistletoe."

"Yeah."

Luke pictured the two of them pressed against the jamb, leaning into each other, their hands raking and groping, their mouths messily joined. Probably twenty or thirty other French Quarter scene-kiddies were in the room, some more concerned with their own sordid pawings, some looking on, blearily marking the fact that Luke Ransom's boyfriend was swapping spit with one of the biggest sluts in town, and many of them probably finding that fact maliciously funny. Luke had a talent for making himself unpopular among posers.

Part of him wanted to throw himself sobbing on Tran's mercy, beg Tran to say it wasn't true, could never be true. Part of him wanted to murder the stupid brat, tear his cheating bones apart, then breathe life back into him for the sheer joy of killing him again. The image of the two boys kissing in the doorway was indelibly branded on Luke's mind, a fresh hot wound searing its way deep into the steaming meat of his brain, making a scar that would last forever.

"So then what happened?"

"Well, he dragged me off into a . . . bedroom, I think, and . . . Luke, do you really want to hear this?"

"No," Luke told him truthfully. "But you made me go this far. Now I have to hear it all."

"Why? I just needed to be honest with you. We never have to talk about this again if you don't want to."

"And I'm just supposed to stop thinking about it, huh? Maybe you can gloss things over so easily. In fact, I'm sure you can. But my mind doesn't work like that. *Even if I could wipe this shit out of my head right now, I wouldn't dare . . . because I might need it someday.* You want to be a writer, Tran? Then you better start saving up too . . ."

He had ranted in this vein for a while. There had been more, much more, but Luke decided to end the flashback there. He didn't want to relive Tran's hesitant description of a blowjob received and reciprocated in a stranger's dark bedroom while the party roared on beyond a half-closed door, or his own wretchedly furious reaction. He opened his eyes and shook his head a couple of times, and it was the present again. Sort of.

That had happened six months after they met, nearly a year before Luke's test came up positive. Luke's own sexual conduct had been blameless during those six months, a first for him. Still, he had to admit that a good part of his anger came from a petty sense of missed opportunity. He'd only been in Baton Rouge to sign at the Hibiscus Bookstore, which he had done several times without event when he was single. But this time, for some reason, the signing was attended by any number of slender, dark-haired, dark-eyed boys so pretty they made Luke's hand shake a bit as he inscribed their books.

One in particular, a self-described poet named Michel, stayed around to talk to him throughout the signing. They had a drink afterward, then two, and when Michel asked him to stay overnight, Luke badly wanted to. Instead he thought of the difficult conversation he and Tran had had the week before. They had talked out their various fears and jealousies, and Luke thought they had decided on some sort of faith to each other. He wanted to spend the night devouring the self-described poet like a sweet bonbon offered up on the altar of his twin gods, talent and lust. That was what such boys were *for.* Instead he found himself horny and half-drunk on I-10, searching the dial for shitty talk radio, the hour way past midnight, the industrial panorama of Baton Rouge dazzling his eyes in the rearview mirror.

When he found out Tran had cheated on him anyway, Luke wished he'd gone ahead and fucked Michel. Never mind that Michel had been a pretentious airhead not half as beautiful as Tran. Luke had an ugly sense of having missed out on an easy, sweet piece of ass while Tran got one, of having failed to put a notch in his barrel to match Tran's new notch. He also had an idea that Tran had tricked him into feeling this way.

Ah, relationships. If he was lucky, Luke thought, he would never have another one. And he was feeling awfully lucky lately. Just waking up alive every day, that made him feel his luck like a ten-ton weight sitting on his chest.

He pulled on a T-shirt and jeans, shoved his feet into a pair of pointy-toed black cowboy boots, slung his ancient motorcycle jacket around his shoulders. This had been Luke's unvarying cold-weather uniform for the past ten years. Now the jeans felt too loose and his biceps no longer filled out the sleeves of the jacket, but the boots were still fine. A good pair of boots was a friend forever, till death do us part. Idly he wondered whether this pair would outlast him. One of the soles was beginning to crack and peel, but then so was his.

Outside, the early morning air caressed his skin like a cool, damp hand. The sky was full of pale blue-gray light, the color of Louisiana dawn. No one had broken into his car during the night, and the engine cranked on the first try. Maybe this was going to be a good day. The flashback had leached some of the self-pity out of him, and he was no longer in the masochistic mood necessary to enjoy the maudlin love songs of WBYU. Instead he slapped on a Coil tape, cranked it up to full volume—which wasn't much, coming from his cheap-ass speakers—and pulled out onto the highway.

Coil's version of "Tainted Love" was just the thing to fuel righteous anger in him, and righteous anger was what he needed to pump himself up for the show. "GAVE YOU—ALL—A BOY COULD—GIVE YOU," he sang, pounding the dashboard. Tran's face floated up in front of him, and Luke hated its effortless beauty, hated the callow, manipulative mind that lay behind those smooth-lidded eyes. He thought of the truth he had poured into his books, all the truth he knew, and he hated every critic who had ever savaged him, every reader who had missed the point.

When he ran out of specific targets for his animosity, Luke hated the world because it would go on after he was dead. The raw emotion coursed through him, as icy-pure as the finest junk, giving him the strength to be insane.

By the time he reached the turnoff to the bayou, stashed his car in a ramshackle wooden building that served as a covert garage, and walked out to the dock where the pirogue would pick him up to take him to the showboat, he could feel Lush Rimbaud stirring inside him, ready to rage.

"The rest of the world could get a fucking clue from China. One kid per family, severe penalties for extras, and mandatory sterilization. Zero population growth is their goal, and they've damn near reached it. A mess of abortion goes on in the People's Republic. A *whole* damn mess of abortion. Scraping fetus has become a way of life to the Chinese. Not to let 'em off the hook, so to speak. Extreme measures are called for because they've been world-champion breeders since the fucking Han dynasty. One out of every five people in the *world* is Chinese. But what percentage of resources do you think all those Chinese people are using? No percentage at all, compared to *your* greedy little American ass.

"Americans comprise less than five percent of the world's population, yet we suck up thirty-three percent of the world's resources. And we can breed as many rug rats as we want. Hey, it's a free country! We don't even have to be able to feed 'em. If you can't keep the little fuckers alive, the government will do it for you! MY tax dollars—YOUR tax dollars—pay breeders to stay home and make MORE breeders! AND RESEARCH TOWARD THE CURE OF AN EPIDEMIC GOES UNFUNDED BECAUSE THE PEOPLE DYING FROM IT SUCKED TOO MUCH *COCK!!!*"

He'd been on the air for several hours now, and he was rolling. Luke leaned away from the microphone and slurped at a vile-tasting protein drink that Soren, the founder, financer, and engineer of WHIV, had stashed in the cooler for him. It was as thick as a McDonald's milk shake, and slightly viscous. The flavor was part strawberry, part Pepto-Bismol, part liver: chalky-bland, sickly sweet, yet somehow meaty. It was among the more disgusting things he'd ever put in his mouth. But Soren swore it would put two pounds on him. He could use two pounds.

He returned to the mike. "They may hate us for sucking cock, but at least they can't accuse us of making more little cocksuckers. At least the biological reproduction of our own DNA in the form of a slimy, squalling lump of meat isn't the greatest satisfaction most of us will ever know in life. Now is it? I'm Lush Rimbaud coming to you on WHIV, your source of aural infection . . . and this one goes out to the one I love."

He cued up Nine Inch Nails' "Something I Can Never Have." Trent Reznor's voice burned like a hot wire into his skull, stealthy and sharp, laced with deadly pain. It might as well be the theme song of this show, this radio station, everything he had ever written, his desperate love for Tran, his whole miserable life.

And yet there was something that kept him kicking despite all the good reasons he had to go ahead and die. He could bow out any time now: it would be easy to score enough junk, and an opiate OD was the ideal way to go as far as Luke was concerned. If the straights found you with a needle hanging out of your arm and wished you good riddance, so what? You'd cashed it in easy and sweet.

If he kept fighting for that extra day, week, month of life, he might end up too sick to let himself out gracefully. Then he would face a hard, protracted death. In the final days his lungs might fail, and he would drown in his own phlegm. He might go blind and no longer be able to see death stealing up on him. His basic functions might go, and he would die in puddles of his own shit (perhaps scrawling a last scatological sentence or two on the wall).

There were any number of colorful horrors to consider. Luke often nibbled his way through them like a cornucopia of rotting fruits, choosing one for its bittersweet ripeness, another for the worm in its core.

So what kept him going? For a while it had been his conviction that he and Tran would return to each other somehow, someday, simply because it was their destiny. Luke could not conceive of dying until this had happened. But slowly he came to realize that for most of his life, *destiny* had equaled anything he wanted at any given time. It wasn't going to work that way anymore. Tran apparently had his own ideas about destiny, a destiny that no longer included Lucas Ransom. Rather than consider the possibility that he had been wrong, Luke stopped believing in destiny altogether. And he kept on living.

A tiny flame of nausea licked at the pit of his stomach, and Luke decided to give the protein drink a rest. He'd grab a sandwich from the cooler in a while, after dark, maybe even manage a cup of coffee out of the thermos. Maybe.

The Nine Inch Nails song was winding to a slow, sinister close. "Now that one," he said into the microphone, "that one's for my lost love, wherever he is. Are you out there, are you listening, do you still hate the sound of my voice? I guess I'll never know. Here's another one for you, my little heartworm."

Lush Rimbaud seldom played two tunes in a row with no rant in between, but he saw Soren heading across the deck with smoldering joint in hand and he was getting maudlin anyway, so he put on a Billie Holiday CD. As the first mournful strains of "Gloomy Sunday" drifted out across the swamp, Soren passed Luke the joint. Luke sucked at the tarry twist of paper, damp with bayou fog and Soren's spit, and felt the little flame of nausea recede.

"Christ, Luke." Soren grimaced at the speakers. "Spin a couple of bummers, why don't you?"

"I thought I would." Luke toked on the joint again and handed it back. The spicy green taste of the weed lingered on his lips, on his tongue. He watched Soren draw deep, sucking the smoke up hungrily. The young engineer was a white-bleached blond with a spare, elegant face and a wardrobe straight out of *Details*. In another life, in his old life, Luke would have dismissed Soren as a clubby bitch. That had been his term for a certain type of well-dressed prettyboy who haunted hipster hangouts everywhere, looking like the bastard offspring of Bauhaus and Duran Duran, sucking up cappuccinos and bragging about art.

In another life, in his own old life, Soren might have been one of those clubby bitches. But in this life he had tested positive for the HIV virus a year ago, one week after his eighteenth birthday. *Welcome to the real world, kid. How do you like being a grownup? Don't worry—you won't be one for long.* Though he hadn't had any symptoms yet, a shell-shocked glaze shone through the obvious intelligence in his eyes, which were gray and huge in his fine-boned face. His natural quietness had taken on a stunned quality. His radio handle was Stigmata Martyr.

Despite his sleek appearance, Soren was a technogeek extraordinaire who could get any recalcitrant piece of equipment on the showboat working inside of an hour. He'd been beaming pirate signals onto FM stations for years, but had started WHIV several months ago after after hearing a right-wing talk radio host shout down a hospitalized AIDS patient who'd called to protest the misinformation being spread.

Soren wanted a front man as strident as the ones on the other side. He'd contacted Luke through a tenuous network of acquaintances. Though Luke had never worked in radio, and though he had been put off by Soren's appearance and demeanor at first, the idea seized him. Here was his chance to let Lush Rimbaud rant freely, without having to edit him later. Here was his chance to decant some of the constant anger. It fueled him, yes; but when it built up past a certain point, it began to gnaw at his heart until he could scarcely think.

Soren was right about "Gloomy Sunday." Billie poured all her loneliness, all her might-have-beens, all the sorrow of her junkie heart into this love song to a dead lover, and the result was devastating.

"Don't you know the story of this song?" Luke asked. Soren shook his head. The side was just ending, so Luke leaned over and spoke into the mike. "Bit of history attached to that one. It was written by a Hungarian composer who killed himself afterward, leaving the world his sheet music. The first recording inspired so many suicides that it was banned in Hungary. Then they translated it and gave it to Billie . . . *good idea, folks*. Whenever you need a little cheerer-upper, just slap old Billie on. People would dive off a roof or blow their brains out, and the cops would find the side on the turntable. Eventually they had to quit playing it on commercial radio. It was the only song that ever got banned for being too sad . . . *twice*."

Luke accepted the joint from Soren, inhaled loudly and sibilantly into the microphone. "Tasty shit," he said in a breathless pothead croak. "What is it, Mississippi home-grown? At least that fucking wasteland turns out one useful product." He exhaled extravagantly. "Hey, Martyr, guess why the governor of Mississippi refused state funding to AIDS research clinics! This is a good one. He said it was a *behaviorally caused disease* and normal taxpayers shouldn't have to foot the bill. Why waste good American money on faggot germs?"

He paused a beat to let that sink in. "So I wrote to my legislators and said I wanted a refund of all my tax dollars that went toward research on birth defects, fertility drugs, miscarriage . . . anything related to the production of the healthy human fetus. I figured, since pregnancy is a *behaviorally caused condition* whose morality—or lack thereof—I deplore, I shouldn't have to finance the disgusting problems of breeders. And guess what!"

Luke pushed the PLAY button on the cassette deck. A snarl of guitars heralded his favorite New Orleans dykecore band, Service with a Smile. *"I got fucked, fucked, FUCKED!!!"* the lead singer spat over a staticky wall of guitar. Though she covered topics as diverse as penile mutilations and IRS audits, the song only lasted a minute and a half. When it slammed to a halt, Luke was right there.

"Goddamn RIGHT I got fucked, you got fucked, anybody who ever got fucked . . . got fucked! You tested negative last week? Congratufuckalations! You don't have to worry about it again for at least six months! Doesn't that just take a load off your mind? Doesn't that just gladden your heart?

"I'm Lush Rimbaud, and I refuse to shut up or die. But my guts are churnin' and my lymph nodes a-throbbin', so I'm gonna take a break and get stoned out of my mind with Stigmata Martyr and the Skipper. Here's a whole CD for you. Something to lighten the mood a little."

He slapped on Pink Floyd's *The Wall,* pushed back his cheap aluminum lawn chair, and left the controls. Soren and the skipper, Johnnie Boudreaux, leaned on the deck rail passing the joint back and forth. The showboat was Johnnie's creation. He'd cobbled it together from a small barge, adding an outboard engine for mobility, a railing in case anyone started getting dizzy spells, and a waterproof shell to protect Soren's radio equipment.

Soren came from old-blood New Orleans, a family with nine aunts all named Marie and loads of money, at least by New Orleans boho standards. Now whatever part of his income didn't go into the station went for preventive health care. He had great faith in folk remedies. Luke sometimes wondered how Soren's herbs and amulets would hold up to a bout of crypto, but the etiquette of the infected allowed no disre-

spect of others' delusions. Whatever got you through the
night—megavitamins, creative visualization, the slow poison
of AZT—was supposed to be inviolate to criticism or mock-
ery. It didn't always work that way, of course, but Luke was
willing to let his friends kid themselves as long as they allowed him the same courtesy.

The boat was adrift on the still waters of the bayou, and the
sun was beginning to melt into the treetops, filling the swamp
with buttery green-gold light. It was one of those moments
when Luke suffered from the delusion that somehow everything could still be all right. Soren ruined it by nudging his elbow and saying, "There's a new guy in my counseling group
who wants to meet you. He's read all your books."

"What'd you do, tell him I was the DJ for your pirate radio
station?"

"Of course not, *Lucas*." It was amazing how bitchy Soren
could make someone's given name sound when he wanted to.
"No one in the group knows I run WHIV. I don't go around
bragging about my illegal activities. I simply happened to
mention that I knew you."

"Tell him to go to the Faubourg Marigny Bookstore. They
have signed copies of all my stuff."

"He wants to *meet* you, Luke. He wants to invite you out
for a cocktail in the Quarter. He's twenty, healthy, and half
Japanese, and since I know what a rice queen you are—"

Luke hunched his shoulders and scowled at Soren. "I'm not
a fucking rice queen. Quit calling me that."

"Riiiight." Soren drew the syllable out, made it rich with
cynicism. "Just because the last guy you dated was Vietnamese, and the one before that was *Laotian,* and you told the
Times-Picayune your favorite vacation spot was *Bangkok*—"

"I've never even *been* to Bangkok, you moron. It was a
joke."

"Wishful thinking, you mean."

"Y'all shut up and pass that doobie," interrupted Johnnie

Boudreaux. He was a big sweet-natured Cajun kid who knew the bayous and waterways of the swamp country as well as Luke knew the French Quarter or the Castro. Like most Cajuns, Johnnie was dark-haired and fair-skinned, though his flush of sunburn offered scant disguise for the small purple KS lesions that speckled his face, upper chest, and arms.

Although Luke wouldn't admit as much to anyone, he had an obsessive, vanity-fueled dread of KS. Johnnie didn't seem to care. Even after a lesion came up on his forehead, he kept scraping his long hair back in a careless ponytail instead of letting it hang over his face the way Luke would have done. His only concession to the lesions was to wear his gimme cap with the bill forward, to keep the sun off his face a little. Eventually the cancer would get a grip on his viscera, and he would have a choice of blistering chemotherapy, slow death, or the barrel of the antique pearl-handled revolver he always kept nearby.

"So anyway," said Soren, abandoning the rice-queen gibe for the moment, "what should I tell Tomiko?"

"Tell him I hope he stays healthy. Meeting me isn't a good way to do that."

Soren shrugged. "Your loss."

Too true, thought Luke, *my loss. But Tomiko's gain. Tran could testify to that.*

The three of them stood for a while in companionable stoned silence, elbows propped on the railing, looking out over the bayou. Roger Waters' voice twined softly round them, now furious, now wry, now stagily seductive. The day was gone. The sky had darkened to an eerie twilight purple, the water to a luminous black. Pale insects sketched ephemeral mandalas in the air. Luke heard the slither and splash of a small gator sliding off the bank into the shining water.

It was at times like this that his sorrow overtook his fury for a little while. He spent most of his days simmering in a brew of helplessness and rage, always conscious of his slow inexorable movement through a bitter life, toward a lonely death.

But here in the swamp it was easy to observe the random laziness of the universe. A virus was such a stupid thing, without meaning or purpose, yet as tenacious as life could be. How difficult it was to believe a parasite that looked like a badly molded golf ball could live in your blood and your lymph, cannibalizing the fragile helix strands of your RNA and DNA, making dissonant music with your nucleotides, turning your cells into its yes-men. A parasite so simple it made a structural marvel of the tapeworm, utterly useless, deathproof as long as its host could still draw breath and feel pain.

Yet it was in Luke and Soren and Johnnie, possibly the only thing that had brought the three of them together, possibly the only thing that could have done so. It was probably in Tran too, despite his observance of safe sex that had bordered on the fetishistic. Luke had worshiped and tormented that lithe body in every way Tran would allow . . . and then some.

He had never ejaculated inside Tran, had been expressly forbidden to do so long before he'd tested positive. But once during a languid afternoon of summer rain and shared junk, they had nodded out together, then made a clumsy but tender attempt at fucking. When Tran dozed again, sprawled on his belly with his spine arched and his smooth rump in the air, Luke stayed awake. He'd rubbed his mouth across those velvety muscular globes, licked a wet stripe down the center, teased the sweet bud of the asshole until it opened to his tongue. Forbidden fruit . . . well, mostly.

Loving Tran's passivity, he had rolled on top and rubbed himself to orgasm in the spit-damp crack of Tran's ass, then wallowed in the wet warmth of his own come for a long time before getting them both cleaned up.

There had been any number of little moments like that. And Luke, of course, had sucked up Tran's bodily fluids whenever and wherever he could get them: swallowed sperm, devoured the tender asshole, kissed the dark bead of blood from the skin of his inner elbow. They could have infected and reinfected one another dozens of times. Luke knew it; he knew Tran knew it. In the end there was no apology Luke could make for his disease.

When *The Wall* had threatened, cajoled, and suffered its way to the last song, Luke went back on the air for a while, but he was getting tired. He read some clippings he'd saved from the paper, mostly pointless statistics. One out of every eight people in Uganda was HIV-positive. AIDS approached random accidents as the top killer of American men aged twenty-five to forty-four. Here was something he could get his teeth into: the Miami dentist with AIDS had deliberately murdered his patients by shooting them up with his infected blood, said his ex-lover on a TV tabloid show. He'd wanted to change the public perception that AIDS was a gay disease.

"Dr. David Acer, leering fag demon menacing home, family, and America with a dripping syringeful of his own foul juices. Nobody would say he did the right thing, not when they first thought about it. But think about it, huh? Imagine him standing there staring down some breeder bimbo's sticky little throat, replaying in his head her idiotic chitchat with the hygienist, realizing that in a year or two he'll be dead and this cunt will be squatting out her third kid, and society will adore her as fertility goddess, pillar of blandness, ROLE MODEL, even as he rots in a pariah's grave. And just try to imagine . . . how the hypo of novocaine and the hypo that just happens to be full of his blood . . . might . . . get . . . mixed . . . up.

"Call it AIDS dementia if it makes you feel better.

"I'm Lush Rimbaud and that's it for tonight. I'll be taking calls on next week's show, same time, whatever frequency we can get, so listen up . . . unless, of course, one of us is dead by next week, or you are. And we all could be. And they don't give a fuck.

"Thank you and good night."

7

Tran shifted from foot to foot in front of the wrought-iron gate on Royal Street, then rang the buzzer again. The pavement felt terribly hard beneath the thin soles of his sneakers. He'd been pounding it for a while, and if he struck out now, he'd be pounding it some more.

He'd left his car and all his belongings in the pay lot over by Jax Brewery, forced down coffee and a single beignet, then skulked around the Quarter for hours until he worked up the nerve to come here. The sugar and caffeine made last night's drugs go swarming through his system anew, and he had to sit and stare at the river for a while just to calm down.

He'd walked past the gate once, around noon, but that was ridiculously early to drop in on a Quarter resident he barely knew. He had no idea what sort of hours Jay Byrne kept, but somehow he doubted Jay was a morning person.

Now the afternoon shadows were beginning to lengthen. Through the gate he could see into Jay's courtyard, a dark jungle of tranquility. Half-swathed in foliage, the little white house revealed nothing.

He wrapped his fingers around the black swirls of iron. "Please be there," he murmured. "Please let me in."

He wasn't even sure what he wanted here. He'd been attracted to Jay for a long time, though before yesterday they had scarcely exchanged ten sentences that weren't about buying drugs. Something about Jay's face had initially fascinated him, a pallid and dissolute gauntness he admired, though most of the other kids found it creepy. He longed to touch Jay's lank blond hair, which looked infinitely soft to him. He liked the gray shadows in Jay's eye sockets and beneath his cheekbones, his sensual lips, his pale eyes of indeterminate color. He fantasized about Jay's willowy body, so different from Luke's sturdy muscular build. The only other person he had been with was the kid at the Christmas party, Zach, whose body was like a mirror image of his own, slight and bony (and who had given Tran a cold-blooded brush-off the next time they met). He dreamed of a tall, slender man with smooth pale skin. He dreamed of Jay, masturbated to memories of Jay's face and projections of his body, found himself hoping Jay would show up to place an order at his weekly acid bazaar in a rotating series of coffeeshops. This week, Jay had.

When he asked Tran to pose for him, Tran nearly got a boner on the spot. But it wasn't as if Jay had specifically invited him here; it wasn't as if he could call Jay a friend. Tran had plenty of friends in the Quarter, but he didn't want to see any of them today.

The scene this morning had gotten to him in ways not apparent at first. Bits of it kept coming back to him all day: a florid phrase from one of Luke's letters, read aloud in his father's precise, heavily accented voice; a memory of standing in the living room, taking a last look at the empty house, wondering when he would see his mother or his little brothers again. Tran couldn't remember ever feeling so lonely, not even in the terrible twilight weeks after the breakup with Luke. He just wanted someone to wrap strong arms around him, to whisper meaningless words of comfort, to ease some of the pain.

All his French Quarter friends were young, bizarre, alienated from their families. They'd be instantly sympathetic to his problem; they would tell him his father was an asshole, and that would be that. Trouble was, Tran could see his father's point of view all too clearly. There just wasn't a damn thing he could do about it. He got so sick of people his own age sometimes.

Jay wasn't home, wasn't answering. With a sudden sense of desperation, Tran leaned on the buzzer. He didn't even know why it felt so necessary to see Jay, except that he had no other plan. He was carrying enough money to check into a hotel, but he couldn't stand the thought of sleeping by himself in an anonymous room. *Answer,* he thought, trying to send his message through the buzzer. *Please answer, please let me in, I promise you won't be sorry.*

He was about to give up and slump against the gate in despair when the intercom crackled. "Yes?" asked Jay's voice, sounding tired and dry and distant.

"It's Tran."

"I know. I can see you."

Tran glanced up at the high brick wall that fronted Jay's property. Its top was inlaid with iron spikes and decorated with coils of razor wire. At one corner of the gate was a small video camera unobtrusively pointed at the sidewalk.

"Well . . ." What to say now? Why had he even come? "I saw you yesterday. You asked me to pose for you."

A long pause, then: "Oh . . . yeah." Tran felt a lump rising in his throat. Jay could not have sounded less enthusiastic if he'd tried.

"Could you : . ." Jay's soft voice trailed off. Now he sounded disoriented, and Tran wondered if he might still be tripping. "Uh, could you come back in an hour? I'm kind of busy."

He was with another person. Tran knew it as surely as a divine revelation. He was with another person and Tran had interrupted their lovemaking. His eyes blurred with tears. He'd thought he was lonely before; now he *knew* what lonely was. "Sorry to bother you." He spun away from the intercom.

Jay's voice followed him. "No, wait! Don't go. I want to see you." Its new urgency made Tran stop and turn back toward the gate. "I'd like to take your picture tonight. I'm just sort of . . . in the middle of something. Won't you come back in an hour?"

Now Jay's voice was coaxing, almost caressing. The change was so abrupt it sent a little chill down Tran's spine. How could the man shift gears so quickly, so effortlessly? But the voice itself lured him, reminded him why he had come here. "If you're sure it will be OK," he said.

"It will be better than OK," Jay told him, and the intercom went dead. Tran was left standing on the sidewalk, his eyes still stinging with tears of embarrassment, his body suddenly, ridiculously horny.

He headed back toward Café du Monde. He hadn't slept in thirty hours; there were least five different drugs in his system; he had no current address. It was time for another cup of coffee. Tran needed to get wired.

Inside the house on Royal Street, Jay was as wired as he had ever been. Possibly he was as wired as *anyone* had ever been.

Over the course of the night, in teacup-sized increments, he'd polished off a large flask of cognac mixed with Earl Grey. He'd swallowed three hits of the acid Tran had sold him, then dissolved two more in the flask to keep the edge on his buzz. Despite the stimulants, he had managed a nap just after dawn.

But his skull still felt stuffed full of cotton, his penis was as limp and sore as a worm on a fishhook, and his jaw ached from biting again and again into unresisting flesh. The bathroom was a charnelhouse. Most of his guest's body was strewn across his bed, reeking and oozing. And Tran was coming back in an hour.

He collected the materials he would need from the kitchen and went into the bedroom. The boy—Jay could no longer think of him by any name, even the pitiful joke of Fido—lay sideways across the mattress, arms flung above his head, feet trailing on the hardwood floor. The comforter and sheets were splashed with blood from the gaping wound in his belly. Polaroid photographs littered the bed and the nightstand, depicting various stages of the guest's devolution from human to property: unconsciousness, reawakening, pain-madness, pain-daze, tranquility. Jay gathered them up, stuffed them into a drawer with hundreds of others.

He spread garbage bags and sections of an old *Times-Picayune* on the floor and lifted the boy onto them. Next to his work area he arranged a bowl of water, a roll of paper towels, several bags, and a large plastic bucket. The knife he preferred was an ordinary kitchen tool, honed very sharp but otherwise unremarkable.

He began by severing the head. The meat of the neck was tender, separating into fleshy layers beneath his blade. When he reached the spine, he inserted the tip of the knife between two vertebrae and levered them apart; at the same time he grabbed a fistful of hair and twisted the head away from the body. The spine parted with a wet click. Jay sliced neatly through the remaining flap of skin, and the head was free.

The hair was a gory scruff, the face swollen, unrecognizable. The tip of the tongue protruded between blood-smeared front teeth, nearly bitten off in some ecstasy of pain. He'd seen that before. Jay put the head in a purple plastic shopping bag from the K&B drugstore and moved on to the extremities. The hands and feet went in drugstore bags as well, rinsed in the bowl to remove the first wash of blood, then tied up neat as Christmas gifts.

Now came what ought to be the best part, the part he hated to rush through. Jay pressed his thumbs into the soft V of skin at the base of the breastbone, ran them down the line bisecting the torso until they slipped into the gaping abdominal wound. He spread the wound tenderly, pulling its edges up and apart until the skin began to tear. It was very slippery going, and he had to use the knife in places, but soon he had the body split wide open from crotch to thorax, a wet festival of scarlet.

The heat of freshly exposed organs wafted up at him. Jay lowered his face into the visceral stink, the stew of blood and shit and secret gases, the innards' rare perfume. His eyelids fluttered and his nostrils flared with pleasure. But there was no time to enjoy himself. He'd had his fun while this one was still alive. The dissection was going to be a total loss.

He pulled out yards of intestines that felt like soft boudin sausages in his hands, the shrunken pouch of the stomach, the hard little kidneys, the sluttish liver, big and gaudy as some flamboyant subtropical blossom. All went into the plastic bucket. He reached up under the ribs and slit the diaphragm, stuck his hands in the chest cavity and raked out both spongy lungs, then the rubber-textured, veined knot of muscle that was the heart.

Jay would have cracked the chest open if he'd had time; it was hard work requiring sweat and a hacksaw, but he liked the symmetrical arrangement of its various muscles and sacs, so different from the slick jumble of the belly. And the ribs, their connective cartilage severed, spread open like wings of scarlet streaked with snow.

But he was in a hurry here, and working blind. Though he could easily cut himself with the knife and risk mingling the guest's blood with his own, the worry that always plagued Jay at these moments was more arcane.

As a child, somewhere on his family's swampland, he'd stuck his hand down an enticing hollow in the roots of a live oak and something had sunk small needle-sharp teeth into his hand. Jay had seized the creature (some sort of mouse or vole) and crushed the life out of it. Then, fascinated by the way the bones felt grinding together, he had torn the soft little body to bits. But he had never forgotten the lancing pain, the panic shot through with loathing, the surety that something poisonous had hold of him. It came unbidden to his mind every time he reached inside a chest cavity.

He wore condoms during the sex he had with his guests, but that was almost incidental. He had tried wearing rubber gloves while cutting them open, unraveling them, and taking them apart, but found that he couldn't bear to. He could sheath his cock, but his hands needed to feel the silken textures of their wounds, their slick interiors. And considering the other ways in which he used their meat, he supposed it was silly to bother taking any precautions at all.

Now the body was a scooped-out shell. Shining nubs of vertebrae were visible beneath a thin layer of pearly pink tissue. Stray rags of flesh hung off the hipbones and dangled in the hollow of the abdomen, reminding Jay of the shreds of pulp left inside a jack-o'-lantern. Only the arc of the ribs seemed to retain any strength, and Jay was glad he'd left the chest intact.

He began at what had been the waist and drew his knife through flesh again and again until only the spine joined the two halves of the body. Again he inserted his knife between vertebrae, twisted, and yanked. The boy parted from himself easily, still leaking various ichors, but not in great quantity. Jay had done his work well.

He wrapped the halves in separate bags, the organs in a third—big black plastic bags designed to hold heavy, wet, stinking garbage. One by one he lugged these bags through the house, through the rear courtyard, and into the former slave quarters that ran along the back wall of his property. This building was a long, low shed with a forward-slanting roof, cramped and hot inside. Thanks to a dalliance with cocaine in his early twenties, Jay's sense of smell was not what it had once been, but even he could detect an odor in here. He propped the bags in a corner with several others in various stages of marination. Left for days or weeks, they produced amazing juices.

That had taken a little more than thirty minutes. Though he preferred to make it an art, he could get it down to a science when he had to. Back in the house, he scoured all the surfaces of the bathroom, then went through the other rooms lighting sticks of incense and every sort of candle: elegant golden tapers, fruit-scented votives, trendy voodoo fetishes of skulls and penises in black wax, Fast Luck Money Candles from the corner grocery that also sold Lotto tickets and John the Conqueror roots, religious candles with pretty young saints and lurid bleeding hearts painted on the glass holders.

Finally he wiped the floors down, changed the sheets, took a fast shower, put on some soft music, and sat down to wait for Tran. When the doorbell rang twenty minutes later, Glenn Miller was swinging on the radio and Jay was drifting in and out of uneasy consciousness. He sometimes went three or four days without real sleep, but just now he was starting to feel a bit punchy.

He buzzed Tran into the courtyard and met him at the front door, vaguely surprised to see dusk outside: where had the day gone? The kid was dressed entirely in black, tight leggings, hightop sneakers, a low-cut silk shirt that left most of his smooth chest exposed. His shiny mop of hair was pulled back in a ponytail, but long strands of it hung around his face. And the smile on that face was pure relief, as if there were no one in the world he'd rather see than creepy old French Quarter pervert Jay Byrne. *Definitely* this had been worth the whirlwind cleanup.

Tran stood at the door making no effort to enter. Jay watched him, curious to see what he would do. But he didn't do anything, just kept grinning like a fool, staring straight into Jay's eyes as if hypnotized. Normally, no one could stare Jay down; it was a game he played in the bars sometimes. But Tran held the gaze for so long that Jay finally glanced back over his shoulder, into the house. "Would you like to come in?"

"Oh! Yeah, sorry," said Tran, brushing past him into the foyer. "I did acid and X last night and I just drank three cups of coffee. I'm a little out of it."

You always seem a little out of it, Jay thought of saying. But that was no way to speak to a guest. Anyway, he had to admit that the kid's brand of spaciness was attractive. Along with the Asian androgyny of his face, it gave him an air of innocence, made him seem younger than he probably was.

They went into the parlor. The room was full of incense smoke and candleglow, dizzyingly fragrant. Jay glanced about for evidence of last night's revelry. There was Fido's coffee cup on a little side table, probably with the residue of four Halcions and three acid tabs still silting the bottom. But in the midst of all the lurid rose-gold opulence, Tran wouldn't notice a stray cup.

"Wow! What a great room!"

"Do you like it?"

"Yeah. It's so *romantic.*" Tran turned to him. Those Oriental eyes transfixed Jay with their coffee-brightness. This kid was so beautiful . . . but local, Jay reminded himself; take pictures, but don't touch him, because if you do, you might not be able to stop.

"But you know what? This music sucks."

Jay had forgotten all about the radio. Now it was blaring an instrumental version of "Seasons in the Sun" arranged for marimba and vibraphone. How embarrassing.

He waved a dismissive hand. "I don't know what that is. Change it if you like."

Tran went to the standing cabinet and twirled the dial. He found something he liked right away, a lone male voice over slow, grinding synthesizer. "Cool. This must be the LSU station from Baton Rouge. You like Nine Inch Nails?"

"Oh yes." Jay hadn't a clue who Nine Inch Nails were. He listened to music a lot, but had no discernment, no individual taste. He supposed he had been born without it. He could enjoy "Seasons in the Sun" or some other tinkling abomination; he could enjoy the bone-stirring vibrations of a Bach fugue; he could enjoy the song that was on the radio now. But he made no real distinction between these musics. He liked them all in the same uncomplaining way, and none made him feel much of anything. When he socialized with kids Tran's age, it was a constant chore figuring out which music was supposed to be cool and which was hopelessly lame.

Tran sat on one end of a purple love seat, obviously leaving enough room for Jay to join him. Jay considered it for a moment, then sat opposite instead. If this was going to lead anywhere, it would be photographs only.

"So," he said, casting about. "How was the rave?"

"The . . . ?" Tran's voice trailed off. He looked stunned, as if he had no idea how he had spent the last twenty-four hours. Then he began to laugh. "The rave. Right. If you knew how bad I wish I'd never heard about that stupid rave . . . but it would have happened some other time, sooner or later. It had to happen."

"What?" Jay asked, a little annoyed, wishing the kid would start making sense. Spaciness was attractive to a point, but manic hysteria was less so.

"Oh . . . my filial disgrace . . . my rising corpses . . . the poison in my blood. Take your pick." Tran laughed again. The sound was eerie, childish, detached. "I got kicked out of my parents' house this morning. My dad found out I'm gay and thinks I have AIDS."

"Do you?"

"Not last time I checked."

"So what's the problem?"

"The problem is . . . nobody loves me now." He scowled at the pathos of his own words, tucked a glossy lock of hair behind the multipierced curve of his ear. "I mean, I have nowhere to go. I thought . . ."

"You thought what?"

"Don't you sometimes . . ." Tran looked helplessly at Jay, who refused to help him out. He was rather enjoying the naked hope in Tran's eyes. "I had the impression you took in visitors."

"Well, I suppose I do. Sometimes. But usually they're out-of-town visitors, and they don't stay long." Jay considered his next words carefully. He was still determined to leave Tran alone. But if he let Tran stay overnight, he was sure to get some good photographs. Just possibly they would jack off together, but Jay would keep his hands to himself no matter what.

"Do you want to visit me?" he asked.

"Yes. Very much." Tran smiled that heartbreaking smile again. Then, in one fluid movement, he slid off the love seat and landed on Jay's lap. "I've wanted to visit you for a long time," he said, and covered Jay's dry lips with his own.

Jay was caught utterly off guard. By the time he realized what was going on, his hands had locked behind Tran's back and their tongues had melted together like warm chocolate. His sore cock twitched and chafed against the inside of his zipper. Tran's fingers brushed it, paused, then moved more purposefully. Jay's moan was part arousal, part pain, part thwarted resolve. He slid his right hand up under Tran's shirt and along the silken ridge of his spine, dipped his left hand beneath the waistband of Tran's leggings, and fingered the downy cleft of his ass.

Tran broke the kiss to suck in air. His eyes glittered with hectic emotion. His lips were wet, and curved in a faint smile. The pink tip of his tongue flickered out, tasting their mingled saliva.

The song on the radio ended and the DJ's voice filled the

room, low, hoarse, and hostile. "Now that one . . . that one's for my lost love, wherever he is. Are you out there, are you listening, do you still hate the sound of my voice? I guess I'll never know. Here's another one for you, my little heartworm."

In the instant before Tran's body went stiff in his arms, Jay didn't know whether he wanted to split this boy open slowly or just throw him on the floor and dive in. But suddenly Tran was off Jay's lap and hurtling across the room, yelling an unintelligible curse, snapping off a sultry female singer in midphrase.

"YOU FUCKER!!!" Tran shrieked at the ceiling. "WHY NOW? WHY HERE? HOW DID YOU FIND ME?" He raked mad claws through his hair, unraveling his ponytail, pulling strands into his stricken face. "My life . . ." Now he appeared to be hyperventilating. ". . . is . . ." He crashed to his knees on the Chinese rug, sending a subliminal shiver through all the glass and crystal in the room. ". . . SO . . . FUCKED . . . UP!"

He sprawled on the rug, sobbing. Jay had no idea what to do. He had seen plenty of boys cry before, but only at his own behest. He watched, dumbfounded. Eventually Tran's shoulders stopped convulsing; the deep raw sobs quit wrenching their way out of his gut; he rolled onto his side and lay curled in a semifetal position, facing away from Jay. Against the rug's red-and-gold pattern, his hair had the black luster of obsidian.

If Jay sat on the floor beside him, Tran would allow him to run gentle fingers through that heavy mass of hair, to lick the tears from his face, to undress him and have him right there on the floor, rug burns and all. Jay knew this as surely as he knew human anatomy. But he couldn't make himself do it, not after a display like that. Tran had revealed himself to be unpredictable, and unpredictable people were dangerous.

So he sat in his chair, still feeling Tran's phantom weight on his thighs, and he let his mind wander. It wandered naturally to the things he had done last night, and by the time Tran spoke, Jay had nearly forgotten he was there.

"I'm sorry," said Tran softly. Then, rolling over on his back and fixing his eyes on the ceiling: "No, fuck it. I'm not sorry at all. I'm sick of apologizing to everyone for stuff I have no choice about. I came here hoping you'd let me cry on your shoulder, maybe take my mind off my troubles with a good orgasm." He tilted his head to look at Jay. Jay watched him, but did not speak or move, and after a moment Tran continued. "But I knew I was gonna lose it sooner or later. See, ever since spring of this year, nothing in my life has made any sense at all. The guy whose voice you just heard on the radio, he's the reason why. He was my boyfriend for a year and a half. My *first* boyfriend. My first lover. Then he . . ." Tears threatened again, but Tran swallowed them; Jay could hear them going down the smooth passage of his throat. "He got sick. And he tried to kill me."

This stirred Jay out of his torpor. "He tried to *kill* you?"

"He tried to inject me with his blood." Tran hitched in a deep breath, then blew it out. "We used to shoot up heroin together. No big deal, just a couple times. We'd stopped by the time our HIV tests came back. His was positive, and mine . . . wasn't. We were always real careful. But I woke up one day and he'd gotten his works out . . . and drawn a syringe of blood from his arm . . . and he was about to jab it into me.

"I just looked at him, and I said, 'Luke, what are you doing?' and he said, 'I want you to love me forever,' and then he started to cry. I was afraid to reach out to him because he still had the needle in his hand. So I just sat there and watched him cry. After a while he let me take it away from him. I didn't know what to do with it, so I put it in an empty Coke bottle, the kind with the screw-on top, and I sealed up the neck with black electrical tape. I've still got it."

"Why?" Jay asked, though he was sure he knew.

"Because it was his. It was almost the last thing he gave me. I couldn't just throw it out. And because it's toxic waste."

"You never know when you'll need a weapon."

Tran acknowledged this with a small smile. "Luke always kept a razor in his boot. After he got sick, he said if anyone fucked with him, he'd slash his wrist and throw blood in their eyes."

"Would he have done it?"

"Absolutely."

Jay didn't know how to follow that up, so he said nothing. After a moment Tran said, "I guess you're wondering why I ever got involved with him."

"No, not really."

Tran didn't seem to hear. "I used to tell myself he wasn't always like that, that he changed after he got sick. But it isn't true. Luke was always crazy. There was always this undercurrent of violence in him. He's a brilliant writer, a brilliant *talker.* He always knows how to make things sound good. But even before he tested positive, every day of his *life,* he was pissed off at the world. He used to say he wished he could wake up one day and not be angry—just for one day. But he couldn't.

"Now he has this pirate radio show. That happened after we broke up, so I don't know where they do it or who the other people are. But he's the one everybody knows about. He calls himself Lush Rimbaud. I hear people around the Quarter talking about him, and I'm scared to say anything in case they realize who it is. Sometimes he advocates killing people, killing straights. Breeders, he calls them. Politicians, evangelists and stuff—but regular people too, anybody who pisses him off. The FCC would go after him in a second. I don't want him to get busted. I don't want him to die in prison."

"You still care?"

Tran thought about it, then nodded. "Yeah. I don't ever want to see Luke again, but I care what happens to him. He's the smartest person I've ever met, and the only one I've ever been in love with. I'd like him to have a good life . . . but all I can wish him now is a decent death."

A decent death. The phrase struck Jay as odd. He supposed

all the deaths he delivered were flagrantly indecent, yet that was why he enjoyed them. These were unusual thoughts for him. He spent most of his time planning how to get boys, engaging them in slow torture until they died, then playing with their components and reliving the details. But he seldom dwelled on his motivations. It was simply something he needed to do, had needed to do most of his life, had been doing for nearly ten years now. Sometimes the craving increased, and he had to have two or three in as many weeks. Sometimes it calmed, and for months he would take boys' pictures and let them leave unharmed with money in their pockets. But sooner or later the need returned, and for a long time all his guests became permanent residents.

Tran stood up and stretched. Between the hem of his shirt and the band of his leggings, Jay saw a smooth hollow of golden, hairless skin. He thought of pressing his lips to that hollow, teasing it with his tongue, then sinking his teeth in and ripping until he tasted blood, rich steaming meat, the jellied essence of life. The urge flared in his belly, sucked at his innards, made his testicles crawl. He did not move, barely dared to breathe.

"Do you mind if I wash my face? I must look awful."

Jay managed to speak through rigid lips. "Down the hall."

Tran left the room. The urge abated a little. Jay felt a sharp pain in his hands, realized he had curled them into fists and was digging his nails deep into the palms. He rubbed his eyes, dabbed sweat off his forehead and upper lip. *Just what is going on here?* he wondered. This was the most dangerous guest he'd ever allowed in his house. Tran's parents might have kicked him out this morning, but they could easily be looking for him in a few days, if not a few hours.

The craving to possess such a beautiful creature was unavoidable. But listening to Tran's anguished story, Jay had almost found himself *liking* the kid. No one had ever talked so honestly to him before. He'd had boys who trusted him unquestioningly out of stupidity, desperation, or both. He'd had boys who were openly suspicious of him from the moment they made contact until the moment they lost consciousness. But no one had ever weighed the options and made a conscious decision to trust him the way Tran seemed to have done.

Tran hadn't treated Jay like an easy trick or a potential sugar daddy, as most of the boys did. He had acted as if he were in the company of a friend. Jay had never had a live friend before, and he wasn't sure what to do with one. All his childhood playmates had shied away early, forced by their mothers to include him because he came from a good Uptown family, but always wary and frequently cruel.

His guests turned into friends after they were dead, but those friends were fathomable: they would always belong to him, because they could never leave. A living person had the option of walking away. Mummified heads and bleached bones couldn't even dream of such disloyalty. All Jay's boys became part of him. They would be with him forever, flesh of his flesh, loving him from the inside.

He sat quietly and waited for Tran to return.

Tran splashed cold water on his face and let it drip while he stared at himself in the huge mirror above the sink. Jay's bathroom was decorated entirely in black-and-white squares, tiny ones on the walls, big ones on the floor. The counter, sink, towels, shower curtain, and Jay's toothbrush (draining in a crystal glass) were black; the toilet and tub were of spotless white porcelain. The bottom of the sink was lightly beaded with water, but not so much as a stray hair sullied its gleaming surface. The bathroom contained no reading material, no visible grooming products except a bar of white soap, a roll of white toilet paper, and a matte-black shampoo bottle.

Tran thought of the family bathroom back home, its counter littered with his various hair products, skin potions, stray eye-liner pencils, and the twins' bubblegum-flavored sparkle toothpaste. There were colorful towels, discarded T-shirts and underwear, an old foam cooler full of his brothers' tub toys in the corner. It looked decidedly lived in. But Tran could see no indications that a human being used this bathroom every day.

There were three drawers beneath the sink. Tran slid them open one by one. The top drawer contained toothpaste, a safety razor and a pricey-looking tube of shaving gel, a silver brush and comb, scissors, a deodorant stone. The middle one was empty. In the bottom drawer was a Ziploc bag full of something soft and multicolored. When Tran picked it up, he realized it was human hair of all shades and textures, some obviously dyed. He put it back hurriedly, feeling as if he'd stumbled onto a seedy secret.

There was a cabinet tucked away beneath the sink too, its edges flush with the rest of the wood, barely visible. He slipped his fingers into the recessed groove of its handle and it whispered open. Inside was a bucket full of water that smelled vaguely of disinfectant. Immersed in the water were several evil-looking sex toys: fleshy pink and glossy black, jellied latex and molded plastic, double-headed, double-pronged, ribbed, nubbed, and flared. After the bag of hair, the shock value of these was minimal. Still, Tran couldn't help but imagine Jay using one of the toys on him, murmuring in his ear, stroking the curve of his back, working the strange shape deep into his intestine.

He rinsed his mouth out with Jay's toothpaste and left the bathroom. Across the hall was the bedroom, a few candles flickering in its shadowed depths. He could see little more than an expanse of gleaming hardwood floor and a very large bed. As he came back down the hall, he noticed the arched entryway to the kitchen on his left. It too was dark, but looked as spotless and shiny as the bath.

He reentered the parlor, where Jay sat as rigid and motionless as Tran had left him. The candles bathed his face in golden light. The smoke from the incense sticks swathed his head and upper body, made him look ethereal. His face in profile was as sternly serene as an angel's. Tran wanted to go to him, sit with him, continue what Luke had interrupted. But he couldn't make himself do it; he had no idea what Jay had thought of his outburst, or whether he was even welcome here.

He leaned against the doorjamb. Sudden shyness rose in his throat, threatened to choke him. "Do you still want me to pose for you?" he asked, so softly he wasn't sure Jay had heard him at first.

Jay stirred, but did not look at Tran. "No . . . not just now."

"Do you want me to leave?"

"That might be best."

Not for me, Tran thought. His heart sank; his balls ached. The bathroom had creeped him out a little—not the strange items in the drawer and cabinet so much as the total sterility of it, the difficulty of believing a man washed, shaved, crapped here every day. He'd heard the word on the street about Jay: the guy was an odd, cold fish; he would suck you off without ever looking you in the eyes; his house smelled funny. He was said to be very rich, with all the accompanying eccentricities. But Tran didn't care about that. The few times he'd spoken to Jay, he had sensed an aura of power under wraps, of utter control. This man would find out his deepest desires, and would be capable of twisting them into pain as well as pleasure.

He'd experienced a similar certainty when he met Luke, and he had been right. But while Luke's power was alpha-male raw, Jay's seemed infinitely refined.

He didn't want to leave. He wasn't sure he could stand to be turned out of another place today. The picture of himself nestled in the pale curve of Jay's arms, sated with sex and ready for sleep, had sustained him for so long that now he could not imagine spending the night any other way.

Feeling like a manipulative little shit—an epithet Luke had once blessed him with—Tran stepped in front of Jay's chair, unbuttoned his shirt, and let it whisper off his shoulders onto the rug. He felt Jay's eyes honing in on his bare chest. "I don't care if you take my picture," he said. "I'll do anything you like. I just want to know you. Please don't make me go."

Jay stood. He was about six inches taller than Tran, and his lankiness disguised a strong, wiry build. Tran wanted nothing more than to step into Jay's arms, press his face into Jay's chest, and wait to be ravished. But Jay only grasped Tran by the shoulders and stared into his face, looking half angry, half puzzled. "What is it you want here? What do you mean, you want to know me? *Why?*"

"Because you fascinate me," Tran told him honestly.

Jay sighed, let his hands drop, then slowly slid them back up Tran's bare ribcage. Tran's skin shuddered into gooseflesh at the touch. He forced himself to remain still, to let Jay do the touching for now. Jay wanted to be in charge, just as Luke always had.

Jay's thumbs grazed Tran's nipples, paused, then traced lazy circles around them. A small ecstatic whimper escaped Tran's throat. He let his head fall back, offering the smooth line of his throat to Jay in supplication. Jay's lips fastened on the V of his collarbone, moved up his throat and along his jawline, brushed his mouth. Then Jay pulled back, and his eyes were terrifying in their intensity, flecked with bright candlepoints, hazed with lust so urgent it bordered on pain.

"You better be ready for whatever happens," he told Tran. His voice was full of dark promise.

"Anything," Tran whispered.

In the candle-dark bedroom they kicked off their shoes, grabbed each other, and fell roughly onto the bed, wrestling, attacking, surrendering. Jay hooked his thumbs under the waistband of Tran's leggings and yanked them halfway down. They snagged on Tran's hard-on, then slipped over it.

He got his own pants undone, struggled out of them, and
rolled on top of Tran, enfolding the boy's sleek limbs with his
clumsy ones. "Your body feels so good," Tran breathed in his
ear. This threw Jay for a second: most boys didn't talk to him
in bed, even when they were still conscious. He didn't know if
he should answer or not.

He sought Tran's mouth and sealed it with his own, evad-
ing the issue entirely. Jay liked to kiss deep and rough; the
slick membranes of a boy's mouth made him hungry. He
sucked on Tran's lips until they were raw, invaded Tran's
throat with his tongue. Tran wrapped skinny arms around him,
scratched lightly at his back with sharp little nails. Their hips
nudged and their legs intertwined. Jay's cock was so hard he
thought it might rupture. What a boy, what a fabulously exquisite creature had come to him willingly, *willfully.* This must
be a gift from whatever dark gods he appeased with his ob-
sessions, a perfect bonbon he could rip into as he pleased . . .

Jay shied away from that line of thought. This boy was no
gift. He was a drug dealer, for Christ's sake, a well-known
face in the Quarter, a New Orleans native with family here.
Harming him would be sheer folly. Never mind the entrancing
fragility of his bones. Never mind how the taut expanse of his
belly felt beneath Jay's hands, trembling with the secret move-
ments of organs just below the surface.

Tran raised his arms above his head and arched his back,
thrusting his ribcage up at Jay. The expression on his face was
part fear, part naked arousal. His eyes and his wet mouth glittered in the semidarkness. As far as Jay was concerned, the kid
might as well have the words PLEASE RIP ME OPEN scrawled
on his chest in Magic Marker.

To distract himself from fantasies of viscera, Jay lowered
his head and sucked one of Tran's nipples. It was as hard and
brown as a cinnamon candy under his tongue. Tran's skin
smelled of soap and some faint musk. Tran's fingers wandered
through Jay's hair, urging his head lower. Jay avoided touch-

ing the underside of the ribcage or any part of the abdomen.
Instead he grabbed Tran by the hipbones, nature's perfect handles, and buried his face between Tran's legs. At once he was
lost in a world of fragrant sweat, soft black hair tickling his
eyelids, silk-rippled flesh throbbing against his lips. He licked
a wet swath from the base of Tran's balls all the way to the
head of his cock, then took the cock deep into his mouth.

The sensation of engorged tissue sliding over his tongue
and filling up his throat was nearly too much to bear. Jay
clawed at Tran's ass, at the scant meat of his thighs. Tran went
very still; then a long shudder went through his body. "Jay—
oh Jay I'm gonna come—don't swallow—ah—"

Tran tried to pull away. Jay seized those sharp hipbones
again, forced his throat around the shaft of Tran's cock, getting
it as deep in his mouth as it would go. When his gag reflex
challenged him, Jay took a deep breath and willed it away. He
might never taste this boy's blood or meat, but he would not
be denied the salty savor of his sperm.

Here it came, spilling over the back of his tongue, dripping warm and faintly caustic down his throat. Tran was
making unbelievable sounds: gasps, sobs, little shrieks. Jay
swallowed again and again. Tran's come was thick, copious,
and ever so slightly bitter. Jay imagined it brewing in the secret sacs and tubes of his testicles, rich with all the chemicals
Tran had recently ingested, a heady concentrate. Spermato-
zoa, proteins, intoxicating extracts from the prostate and the
Cowper's gland . . .

His erection was plaguing him again, shouting for attention.
He moved up beside Tran, kissed his mouth and his eyelids,
guided Tran's hand to his cock. Tran's fingers closed around it
gratefully and moved up and down, gentle at first, then a little
rough, squeezing, eager . . . then gentle again, painfully so.
Whatever else this Luke character may have done to Tran, he had
taught the kid to handle another man's penis with care and skill.

"You shouldn't have swallowed my come," Tran murmured. "I told you . . ."

"I needed it."

Something in Jay's tone shut Tran up. His hand kept rubbing, sliding, stroking. In another minute or two Jay would be on the verge of orgasm, and this worried him. Most of the boys who left his house unharmed were those he had only photographed. He had ended up in bed with a few, giving them what they wanted, sucking them off and letting them go. But no one ever survived once Jay had come.

A bloody haze began to creep into the edges of his vision. Waves of pleasure foamed in his brain. A dark gobbet of tissue hung from his mouth, slapping his chin . . . no, that was last night, that was memory.

"Fuck me," Tran gasped. "I want you inside me." He was up off the mattress, instinct leading him to the nightstand drawer and the box of lubricated condoms there (though not the gore-encrusted shrimp deveiner tucked away deep in the back). In a single practiced movement he tore one of the foil squares open, extracted the condom, and sheathed Jay's hard-on in a thin layer of latex.

Then Tran was on his back again, pulling his knees up to expose two heartbreaking half-moons of flesh with a molten pink eye at their center. The asshole hypnotized Jay, drew him in like a vortex. No one had ever voluntarily shown him their asshole before. The gesture impressed him as one of trust . . . of *choosing* to trust, like Tran's decision to talk to him in the first place.

But what had he told himself after Tran talked to him? Unpredictable. Dangerous. Off-limits. If he fucked this boy, he would surely kill him. And that would be so very bad for so many reasons.

He found himself half on top of Tran, straddling the boy's narrow hips, the head of his cock easing into the tight heat of Tran's ass. "Put it in, put it *in!*" Tran begged, rocking under him. How easy it would be to plunge into that slick sleeve of muscle and membrane, to lose himself in that welcoming maze with no thought for the consequences. Maybe he could do it. Maybe Tran was the one boy who could survive his orgasm. Maybe it would be nice to share an afterglow with someone who still breathed.

Jay felt his eyes blur with tears. He *wanted* Tran to stay alive, he wanted that so much. He never used to want his lovers dead. In the beginning he had only wanted them to stay with him, and it seemed no one ever would, not if given a choice in the matter. Somewhere along the way, control became a pleasure in itself. Then it became the main pleasure. He drugged boys and took pictures of their slack, helpless bodies and stared into their unknowing faces as he strangled them.

Eventually strangulation wasn't enough; he wanted them to *react,* and he began waking them before they died, hurting them a little, then hurting them a lot. He fell in love with the insides of their bodies, found that he preferred them to the outsides.

But for all his desire to worship Tran's insides, there was equal longing not to hurt him at all, to slide into him and move with him and make him feel good, to hold him afterwards and listen to his breathing, to bask in his warmth that would not leach away.

"Jay! *Fuck* me!" Tran slid his hands down to Jay's ass and tried to pull Jay forward, into him. Jay's cock slid in a little deeper; Tran groaned, a hoarse, wildly erotic sound; and Jay understood without a doubt that if he penetrated Tran's body in this way, he wouldn't stop until Tran was split wide open.

He made a conscious decision to stop, something he had never done before. It took every ounce of his will to make himself pull back, pull out. Luckily, his reserves of will were considerable. "I can't possibly fuck you," he told Tran. "You really ought to leave."

Tran's face was a study in shock. His eyes glittered black with tears of frustration. "What do you *mean* you can't fuck me?" he demanded.

"I just can't. I'm not in the mood anymore. Forget it."

He pulled the condom off his softening penis, deposited it in a sticky little heap on the nightstand, and lay waiting for something else to happen. If nothing did, he could easily lie here all night. A lovely numbness was beginning to steal over him. His bones felt soft, his tissues steeped in liquid opium.

He thought of Tran's legs drawn up, offering himself. He thought of Luke (a bulky faceless figure) on top of Tran as he had just been, but treating the poor kid right, screwing him deep and hard, giving him everything he wanted and maybe a little more.

Neither image affected Jay at all.

Something brushed his hand. Tran's fingers, sweaty and timid, sliding into his grasp. "It's OK," Tran said. "Let me know if you change your mind. Maybe if we get to know each other a little better . . ."

Right, thought Jay. *I'm sure you'd be thrilled if you really got to know me, saw how I spend my evenings, met some of my friends.* But he only said, "Maybe so."

Tran sighed. "Look, I hate to ask . . ."

"What?"

"Can I still stay here? Just for tonight? I really don't have anywhere else to go."

"Sure."

"I'll sleep on the couch if you want."

"Don't worry about it." Jay realized he no longer felt any attraction to Tran, though he liked having the lithe, warm body in bed with him. He had turned off those feelings, and there was no danger now. Hurting Tran at this point was no more likely than ripping his pillow to shreds. The boy was only a comfort, a fleeting one that would be gone tomorrow.

The drugs were completely flushed out of his system now, and Jay found that he was exhausted. He squeezed Tran's hand once, a gesture as unfamiliar to him as friendship itself. Then he rolled over and fell at once into a deep, dreamless sleep.

• • •

Tran lay staring at Jay's smooth back, aching with horniness
and disappointment. He could not fathom what had happened.
He'd been reveling in Jay's touch and taste, anticipating the
delicious sensation of Jay's cock filling his ass. They had
come so close to losing themselves in each other. Then, this.

He had been with no one since the breakup, nearly eight
months now, and there had been moments when he wondered
if Luke had ruined him for sex altogether. When Jay led him
to the bedroom, Tran thought that notion was about to be laid
to rest. Now he felt worse than ever.

There was no way he was going to sleep anytime soon. He
sat up, swung his legs over the side of the bed, balanced shak-
ily on his feet. Blood rushed to his head, making him dizzy
and momentarily obscuring his vision. He felt his way to the
bedroom door and down the hall.

When he reached the kitchen, he realized he was ravenous.
Surely Jay wouldn't mind if he fixed himself a snack. The
floor and countertops were spanking clean, as was the inside
of the refrigerator. Tran found bread, mustard and mayon-
naise, some kind of thinly sliced meat on a Saran-Wrapped
plate. He made a sandwich and poured himself a glass of milk.
His stomach growled at the rich scents, and he realized he had
eaten nothing but a beignet since yesterday afternoon.

He took his snack into the parlor and sat cross-legged in the
center of the rug, scene of his freakout. The meat was rare and
tender, like a special kind of beef his mother sometimes
bought from the Vietnamese butcher. The milk was cold and
fresh. He finished everything, carried his dishes back into the
kitchen and rinsed them, set them in the rack to dry.

He felt better now, but he was still ridiculously horny.

He found himself in the bathroom without quite knowing
how he had gotten there. The cabinet below the sink was open,
the bucket of sex toys before him, singing its siren song. Tran
watched his hands dip into the bleachy-smelling water, select
a long, slender jelly-pink dildo that closely resembled Jay's

cock in size and shape, rinse the thing in warm tap water. He glanced at the door, then walked over and closed it.

His prostate throbbed, demanding attention. Before he met Luke, Tran hadn't even known where his prostate gland was. The idea of getting fucked in the ass seemed vaguely embarrassing until he tried it. Luke had taken his virginity gently, but not too gently. There was a spot about four inches up his ass that felt heavenly when Luke's cock pressed against it, and from the first internal orgasm that traveled up his spine and spread in ever-expanding circles through his body, Tran was hooked.

He couldn't find any lubricant, so he climbed into the tub, soaped up the dildo, and eased it in. As he rode it, he played with his nipples, pinching and pulling, thinking of Jay's mouth on them. But Jay had refused to play rough with him, almost as if he were afraid he might hurt Tran. Tran wouldn't have minded being hurt a little. Luke had always left his nipples sore. Luke had fucked him so deep it made him scream, so deep he could feel Luke's cock hitting the upper curve of his intestine.

As he arched his back and came from the inside, Tran reflected that for someone he never wanted to see again, Luke certainly turned up in his thoughts a lot. It bothered him, but there didn't seem to be much he could do about it.

So he gave in to his fantasies, and as he lay clutching himself in the tub where another boy had met an agonizing death just hours ago, he imagined himself back in Luke's arms, his cheek pressed against Luke's chest, and all Luke's perverse power flowing into him, making him feel safe, strong, loved.

8

Back at the motel, Luke scrolled a piece of paper into his typewriter, stared at it for a while, then centered the carriage and began to type. He worked at a tiny table barely large enough to hold a bottle, a glass, and the Smith-Corona electric; the ice bucket and the accumulating stack of pages had to go on the dresser behind him. He soaked up cheap whiskey as he worked, pouring himself a half-inch every hour or so, occasionally wetting his lips with its amber burn, chasing a vague buzz but never quite getting drunk. The pages came slowly. The constant ache somewhere deep in his core was kept at bay.

This book was the story of his and Tran's collapse in flames, of course, mutated and tortured until only the raw nerves of it were recognizable. Luke knew these wounds were too fresh to write about, but it wasn't as if he could return to them in times of tranquility; he had no more hope of tranquility in this life. Too much of the story was told in second person accusatory, more paean than plot, more character assassination than character development. He was pretty sure it sucked, and he doubted he would ever finish it. Still the pages piled up on the dresser. He could not abandon this spiritual autopsy any more than he could shut up Lush Rimbaud.

His radio persona had been conceived in the glory days of early junk use. Lush Rimbaud was a name he gave his heroin-induced self, a brain of utter clarity tethered to a body like an exquisite vessel brimming with pleasure, spiked with fury, a personality composed of liquids that could not mix.

He was twenty-five then, and had just published his first novel, *Faith in Poison*. The book was a distillation of his adolescence in small-town Georgia, his abortive Baptist upbringing, his escape. For some reason, seeing his own name on the cover had compelled him to invent an alias. Rimbaud was for the mad boy poet who had scrawled scatological letters to Paul Verlaine in Paris cafés. Blood and shit were among his greatest passions. At nineteen he'd tormented Verlaine into shooting him, but escaped with a flesh wound, drank up every franc he ever made, later ran off to Africa, lost a leg, and died of a fever at thirty-seven. The title of Luke's novel came from Rimbaud's poem "Drunken Morning." *We have faith in poison. We will give our lives completely, every day . . .*

The book was universally revered or reviled. The praise was lavish and slightly shell-shocked, as if Lucas Ransom had begun by massaging the reader's brain stem, then delivered a quick sharp blow to the back of the neck. The disparagement was similar, but with an aggrieved tone, as if the novel had deeply and personally offended the revilers. Luke was pleased by both reactions. He had no use for middle ground.

It was 1986 in San Francisco and he was riding high on infamy, maintaining a medium-strength junk habit and supplementing it with every other drug that came through the Castro, doing the best work of his life and getting paid for it, feeling as if he'd found the elixir of perfect existence: notoriety, heroin, and as much sex as he could stand, which was a lot. His steady boyfriends tolerated one another with varying degrees of unease; sometimes he could charm two into bed at once. His side dishes were numerous and delectable. There was a recurring Oriental theme to the banquet.

The young gay scene in mid-eighties San Francisco included bloodlines running back to every Asian country Luke had ever heard of, and then some. He sampled them all, a dim sum feast of sweet cocks and smooth asses and skinny bodies and beautiful fine-boned faces. At one point he'd started coloring in a mental map that reflected his sexual history: China, Japan, Korea, India, Thailand, Laos, Bali . . .

He was surprised by this specialization of his tastes, and could not explain it even to himself. He simply craved them, the perfect single folds of their eyelids, the slippery coarseness of their hair, the sandalwood taste of their skin, their skinny ivory bones. Eventually he became known for it, and they would approach him. To some of them, Luke's dissipated-frat-boy good looks were as exotic as their ebony hair and golden skin were to him. Back then he was too young and too desirable to be called a rice queen.

Lush Rimbaud was embryonic then, just a sybarite seed in the fertile ground of Luke's ego. It had only been a name he used sometimes. It hadn't started developing like some malignant alternate personality until after he tested positive. Lush Rimbaud had been fathered by junk. Seven years later, the HIV virus gave birth to him.

He left San Francisco right after his short story collection *Rack of Enchantments* (titled from the same Rimbaud poem) was published. The backbiting had begun in earnest, and he was sick of other hot young gay writers who didn't think there was room for one more. He was also sick of bitchy queens who cut him dead because he wouldn't fuck them, sick of empty-headed muscle fags who thought he was one of them because he liked working out, even sick of pretty Asian boys who fucked him just because they knew they could.

About the only people he wasn't sick of were other junkies. He spent three and a half years bumming around the country, feeling terribly beat with his motorcycle jacket and his battered boots, his typewriter and his low-grade habit. He found junk in every city he visited, usually within a day or so. Heroin made immediate acquaintances but few friends. This was fine with Luke; he had always preferred to have few friends. He finished another novel, *Liquid Altar,* and made notes on a related work called *Raw Shrine.*

One of the things that had soured him on San Francisco was the death pall that seemed to hang over the city. It was the queerest town in America, and by the late eighties it felt like a plague zone. AIDS had eaten huge holes in the older gay population, levying an outrageous surcharge for the revels of the preceding decade. He saw healthy, HIV-negative men in their forties and fifties committing suicide simply because they were so demoralized. They had been the first generation to come out publicly, the first ones to give a big fuck-you to a cold heterocentric world, the first ones to discover and define themselves through sex. Luke could understand their bitterness. They'd tried to celebrate their nascent freedom by throwing themselves a festival of promiscuity, but an uninvited guest had shown up in the guise of a lover and mowed the party down.

New Orleans hadn't seemed as gloomy, not at first. There was a miasma hanging over the city, to be sure. But this miasma was one of dark decadence and sweaty sex, not of death. Luke landed there in 1990 by no particular design, got laid a lot, found a bookstore that stocked his work and was thrilled to have him come in to sign. Soon enough he could think of no real reason to move on. He had his apartment in the Marigny, the signing advance for his next two books, and a whole French Quarter full of cheap booze and lissome queer boys.

The city's atmosphere was such an opiate to his soul that he decided to kick for a while, and did, enduring the sickness as he would a bout of flu or a really bad hangover. He loved heroin, but he abhorred the idea of needing a drug nearly as much as that of needing another person.

A year later he met Tran, and everything changed forever.

They turned up at the same party, a cruisy catered affair given by friends of another writer Luke didn't particularly like. He almost hadn't gone. Some Quarter kids crashed the party looking for free alcohol, which was tolerated because they were mostly young and cute. They brought along the silent, scared-looking, drop-dead-beautiful Vietnamese boy they'd met in Jackson Square earlier that night. Tran was an extremely young nineteen, a good shorthaired Oriental son making his first hesitant attempts at being bad. He was drunk on the sweet pink wine the kids had been passing around, and sat in a corner holding his head, his thin body jerking with an occasional hiccup, looking so sick that even the most avid prowlers stayed away.

Luke had just turned thirty, and was wondering if he could still trust himself. He didn't want to watch this beautiful kid puke his guts up in front of everyone, or pass out and get groped by a stranger. But the kid looked like jailbait and Luke had no idea if he was gay.

He'd gotten Tran up and out of the party, walked him around the block, waited a discreet distance away while Tran vomited pink wine into some banana plants. After that, Tran staggered into Luke's arms and tried to kiss him, which clarified one aspect of the situation. The kiss landed on the side of Luke's neck, sloppy and wine-scented, making his cock and his nipples harden nonetheless. They stood on the street corner, just outside the circle of a gas lamp's glow, their arms wrapped loosely around each other, Luke supporting the full weight of the frail, shaky body.

"How old are you?" he asked Tran.

"How old do I have to be?" Tran mumbled into his shoulder.

Luke liked that answer a lot. Even in extremis, this kid

seemed fairly perverse. Luke helped him find his car and loaded him into it, drove him all the way out to East New Orleans, kissed his cheek and watched him stumble into the house. He left the car parked in the driveway and sat on the curb until dawn, then walked back to the highway and caught a bus downtown. People waiting for buses were routinely held up at gunpoint out here. Luke didn't care. Tran's phone number was scrawled on a piece of paper in his pocket, giving him a warm feeling when he reached into his jacket and touched it.

When he finally got home, he sat down at the typewriter and started writing Tran a letter, the first of a hundred or more. *Through your haze of drunkenness I saw a fierce and obvious intelligence, and no drug could hide your beauty . . .*

He never thought he would mail it. As it turned out, he didn't have to. The next day, he dialed the number Tran had given him, half expecting it to be a fake. Tran answered, sounding slightly embarrassed, vastly grateful, and not at all hung over. They arranged to meet that night in a French Quarter coffeehouse. Luke bought Tran three iced lattes and gave him the letter, along with inscribed copies of his four books. Back at Luke's apartment, they spent a delicious hour kissing, nuzzling, rolling around on the bed fully clothed, pressing their hard-ons together through maddening layers of fabric. Toward the end of the hour, Tran finally admitted that he was a virgin.

The next week was the longest of Luke's life, and the most sweetly excruciating. He saw Tran every day, and he knew they were going to fuck soon, but he didn't know when. It was like being in high school: first base, second base, and so forth. When he sat down to write, his train of thought wandered—*he let me kiss his nipples last night, and his belly, I got all the way down to the top of his pants and I could feel what a raging boner he had, will he let me touch it tonight, strip him naked, suck his dick, at least put his hand on mine, OH GOD I WANNA BE INSIDE HIM SO BAD . . .*

He had to masturbate before he could get any work done.

The situation was untenable but exquisite. Luke wondered if he was in love. He had been in love a few times, but never with someone he hadn't fucked first, and never so *helplessly*. He felt as if he would do anything for Tran, even wait.

He didn't have to wait long. A week after the night of the party, Tran showed up at the apartment with a wicked little gleam in his eye. He'd told his parents he would be sleeping elsewhere that night, and not to worry, though of course they would. *I want you to show me everything,* Tran whispered as they got naked and slipped into bed. *Just be careful.*

Looking back on it, Luke thought that had been the theme of their entire relationship. *Show me the heights of experience, and their seedy depths. Drive me mad with pleasure, then tease me with pain. Take me to the edge, share your joy and fury, know my body like you know your own. But don't forget to wrap it all in latex.* Back then, though, he probably would have sprayed his dick with Lysol and worn two condoms if that was what it took to breach the virgin sanctity of Tran's perfect ass.

At first Luke couldn't figure out what was different about Tran, why he'd fallen so hard for this particular cute Asian boy when there were so many in the world. Part of it was the fact that Tran hadn't been instantly attainable. He had presented a challenge. But the thrill of the chase couldn't account for their intimate, intense conversations, or the part-protective, part-voracious gnawing deep in Luke's gut when their bodies interlocked, or the sense of completion they felt in each other's company.

Spending so much time with Tran reminded Luke what it was like to be nineteen: poised on the brink of your own life, wanting to know everything, to experience all sensations. Tran was like a raw nerve cell in a world of constant sensory input. He felt things deeply, laughed easily, got his feelings hurt often. He was at once elated and terrified by his emergent sexuality, and Luke found the combination exhilarating.

Tran was also very smart, and curious about everything. He was talented at intricate pastimes that left Luke mystified: computer programming, cooking, reading the *I Ching*. He said he wanted to be a writer, which made Luke slightly nervous, but so far he seemed to be stuck in the notebook-hoarding stage. Eventually he let Luke read some of these notebooks, the same kind Luke had kept at nineteen with their tattered, soft-cornered covers, their spiral bindings full of the shredded leavings of ripped-out pages. It was mostly diary stuff—Tran was still his own main character—but the voice was clear and engaging, with traces of stylistic extravagance.

All in all, Tran's company made Luke feel as if he'd been getting intellectually and emotionally lazy prior to their meeting. The relationship inspired him to cram his brain with information, to stretch the possibilities of his intelligence, to read and write whenever he wasn't having blissful sex with his new lover.

Six months in, they weathered the Christmas party affair with minimal damage. Luke suspected that incident had been Tran's way of testing him, a venture into dangerous territory to see how much shit he would brook. He brooked none, but how strange it felt to be on the other side of infidelity! He wished he could apologize to all the boys who'd ever had to listen to his antimonogamy riff: *I refuse to limit my range of experiences; you can deal with it or walk, your choice, but I'm not changing.* He cringed to think of that now, because if any of those boys had cared for him a tenth as much as he cared for Tran, Luke knew how deeply his smug words must have cut.

It was the longest monogamous relationship Luke had ever had, the only one Tran had ever had, and they were determined to explore all its avenues. Tran was in the process of breaking away from the loving but vastly overprotective confines of a Vietnamese home, and Luke found it fascinating to watch him seek out new thrills. Tran tended to get in trouble when he drank, so they smoked pot, inhaled nitrous oxide, tripped on acid a number of times. Luke had never been crazy about acid—he was already pretty well unfiltered, and all the sensory input made his brain ache—but Tran loved it, and mushrooms too.

Things got a little weird when Tran decided he wanted to try heroin. Luke decided to go along with it. He'd always been able to maintain occasional use without letting it get heavy. Shooting up again now would be like visiting an old friend he hadn't seen in a while; a volatile and temperamental friend, to be sure, but a faithful one.

So he looked up some of his old connections, scored a bag and tested it by himself. The first stuff he got was low-grade; it numbed his fingertips, sent pins and needles up his spine, left a nasty medicinal taste in his mouth. He threw it away and told Tran he hadn't been able to score, but would keep trying. Eventually the sweet payload came through, the gingery stuff that took you down smooth and slow. Injecting Tran, finding the vein in that healthy firm-textured skin and puncturing it with his needle, Luke was as nervous as he had been their first night in bed.

To Luke's relief, Tran enjoyed himself on heroin but seemed unaffected by its more insidious charms. You couldn't get hooked with your first shot, like the straights said, but some people took to a heroin high so strongly that the old saw might as well have been true. Tran said he'd be happy to do it again next week or never. So they toyed with junk occasionally, but Luke didn't get his habit back, and Tran never had anything resembling a habit. They found each other more intoxicating than any drug.

Tran still lived at home, but he spent most nights with Luke, and his parents tolerated his absence as long as they didn't have to think too much about what he might be doing. According to Tran, they thought he was sowing wild oats and would soon settle down, marry a nice Vietnamese girl, and become a partner in the family restaurant. They even had a particular Vietnamese girl in mind, a former high school classmate Tran eloquently characterized as "a brown-nosed dweeb."

Luke wondered how long Tran expected to keep up this slacker's charade, living rent-free, doing what he pleased but committing to nothing, shuttling between two worlds. It seemed a fool's paradise, but of course Luke had abandoned his own family at seventeen. His parents hadn't been so bad: hardscrabble Georgia crackers, barren until late in life, they had always seemed old to him. It was the town that had driven Luke away, the bland contempt in his neighbors' eyes, the rapacious cruelty of his classmates, the smug ignorance, the eternal exhortation to pair off and breed.

But Tran had been lucky enough to grow up in New Orleans instead of rural Georgia, and Luke surely didn't begrudge him the hope of maintaining a relationship with his family. All in all, things were good.

Then they got tested together, and everything fell apart.

Luke had never taken an AIDS test in San Francisco. He knew he would want to kill himself immediately if he turned up positive, and he couldn't afford suicide; there was still too much writing he had to do. If he did have it, he would know the cause of infection, though not its exact source. He had always been obsessively careful with needles. He had never been careful with sex.

He would wear a condom if his partners asked him to, would refrain from coming in their mouths if they insisted. But there was little he wouldn't do with an acquiescent partner. Safe sex struck him as a form of living death. How could you lust after someone without wanting to taste his fluids? How could you love someone without wanting to seek out his innermost membranes and spend your pleasure there?

When Luke tested positive, Tran had tried to deal with it and keep on loving him. Luke realized that now. But at the time, a little over a year ago, it had seemed as if Tran just wanted to get away. Hardly surprising; what twenty-year-old kid could confront the specter of his own death, let alone the reality of a dying lover? It had gone bad, very bad. Luke began to see himself as if from a distance, a writerly part of his brain observing his own madness, storing even this for later. He might have no more tranquility in which to remember this emotion. It didn't matter; the mill never quit grinding away.

They tried to separate, kept peeling apart and slipping back together like the edges of a wound that would not heal. Somewhere along the way, Luke found himself wanting to hurt Tran, to hurt himself and bleed into Tran, to let a condom slip or tear. He caught himself getting physically abusive in small ways, shoving Tran into the pillows, holding him down on the bed, grinding those delicate bones a little too hard.

Tran took every bit of it. He didn't have much choice, since Luke still outweighed him by forty pounds, but his tongue stilled and his eyes flared with resentment. He began finding reasons to stay away. Luke remembered the wretched exultation he'd felt when he first realized Tran was afraid of him: a spasm of self-loathing so great it was almost pride. Soon after that, Tran bailed. A rash of interminable phone calls at odd hours, a plethora of endlessly revised scheming letters, and then nothing. Nothing at all for a very long time.

It was too much to think on now, right after doing a show. He crawled out of the hole in the page, hauling himself on bony knees and bruised elbows. He dragged his fevered brain out last. It was nearly nightfall. He'd been writing all day, hadn't slept in thirty-six hours. Sometimes he thought heroin was the only thing that had ever let him sleep.

Outside, Airline Highway was cracking one bleary eye and shaking off last night's hangover. Luke could hear souped-up engines going by, the subliminal hum of neon, the occasional dull pop of gunfire. He sensed a hive of activity in the rooms around him, comings and goings on the veranda. Cheap sex and business deals of all kinds. There was junk out there, pure and merciful.

He couldn't stay in the room any longer. He slung his jacket over his shoulders, pulled his boots on, went out and sat in his car with the windows rolled up and the tape deck blasting Bauhaus' last album, *Burning from the Inside*. Peter Murphy only sang half the songs on the album, officially because he'd been in hospital recovering from double pneumonia. Rumor had it that his pneumonia symptoms bore a remarkable resemblance to heroin withdrawal. The emaciated, androgynous singer had once bragged about a psychic's prediction that he would die of AIDS in Paris; now he had a kid.

As far as Luke was concerned, Murphy should be here begging to trade places with him. *Sure, breeder,* he'd say, unzipping his pants, *suck my dick, then go buy yourself a ticket to Paris.*

He huddled in the bucket seat and wrapped his arms around himself. His leather jacket creaked softly, familiar as the sound of a lover's breathing. The bulk of it reminded him what it felt like to be strong.

9

I stood staring at the filthy brown surface of the Mississippi River. The water had a slick look, iridescent with a thin film of crude oil. It humped and heaved and rolled as if in peristalsis, a long brown string of viscera endlessly churning. I was near its sphincter, which accounted for the smell.

A line of barges moved slowly upstream in the night, silhouetted against the opposite bank, heaped with some glittering black substance. I imagined them plowing into the gaudily lit bridge that carried traffic across the river, the long silver girders bending and shearing, the roadway crumbling into the water, spilling cars and tiny half-crushed bodies. Unfortunately, I held no sway over barges.

This river was nothing like the Thames, the cold gray vein that snaked through my cold gray city, upon whose banks I had spent most of my life, into which I had flushed through my toilet any number of carefully wrapped, slightly stained parcels. The Thames seemed sterile beside this roiling brown stream.

I wondered what it would do to a corpse. Perhaps I could float one out tied to an empty plastic bottle, then row out to retrieve it in a fortnight. From all the similar bottles sailing past, multicoloured indigestible tidbits, it appeared as if other curious parties might have done just that.

Once I had boarded the flight from London and found myself safely in the air, I raced through the papers I'd bought, suddenly ravenous for news of the world I was rejoining. Aside from myself, it seemed as dull and repetitive as ever: royal scandals, politicians' sex lives, vicious opinions of the willfully ignorant presented as facts and swallowed whole by vacuous readers. One of the front-page articles about the abduction of my corpse had a sidebar entitled THE GAY PLAGUE —ARE YOUR CHILDREN SAFE?

I read every word of these insipid rags, then turned in desperation to the in-flight magazine. Ads targeted at corporate drones with brown noses and fat wallets exhorted me to monogram my briefcase, upgrade my powerbook, emboss my business card on the face of a watch. At last I found a travel article among all the sales pitches. It extolled the humid vices of New Orleans, the jazz, the food, the other delicacies. My interest was piqued by the caption beneath a picture of a blood-red drink in a long-stemmed glass, garnished with a cherry, a slice of orange, and a vivid green paper ruffle: *New Orleans has over 4000 bars and nightclubs . . .*

In London there were half again as many. But surely the city was only a fraction of London's size . . .

I scanned the rest of the article. The population of New Orleans was just over seven hundred thousand. London was home to seven *million* shivering souls. As I worked out the math, I felt an incredulous grin spreading over my face. Londoners had a pub per thousand citizens, a ratio that had always set well with me. But residents of New Orleans had one for every 175.

By the time the plane touched down in Atlanta, I knew where I was headed. Going through U.S. Customs on an American passport, I worried about my accent. I needn't have;

no one required me to look them in the eye, much less to speak. Once I received the government's stamp of approval, I stopped at a currency exchange booth and converted all Sam's pounds back into Uncle Sam's dollars. It seemed the pound was strong; I received a fat handful of unpleasantly furry-feeling green bills.

An underground train carried me from the airport to the bus station, where I discovered I had several times the price of a one-way ticket to New Orleans. I left Atlanta at dawn and spent the next fifteen hours dozing and waking through green countryside, down into the swamps, along a corridor of foetid factories and oil refineries that seemed to go on forever, a nightmare of blackened smokestacks topped with greasy orange flames against weird purple skies.

At last the coach pulled into New Orleans, and I told a cabdriver to take me to the cheapest digs nearby, which turned out to be the Hummingbird Bar, Grill, and Hotel on St. Charles Avenue. I consumed a cheeseburger and two frigid, heavenly American draft beers (can the chill of death itself be more delectable than that of a truly cold beer?), then climbed a narrow flight of stairs to a small square room and slept for twenty-four hours.

Earlier tonight I'd checked out of the Hummingbird and walked bravely to the French Quarter, as a million low-budget tourists before me must have done. ("St. Charles turns into Royal at Canal," the desk clerk told me, and her words seemed an exotic invocation, rich with mystery and promise.)

I conquered the Mississippi in my heart as I stood there on the pier. I had no fear of it, or of this city it churned through. I had seen intestines and sphincters before; I was capable of handling them. Then I went off to have a drink.

Jay sat in his parlor shaking like a spider on a web in a high wind. It was late afternoon, and Tran had left an hour ago.

They hadn't had much to say to each other upon awakening: both were embarrassed, and both felt ill from the ingestion of various substances. There had been no further physical contact.

But as soon as he had seen Tran out of the courtyard and locked the gate behind him, all Jay's compulsions and desires of the past twenty-four hours came rushing back a hundred-fold. He returned to the house in a daze, took the medical text-book down from the shelf and leafed through it, then put it away again. For a few minutes he simply sat, feeling his skeleton rattle and his eyeballs pulse and his heart hammer. He wanted another boy *right now.* The urge had never come this strongly so close on the heels of a kill. The encounter with Tran had short-circuited him somehow, knocked him into a re-peating loop.

He got up, went into the bedroom, and opened the bottom drawer of his dresser. Inside were the images he kept of all the boys, his Polaroid collection. They were good shots: Jay had an eye for composition, a keen sense of pose and angle. Here was a boy with his chest and stomach barely slit open, a shallow Y-cut showing the pale layer of fat inside, but no organs. Here was a close-up of the same boy's face, divinely peaceful. Here were two together in the tub, half on top of each other as if embracing, black skin contrasting with white, alike only in their headlessness. It still wasn't enough. Pictures would do him no good just now.

He unbuttoned his shirt and shrugged out of it, let it fall to the floor, undid his trousers and stepped out of them. Turning in a slow circle in the center of the bedroom, he caught sight of his reflection in the large cheval mirror. His face was impassive, his penis swelling to erection.

He let himself out the kitchen door, walked quickly along the side of the house and into the rear courtyard. The dead over-growth and damp statuary seemed to nod into his path. He could not get to the slave quarters fast enough. Naked and trembling, he wrenched the door open and flung himself inside.

The smell was sweetly rotten, richly vile, stronger than yesterday due to the addition of fresh meat. It was an invisible finger, soft and fat, pushing against the back of Jay's throat.
Instead of gagging, he took a deep breath and let it invade him.
He felt the odor of rotting flesh enter his lungs and seep into
his bloodstream. He opened his mouth and let it rest upon his
tongue like a sacrament.

All the windows were painted black, outside and in. When
Jay flicked a switch by the door, a long row of ceiling-
mounted 120-watt lamps flooded the scene with merciless
white light. He liked it bright in here. He liked to see things
glisten.

The inside of the shed was a single room, long and narrow.
To the right was a stack of black plastic garbage bags bulging
with oddly shaped lumps, distended here and there with gases,
reaching halfway up the wall. To the left, just inside the door,
was a deep freezer large enough to hold a man.

A row of long shelves ran along the back wall, bearing objects carefully arranged and frequently dusted. A number of
polished skulls, their hollow eye sockets packed with dried
roses. A mummified ribcage fragile as an old box kite. A pair
of slender-fingered hands resting at the bottom of a gallon
pickle jar, preserved in grain alcohol. (Jay planned to use this
alcohol to make a cherry liqueur whose recipe had been
passed down through his mother's family, but not until the
hands had steeped for a while.)

To the left of the shelves was a metal hospital table fitted
with leather restraints, and in the left rear corner of the room
was a fifty-gallon drum of hydrochloric acid. When young
Lysander Byrne called the orders division of Byrne Metals
and Chemicals and said he wanted such a drum delivered to
his house in the French Quarter, no one asked questions. The
rest of the left wall was taken up by a huge standing refrigerator he'd bought cheap from a restaurant about to go under.
This had been somewhat more difficult to have delivered. Jay

had allowed them to bring it as far as the rear courtyard, then made them leave it on the dolly, claiming he hadn't cleared a space for it yet. Later he wrestled it into the shed by himself, wrenching his back in the process.

The double doors of the refrigerator were opaque with condensation. Jay wiped a hand across the glass, revealing a pallid swath of what was inside. He touched his fingers to his lips, anointing himself with wetness. Then he grasped both handles and pulled the doors wide.

The young man had been perhaps twenty-five, tall and slender, with long graceful legs and the kind of smooth hairless skin Jay craved. In life his body had been the color of dark chocolate washed with a honey-gold patina, the spoils of a summer spent sleeping naked on Caribbean beaches. He had told Jay of bumming around the islands, hitching rides on whatever crafts were going his way, living on fish, fruit, and sticky ganja. His tissues had soaked up enough warmth to keep that vibrant color for a long time.

But he had been dead and decapitated for more than a week, hanging upside down from a steel meat hook thrust through the tendons of both ankles. As the blood drained from his neck stump into a pan Jay had set to catch it, his skin took on an ashy pallor and a slightly crinkled appearance. He looked as if he had lain too long in a very cold bath. His penis and testicles were purple-black scraps of flesh nearly lost in a thicket of blood-stiffened hair. His arms were trussed at the wrists and pulled up to his sides, the ropes tethered to the meat hook, helping support the weight of the body.

Jay had slit the belly open and removed the entrails as soon as he killed the young man. You had to remove the entrails; otherwise the body would bloat and sometimes rupture in a matter of hours. He'd taken the heart and lungs from this one, too. The empty body cavities were smooth and free of blood, since Jay had hosed the body down before hanging it. Blood rotted fast and had a rich, savory stink. He had known this since the age of sixteen, when he had sliced his thumb open and saved the blood in a bottle so he could smell his own flesh decaying.

He pressed his fingers to the corpse's chest, leaving five indentations in the cold flesh. He stroked the edges of the enormous wound, appreciating the layered textures of skin and flesh and bone, then touched his lips again, licked the frigid moisture off his fingertips. His penis throbbed. His skull felt full of bluebottle flies, razor wire, boiling slag.

Jay threw back his head and shrieked at the ceiling. The echo caromed off the walls and the concrete floor. Whether he shrieked from joy or anguish he could not have said, but the sound poured back into him through every orifice, filling him with his own power.

Then he fell to his knees and buried his face in the hanging man's belly. He sank his teeth into flesh that had gone the consistency of firm pudding. He ripped at the edges of the wound, pulling off strips of skin and meat, swallowing them whole, smearing his face with his own saliva and what little juice remained in this chill tissue. He ran his hands up the spine, between the buttocks, slipped a finger into the asshole and saw it wriggling deep in the hollow inner cavity. At some point he ejaculated, and the semen ran down his thigh almost unnoticed, a small sacrifice to this splendid shrine.

For several minutes Jay kneeled on the hard floor, catching his breath, his cheek resting against the corpse's left pectoral muscle, his hand loosely cupping the smooth curve of its shoulder. Deliciously cold air poured out of the fridge, drawing him into this dream of death. When at last he was able to rise, he felt reborn.

He left the slave quarters and went back to the house to bathe and dress. Soaping himself, he felt various residues draining away: lingering traces of Tran, cold corpse ichor, the dried drug-laced sweat of his own pores. When he stepped out of the shower, Jay was at once calm and terribly excited. Both of these emotions were overlaid with the thin veneer of dread that always accompanied them, like an acid trip with a jittery strychnine edge.

The interlude in the shed had calmed him, helped him regain an unstable equilibrium.

But he still couldn't stop himself from going out tonight.

IF YOU LIVED HERE, YOU'D BE DEAD.

I had just seen this phrase neatly printed in black felt-tip pen on a pastel-pink wall. I could not fathom its meaning, though I suspected it to be ominous. I was not quite reeling drunk, but I was working on it.

The French Quarter didn't feel like the wicked place I had expected. I'd envisioned certain gray alleyways in Soho, furtive porno shops and peep shows, dodgy customers ducking in and out of low dark doorways. But all the sex in the French Quarter seemed cheerful, garishly lit, and highly commercial. The shop windows of Bourbon Street displayed colourful plastic penises and flavoured lubricants, inflatable lovers and leather bondage gear. The strip clubs sent barkers into the streets to extol their seedy array of vices. Sex, or at any rate the ersatz rendering of it, seemed to be a major tourist attraction.

Farther down Bourbon Street the lights dimmed, the music grew louder and more synthesized, the crowd thinned and became mostly male. The drinks were more expensive at these bars than they had been on the tourist strip, but I was already approaching the highest plateau of inebriation I could allow myself. For the next several hours I would pace my intake, twirling in the stream of drunkenness without allowing myself to be swept away on the current. Drunkenness was not the only pleasure I sought tonight.

I moved from bar to bar, soaking up beer and ambience, measuring the tenor of the various crowds. Some places were

young, loud, and frantic. Some were full of older men hungrily eyeing anything under thirty-five. A few were mixed, and
it was these I lingered in longest. No one would remember me
as an odd sort; I would just be one more barfly. No one would
mark me as too young, too old, too trendy, too straight. No one
would play Barbra Streisand on the jukebox.

Several men chatted me up. I chatted back, accepted their
offers of drinks, eventually saw them off alive and well. Some
didn't appeal to me physically, and the attraction of the flesh
was essential. Some seemed too clever, too sober, too much in
control of their faculties.

There was a certain diffidence I always looked for in my
companions, nothing so obvious as a death wish, but a sort of
passivity toward life. There have been offered in recent years
a plethora of "murderer profiles," a series of lists and charts
meant to delineate the character of an habitual killer. What
about the profile of an ideal victim? They exist as surely as we
do, and they move as inexorably toward their given destinies.

(Yes, of course there are victims who are simply in the
wrong place at the wrong time. And then there are waifs who
wander the world without guile, seeming to offer themselves
up to whatever wants them.)

I maintain that ideal victims are actually *more* similar than
their murdering counterparts. An habitual killer needs a vivid
personality, even if all that lies beneath the flash and scintilla-
tion is a howling emptiness. But even before his death, the victim is often more void than substance.

Without knowing what streets I had traversed to get there,
I found myself in a place called the Hand of Glory. I remembered reading someplace that a hand of glory was a magical
talisman made from the mummified severed hand of a murderer. In my drunken state, I saw this as a good omen.

I ordered a maintenance drink, a vodka tonic I could sip
more slowly than beer, and found a table with a view of the
bar. The place was crowded but not overrun. I avoided vast

crowds because someone was always likely to be nearby when you were trying to leave unnoticed.

This bar had the feel of a grotto, cozy and mysterious. The ceiling was a latticework hung with bunches of dusty plastic grapes. The main illumination was provided by a radioactive-looking chartreuse-coloured sign advertising Mickey's Big Mouth Malt Liquor. The jukebox was stocked with crooners, and no hateful television set glowed and flickered as in most American bars. A white marble nude stood sentinel in a corner, blank-eyed, pitifully endowed, rather ghostly.

I scanned the crowd. It was a mixture of young punkish kids, black-clad espresso types, elegant male couples, and single men on the prowl. I wondered if I looked like one of the latter, then decided not. I was too calm, too self-contained. I never approached anyone. It had always been the way with my companions. They saw something in me that they needed, and they came to me.

I supposed I was more a black-clad espresso type, if a bit of an unsteady one. But I felt silly in my jumper and heavy trousers, and I had shucked my good English winter coat altogether. There was a chill in the air, to be sure, a damp cool vapour drifting round corners and rising from drains. But I had just come from London, where November vapours were like ill-intentioned hands sliding beneath your collar to encircle your coat-chafed, chicken-skinned throat, where November winds cut more deeply than my stolen scalpel ever did.

For the first time since I lulled myself to death in Painswick, I felt comfortable, almost contented. Someone would come to me, some perfect boy ripe for the slaughter. I would find a place to take him, and I would take him again and again. I wanted this so badly that I could not make myself care what happened afterward. If they caught me, I would let them kill me; I would never be taken back to prison. If they would not kill me, I would will myself to die again, and this time I would stay dead.

I closed my eyes and felt the room spin pleasantly. When I opened them again, I would see him.

"Excuse me."

The voice was soft but very sharp. It cut through my hazy maundering like a serrated knife through gauze. I opened my eyes, blinked away a brief dazzle of bar lights and unfamiliar spectacles, and beheld the love of my life for the first time.

Of course, I didn't know then that he was the love of my life. All I saw was a tall, rather wispy blond in expensive dark clothes, holding a frosted beer bottle in each hand. Dixie, the brand I'd been drinking.

"I saw you sitting alone over here. You don't look like you know anyone. I thought you might like a cold drink."

Not just a drink, but a *cold* drink. The man had a way with words. How many hours had I lain in my cell, parched beyond any relief the tepid tap water could give, dreaming of a really *cold* drink?

"Certainly," I said. "Thanks very much. Won't you join me?"

He smiled as he slid into the opposite chair, and I noticed two things about his face. First, it was beautiful; long thin nose elegantly squared at the tip, lean smooth jaw, sensuous lips with a twist that might be sardonic or cruel. Second, his eyes were colder than any drink could ever be: cold from the inside out, a weird mint-green colour like glacial ice. The smile did not touch them.

If I hadn't been intoxicated, I think I would have known what he was then. But I only smiled back, and regretted that sooner or later I would have to send this icy beauty on his way, because he was clearly no ideal victim.

"I like your accent. Where you from?"

"London," I said. It seemed safest; an Englishman from London was less remarkable to Americans than any other kind.

"London." He nodded, affirming what I'd said, as Americans do. "Are you homesick?"

"Not at all."

"What brings you to New Orleans?"

"The climate."

"Moral or meteorological?"

"Both."

We paused, offering noncommittal half-smiles, sizing each other up. He wasn't my usual type, and I had a hunch that I wasn't his either. Yet I didn't want him to move on, and he seemed in no hurry to go.

At last he asked me, "What's your name?"

Before, in my previous life, I'd told all my boys my real name. There had never seemed any need to do otherwise. Tonight I had been using Arthur, since none of the men who approached me were interesting. But to this man I said, "Andrew."

"I'm Jay." He reached across the table to shake my hand. His grip was cool, dry, and languid. When I shook hands with a potential companion, I always slid my palm over his palm and grasped his wrist, briefly encircling it with my fingers, gauging his reaction to such an intimate, dominant touch. But now I was shocked to feel Jay doing the same to me. We both snatched our hands away and stared at one another.

Again he broke the silence. "Would you like another drink?"

I hadn't been aware of finishing my first one. I tipped the Dixie bottle to the light: empty. The vodka tonic was gone too.

"No thanks," I said. I wanted one, but I wasn't sure what was going on here, and I knew I would be drunker in ten minutes than I was now.

"Well, I would. Excuse me a minute, will you, Andrew?" He actually waited for my nod of assent before walking away. I watched him wind through the crowd, sinuous as a Siamese cat, and I wondered what such an elegant, tightly wound, oddly *polite* man wanted with me. The bar was well jammed by this time, and I soon lost sight of him.

Ten minutes later he hadn't come back. I shifted in my

chair, wondering if he'd given me the slip, desperately needing a piss. My bladder had shrunk in prison, where aiming
one's cock into the chamber pot and producing a few tainted
drops of urine qualified as a way to relieve the boredom. I
worried that Jay would return first and think I had gone. By
that point I was already deeply intrigued with him, though I
couldn't quite say why.

But nature won out. When I finally got up from the table,
able to hang on no longer, I had to clutch at the back of my
chair to keep from stumbling sideways. The bar tilted at a vicious angle. *Get ahold of yourself,* I thought. *You're an alcoholic and an Englishman. You can sail through this.*

It was more like lurching into a tempest, but I managed to
negotiate my way across the bar and into the men's loo. Mer-
cifully, it was a single tiny room whose door locked from the
inside. After Sam, I wasn't quite ready for another dingy row
of sinks, another dim line of cubicles. I pissed what felt like
several litres, then glanced at myself in the mirror as I was
leaving. Hair spiky and tousled, spectacles askew, eyes faintly
mad: just a nice English tourist out on a bender.

Jay was leaning against the wall outside the door. He
looked as cockeyed as I felt. "I needed to pee," he told me,
"but I had three shots of tequila on the way to the bathroom."

"Why three?"

"Once for every time you've unnerved me." He gave me a
sly sidelong look. "First—when I laid eyes on you. Second—
when you shook my hand. And third—when I looked back at
our table and saw you were gone."

I tried to grasp his shoulder. My hand seemed to float between us for a moment, then wound up on his chest, in the V
of his shirt where cloth gave way to flesh. Jay reached out long
arms and pulled me in. I stumbled, fell against him. He was a
bit taller, and I felt my face crush into his neck, my lips splay
open against his throat. Then somehow we were kissing as
ravenously as I had ever kissed anyone, alive or dead.

My fingers were tangled in his hair, tugging so hard it had to hurt. His tongue was in my mouth, raking against the sharp edges of my teeth, feeling as if it would plunge straight down my throat and choke me. He tasted of blood and rage. His kiss was laced with the slow savour of pain. I knew these tastes; they were the tastes in my own mouth, the flavour of my life.

I did not know what Jay was, not yet; but on some instinctual, almost biological level I *recognized* him. I knew then that this man was infinitely dangerous to me. I also knew that I had to go as deep inside him as he would let me.

When I was able to stop grinding my body against his as if I meant to drive him through the wall, I pulled back and looked him in the face. Trying to read his eyes was like searching for sentience in a pool of murky water: I thought I saw things moving deep down in there, but all I could be sure of was my own faint reflection. "What are we letting ourselves in for?" I whispered.

"An adventure," Jay said, and offered up another of those lovely cold smiles. He told me later that, at that moment, he still believed he would kill me.

There was no question but that we were leaving together. When we quit the Hand of Glory, I didn't know whether to bless the place or curse it. We walked up a side street, stealing glances at each other, occasionally bumping shoulders or brushing hands. The streets were narrow and quiet, the cobbled pavements overhung with lacy iron balconies and Victorian cottages and a curious flat-fronted, shuttered type of house. There were mysterious gates and dark alleyways, through which one occasionally glimpsed a sylvan courtyard with a fountain sparkling at its centre.

Jay pointed at a tall gray building on a corner. "That house is haunted."

"By what?"

"The ghosts of tortured slaves."

An expectant silence lay heavily between us, not as if he

wanted me to inquire further about the ghost story, but more as if he thought I might have some opinion on tortured slaves.

"Fascinating," I said, leaving it ambiguous for now.

Again I wondered what this man wanted from me, and what I expected to get from him. Were we going to fuck? It had been so long since I'd had sex with a breathing body, I wasn't sure I would remember how. Did I think I was going to kill him, on his own territory, with no weapon or means of disposal? The idea appealed to me, but the reality seemed implausible, and more so when I studied Jay's profile. This was no acquiescent brat to the slaughter. This was some other kind of animal.

Jay stopped and unlocked an iron gate with finials wrought in the shape of pineapples. We passed through an overgrown courtyard to a small white house. A series of keys, a sequence of numbers pressed on an electronic keypad, and we were inside. My memory telescoped briefly back to my Brixton flat, the last place I'd lived before being arrested, and the complicated series of locks and bolts I'd had on the door.

My terror had been of someone coming in while I was away and finding something I'd forgotten to dispose of. This was not a terror of arrest or punishment; the fantasy ended abruptly with the nameless intruder's find. It was a terror of *exposure,* of having the lid ripped off my secret world, its vulnerable inner workings laid bare. This was how I actually did feel when they came for me: a blind, shrivelling, sorrowful pain, the sort of pain a garden snail must feel when stepped on and cracked open, its spiralling home crushed to shards, now nothing more than a snotty smear of meat left to dry in harsh sunlight.

Jay led me deeper into the house. The parlour was a marvel of brocade and gilding. I liked the way it smelled, an overlay of sweet incense with a scrim of dust around the edges, a hint of mildew in the cracks.

We entered the kitchen. The floor and all the cupboard tops

were immaculate. Against one wall was a small table made of tubular metal and some glossy white substance with gold flecks embedded in it. The table held a salt cellar, a pepper mill, a bottle of Tabasco sauce, and a wine corkscrew. There were two matching chairs, of which I took one.

"Would you like a drink?" Jay asked.

"Er . . . not just now." The room was still tilting a bit, and I wanted to stay alert for whatever might happen next.

He poured a draught of cognac from an expensive-looking bottle, drank off half of it at once, and came over to me cradling the snifter, a great bubble of thin fragile crystal. The cognac in the bottom was the colour of liquid copper. Jay wafted it under my nose. "Just a taste?"

"Why not?" I took the snifter from him, sipped, and held cognac in my mouth before I swallowed. Its smooth smoky burn blessed my tongue.

"Lovely," I said, looking up into his strange eyes.

"Yes, isn't it?" With one hand on the back of my chair, he leaned over and kissed me. The flavour of the cognac passed between our mouths, warmed and enriched with our saliva. One of Jay's hands grasped mine and I felt something cold slide round my right wrist, a circle of metal that tightened and clicked shut.

I broke the kiss and stared down. Jay had handcuffed me to the chair. Part of what I felt was stark disbelief at being trapped again. Part was utter unsurprise that Jay had done it.

I looked back up at him and smiled.

The slightest shadow of doubt flickered across his face and was gone. He took another sip of cognac, wet his fingers on his tongue, and ran them slowly along my jawbone. He stopped at the juncture where my pulse beat and let his hand rest on my throat.

"So it's a bit of a game you like, Jay?" I asked him. "Well, that's all right, then. I like a game too."

I laid my free hand on his, stroked the length of his arm,

twined my fingers in his hair and pulled his head down to mine. His lips went stiff when I kissed them. His tongue lay in his mouth as if stunned. I was very aware of his teeth, of their hardness and sharp shiny edges. I let go of his hair, kissed the underside of his chin, moved my mouth down to the smooth dip of his collarbone.

"Play with me," I whispered into his skin. "I'm all yours."

My left hand found the corkscrew on the table. I grasped it clumsily and felt the sharp tip bite into my flesh. Jay's body was rigid everywhere it met mine. I swung my legs up and pinned his arms to his sides as best I could. He wasn't very well trapped, but he was too startled to break away at once. The chair tipped backward and hit the table. I pressed the screw's tip against the pulse of his throat, just where his cognac-damp fingers had touched me.

"Come on then," I hissed into his ear. "Let's play your game. What's your next move?"

He tried to jerk his right arm out of my knee hold, and I jabbed the corkscrew harder against his throat. A thin red dot appeared at the point where it dimpled his skin, quickening my blood and my breath. The sight of scarlet on stainless steel has always done this to me.

Jay went very still. "What do you want?"

What did I want? I beg you to recall that the man had a sharp object at his throat; my love did not make a habit of stupid questions. "What the bloody hell do you *think* I want? Take back your jewelry—it doesn't suit me at all!"

"Jewelry?"

I moaned in frustration and rattled the handcuff against the chair's metal frame.

"Oh, those." My legs still pinned his arms to his sides; my blade still lay against his jugular; but I swear I could feel the man considering. "Well, I bet I could get across the room and out of your reach before you could inflict a fatal cut. What would you do then?"

"I'd drag the chair after me and finish you off in a corner."

"What if I told you I had a gun in that drawer over there?" He gestured with his chin. I followed his motion with the corkscrew, which was beginning to seem a slightly ridiculous weapon. My legs were tiring from the awkward position, and I felt drunker than ever.

"I'd say you were lying, Jay. You're not a gun man."

"You'd bet your life on that?"

"I've bet it on less."

We stared at each other, both sizzling with adrenaline, blazing with lust, terrified to move. I realized he was enjoying this as perversely as I was.

"Fine," said Jay at last, "let me go. I'll get you the key."

I unscissored him and slowly took the screw from his throat. I had no choice; I could not remain in that precarious tipped-back position a moment longer. The chair's front legs hit the floor, and I realized that my thigh muscles were trembling.

Jay backed slowly across the kitchen, not toward the drawer he'd indicated, but to the refrigerator. He stood beside the gleaming appliance for a moment, transfixed me with a clear calm gaze. I noticed, as one will mark small details in such moments, that his refrigerator door was unadorned by decorative magnets, sticky notes, snapshots, and other such frippery. Like most of the surfaces in the kitchen, it appeared to have been recently wiped down with a strong disinfectant.

Jay opened the freezer and took out a parcel done up in heavy black plastic. He brought it to the table and began to unwrap it, no longer pretending to worry about the corkscrew I still held in my free hand. He knew he'd caught my interest again.

By the time he had the parcel undone, I had already guessed its contents. I had stored and disposed of many such parcels myself. I knew the shape and heft of a wrapped human head, the distinctive size, the rough egg-shaped bundle it made inside plastic, cloth, or newspaper.

Faces lose much of their personality when frozen. The features harden and take on a shrivelled look. Sometimes it becomes difficult to tell one from another upon unwrapping them. This one had stringy dark hair and cloudy gray marbles for eyes. The nose and left cheek had flattened somehow, perhaps against the bottom of the freezer. The mouth was slightly open, the edges of upper and lower teeth a scant inch apart. Inside was only darkness.

Jay took a small key from his pocket, showed it to me, then dropped it into that frigid black mouth. I only just kept myself from scoffing. So this was his big test, was it?

I took hold of the frost-rimed hair and pulled the head across the table to me. I slid my thumb and forefinger into the narrow gap between the teeth and felt for the key. My nails scraped unpleasantly along the rough surface of the tongue. It was like clawing at a stale brick of ice cream. Something adhered to my fingers: saliva, blood, crystallized epithelial cells. I disliked the sensation of the cold teeth scraping my knuckles. I'd handled plenty of fresh remains, and some not so fresh, but I had avoided this sort of storage whenever possible. I liked the cooling pallor of room-temperature death, not the icy shock of the deep freeze. Still, a show of distaste at this point would be unwise.

The key had slipped to the very back of the tongue. As I scrabbled for it, I felt it disappear into the passage of the throat. I was rapidly becoming annoyed with the whole business. I felt almost certain I could kill Jay even with one wrist cuffed, so why bother proving anything? But I didn't want to kill Jay.

I picked up the head by its hair and gave it a firm shake, then rapped the stump of the neck against the tabletop. A head liberated from its body is heavier than you might expect, but if you have plenty of hair to grip by, it is easily lifted with one hand. The key fell from the ragged end of the oesophagus. I set the head down with a thump, pinched the key off the tabletop with two fingers (the same two I'd put in that frozen mouth), and unlocked the wretched handcuffs.

As I stood and faced him, the expression on Jay's face was something like wonder. "What are you?" he asked.

I touched my fingers to the bead of scarlet on his throat, brought them to my lips and tasted his blood for the first time. "I'm your nightmare. Did you think you were done with nightmares, now you've become one?"

Mutely, he shook his head no.

"Never relinquish your terrors," I told him. "That's when they catch you. What is your greatest terror, Jay?"

There was no hesitation. His voice sounded hollow, flat. "Loneliness."

"Do you think you're lonely now?"

Another nod.

"Imagine, then, a cell with four walls. The ceiling is a map of a terrible country you know by heart. The walls can move and close in on you if you stare at them long enough. There's no blood, no company, nothing but the rasp of your breathing and the stink of your chamber pot." My voice was beginning to shake. "No one comes in, and it seems you never go out, and you've nothing at all to look at, but anyone can look at you. Does it terrify you?"

"Yes."

"Then never give up that terror. Never grow careless of it. They could kill you, Jay; they kill murderers here, don't they? Perhaps that's kindest. Yes, surely it is. What a merciful country. If they catch me again, Jay, make them kill me before they put me back in the coffin!"

"Andrew." Jay's hands were on my shoulders, his thumbs stroking the sides of my throat. The touch soothed me somehow. "I don't know what your story is, but you're not in prison now. Nobody's going to kill you. Stay with me." His eyes shone. "Play with me."

"Yes." I slid my arms around his narrow waist, leaned into him. "I think I can do that."

We stood embracing in the stark light of the kitchen. When we kissed, it was not the sloppy tongue-sparring we'd done at the club; this was more tentative, almost delicate, a rediscovery of each other. Soon, though, Jay broke the kiss and pulled me toward the door. "Come out back. I want to show you my slave quarters."

I had never savoured decay. Handled it, yes; conquered it, yes. But never had I revelled in it.

Never, until now.

As Jay stood by smiling, I savaged the headless body he laid out for me. I gripped its rigid shoulders as I fucked it. I slashed its bloodless flesh with knives, scissors, screwdrivers, everything Jay put into my hand. When I had reduced it to little more than a smear on the ancient bricks, I wallowed in its scraps.

Then Jay joined me, and licked me clean.

I felt a vestigial trace of disgust as his tongue combed shreds of tissue from the hair on my lower belly. But it was nothing I could sustain, not as the world expects a sane man to do. Horror is the badge of humanity, worn proudly, self-righteously, and often falsely. How many of you have lingered over a rendering of my exploits or similar ones, lovingly detailed in its dismemberments, thinly veiled with moral indignation? How many of you have risked a glance at some wretched soul bleeding his life out on a highway shoulder? How many have slowed down for a better look?

It is claimed that habitual murderers must harbour some veiled trauma in their past: some pathetic concatenation of abuse, rape, soul-corrosion. As far as I can remember, this did not hold true for me. No one interfered with me, no one beat me, and the only corpse I saw during childhood was the thoroughly uninteresting one of my grand-auntie. I emerged from the womb with no morals, and no one has been able to instill any in me since. My incarceration was a long dream, a limbo to be endured—not a punishment, for I had done nothing wrong. I had spent my life feeling like a species of one. Monster, mutation, Nietzschean superman—I could perceive no

difference. I had no basis for comparison. Now here was another of my kind, and I wanted to know everything about him.

But he was rummaging in a cabinet, pulling out a bottle of
vodka, guzzling from it and forcing it on me. The glass and the
label were smeared with bloody fingerprints. The neck chat-
tered between my teeth as I drank. I had not feared Jay when
he wanted to kill me. Now that he wanted me alive, the intimacy between us was terrifying.

We drank until we collapsed in the boy's shredded ruins.
When morning light woke us, we rose aching and stinking,
staggered into the house, and leaned on each other in the warm
spray of the shower. Clean as babes, we burrowed into bed
and slept for the rest of the day, half unnerved and half com-
forted by the nearness of each other's breathing body.

10

Luke was clutching him hard, staring into his face and fucking him deep. Tran was on his back, legs wrapped around Luke's waist. Their skin was iridescent with sweat, their muscles pulled tight as violin strings, their bodies utterly in sync. "You like that, baby?" Luke would sometimes groan as he thrust all the way in, and Tran could only gasp his assent as his lover impaled him, deliciously, again and again and again

"Hey, Tran! Tran! Are you OK?"

He turned over, away from the light, and buried his face in something soft. He wanted to keep dreaming. He knew there were a lot of reasons not to wake up, but the feeling of Luke's body on his had helped him forget most of them.

"Come on, wake up. You shouldn't be sleeping here. Some cruddy stewbum might roll you."

Dimly Tran remembered the five hundred dollars folded into his sneaker. He could feel the itchy wad of bills through his sock, still safe, but he didn't want to think about them. They reminded him of his father, his utter failure with Jay, his car full of possessions parked at Jax Brewery, his lack of basic shelter. All of this led directly away from the frangible nirvana of Luke's cock in his ass.

He opened his eyes and found himself gazing up at Soren Carruthers, a kid he knew in a vaguely friendly way from clubs, coffeehouses, and parties. Behind Soren's head loomed the white spires of St. Louis Cathedral. Apparently he had fallen asleep on a bench in Jackson Square. The way he'd been feeling when he left Jay's house, Tran supposed he was lucky to have made it to a bench.

He had managed to get his head into Soren's lap, and Soren was cradling it, gently brushing Tran's hair back with one slender hand. It felt so good to be touched in a kind, nonsexual way that Tran's eyes filled with tears. He remembered his flood of emotion at Jay's yesterday. Something in him cringed from the memory, and he did not cry.

He hooked an arm over the back of the bench and pulled himself up to a sitting position, ran his hands over his eyes and through his hair, sneaked a sheepish glance at Soren.

"Don't even bother being embarrassed," Soren told him. "I once spent three nights out here."

"Really?" Tran couldn't imagine Soren living on the street, with no mirrors, no mousse, no scented shampoo. Soren seemed the sort of person for whom luxury was essential to the sustenance of life. But apparently he had an underlayer not visible through the polished surface. Tran realized that he barely knew this quiet young man, had never really taken the trouble to know him. He'd spent so much time with Luke that most of his other friendships were either in ruins or dying of terminal shallowness.

"Really," Soren said. "I've been more or less on my own since I was sixteen. My family pays me handsomely to stay away and not associate myself with them. Last year my grandfather offered me a quarter-million dollars to leave New Orleans for good, but I wouldn't go. I have things to do in this city."

Like what? Tran wanted to ask, but didn't.

"Anyway, what are *you* doing here? Did your family kick you out?"

"Yeah, for starters. How'd you guess?"

Soren rolled his eyes. "Gee, I only know about twenty other queers it's happened to. You'll be OK. If they disrespect your basic identity enough to kick you out, they were damaging you anyway."

"They're Vietnamese. They don't understand being gay."

"Bullshit! Queers exist in every culture in the world. It's just that most cultures try to sweep them under the carpet. You can bet there are gay Vietnamese. You're one."

"I'm American."

"There are queers in Vietnam. The government may be willing to kill them in order to hide them, but that doesn't mean they aren't there."

"I don't think the Vietnamese government has any special vendetta against queers," Tran said, hoping they could drop the subject. He wondered when Soren had gotten so crypto-mysto-political, and why.

"Well, do you want to get a cup of coffee and talk?"

Tran's stomach cramped at the very thought. He'd had enough stimulants for a while. "Anything but coffee."

"What would you like?"

Tran thought about it, realized he hadn't eaten anything since the cold meat sandwich last night at Jay's. "What I'd really like is some Vietnamese food."

"Sounds great. Let's do it." Soren pulled Tran up off the bench. Tran still had traces of a dream-boner, but luckily his shirttail was long and loose enough to hide it.

He wasn't about to return to Versailles, where he would almost certainly see someone who knew him in any of the restaurants, and it would get back to his family before nightfall. He hadn't thought much about his family since turning up at Jay's. Now his feelings toward them had begun to crystallize into a stubborn anger. If his father never regretted throwing him out, if his mother and brothers could be brainwashed into despising him, then Tran would let them be equally dead to him.

They drove across the river on the bridge called the Crescent City Connection after the way the Mississippi curves in a half-moon shape around the city. Versailles was populated with North Vietnamese, but there was a large South Vietnamese community over here. They wound up at a dim little café lodged between a seedy bowling alley and a cheap motel. Incense sticks smoldered in a tiny Buddhist shrine below the cash register. Soren had a green curry flavored with sweet basil and coconut milk. This was an Indian-influenced Southern dish, and though Tran liked the savory pieces of chicken and sweet potato stewed in the rich emerald sauce, the flavor was strange to him.

His own meal was more familiar: *phó bò hà nôi,* a huge bowl of clear spicy broth filled with tender shredded meat, chewy beef tripe, and masses of elastic rice noodles. It was served with a platter of fresh greens, lime wedges, and fiery red chilies for seasoning. He'd been surprised to see it on the menu, for this was the signature soup of Hanoi, the northern capital. But he guessed Vietnamese people ate it everywhere.

This revelation made Tran think about how insular life in his community had been. He'd grown up knowing nothing about the lives of these other Vietnamese, and little about the lives of Americans except what he gleaned in school. People in Versailles lived as they would in a middle-sized Vietnamese village; they ventured into the city when they had to, but they ate, worked, and loved among themselves. And they punished their children for wanting to step outside.

He and Soren talked of what it was to leave home, of how sometimes you couldn't go until you had to, even if you knew it was what you needed most; of how you never wanted to return until some tiny random image rose up in your mind. The pitcher of water in the refrigerator, yellow lemons painted on cool green glass; your mother's antique dressing table; the perilous archeology of your own closet. For Tran it was the clutter of the family bathroom, the homey mess he'd thought of when confronting the sterile expanse of Jay's john. He remembered masturbating in there, remembered the bag full of multicolored hair, and a little shudder ran through him.

Soren seemed to comprehend the range and depth of emotions you could feel toward a family who had essentially revoked your membership. By the time the dishes were cleared away, Tran thought they had forged a fragile bond of friendship. It had been a long time since he'd had a friend who didn't want to fuck him or score acid from him; he wasn't sure he'd ever met a Caucasian who didn't want to do one or the other, or both. Halfway through dessert—strong coffee with sweetened condensed milk for Soren, a jackfruit shake for Tran—he felt comfortable enough to ask, "Have you seen Luke Ransom lately?"

Something passed across the gray haze of Soren's eyes, some veil of wariness or pity. Tran had no idea what that might be about. Luke and Soren had scarcely known each other when Tran had been on the scene, and Soren seemed like the type of boy Luke could really get into hating.

"No. Not lately." Soren seemed on the verge of saying something else, but did not.

Tran fidgeted in his chair, toyed with the metal napkin holder, the bottles of fish sauce, vinegar, and the *sriracha* pepper sauce that was a staple of every Vietnamese restaurant he'd ever been in. Soren knew something about Luke. Maybe only that he had tested positive, maybe something more. Finally he couldn't stand it. *"What?"*

"Nothing. It's just that last time I saw Luke, he was in really bad shape over you."

Tran shrugged. "If calling me at three o'clock every morning for a month, sending me twenty-page psycho-love rants, and threatening my life qualifies as being in really bad shape, then I guess he was."

Soren arched one elegant eyebrow. "He threatened your *life?*"

"He once threatened to kidnap me and rape me. He said he'd keep me locked up somewhere for a week, fuck me without a condom, make me swallow his come and his blood." *He also said he'd make me like it . . . but I don't think I can say that out loud.* "Then he'd let me go, and I could turn him in if I wanted, but he would die happy knowing I was infected too."

"Luke is never going to die happy," Soren murmured.

Tran stared at his hands encircling the milk shake tumbler, at his ragged cuticles and grimy knuckles. "I don't even know if you knew Luke was sick," he said.

"Yes, I know. I'm positive too."

Tran nearly choked on the last drops of ice cream sliding up through his straw. He couldn't have anticipated that one in a million years. With Luke it had been so easy to believe; sloppy, hard-partying, pissed-off Luke, his brain always burning, his body and heart wide open to any number of poisons. AIDS seemed no worse than Luke had always expected the world to dole out to him.

And of course, Luke and Tran had been born a decade apart. They were at such different places in their lives. Tran liked spending time with someone so much older than himself, yet clued in. Luke had written, had fucked, had traveled. He *knew* things, not only facts but truths of existence, and he could talk about them for hours. Tran often felt wordless and ignorant in his presence. But Luke drew the intelligence from him, and found people his age amusingly amoral, and worshiped his tender young body.

Still, when Luke tested positive, the difference in their ages allowed Tran to rationalize so many things. He imagined that Luke had had hundreds of lovers in San Francisco and on his cross-country travels. He knew that men Luke's age often got sick; they had been the last generation to experience sex without fear. AIDS was comparatively rare among gay men in their teens and early twenties. And they had always been so careful, Tran and Luke.

He wondered if Soren had been careful too. Tran wasn't sure, but he thought Soren was a year or two younger than him.

He must have looked stunned, because Soren began to laugh. "What, you think we can't get it because we're young and cute? I hope *you've* been tested."

Tran managed to nod.

"Still negative?"

Tran nodded again, but glanced away from Soren. Soren leaned across the table and laid his hand on Tran's wrist. "Forgive me. We get so used to discussing our status, it starts to seem like a kind of small talk. I shouldn't have asked."

The sensation of Soren's skin against his own alarmed him, and Tran slid his wrist out from under Soren's cool, dry palm. Whenever he walked into a Vietnamese restaurant, Tran couldn't help feeling that all eyes in the place had suddenly turned on him, were scrutinizing his behavior for signs of deviance. Usually this small paranoia wasn't all that far from the truth, considering his reputation in Versailles. But it had been a problem the few times he'd eaten Vietnamese food with Luke. Luke knew better than to touch him here as he would in a French Quarter bar, or even on the street; still, Tran couldn't help flinching away every time their hands reached for the same dish or Luke's knee accidentally bumped his under the table, until his flinching made him feel more conspicuous than their touching would have done.

It had hurt Luke's feelings then, and Soren looked faintly injured now, but he hid it well. The infected, as Luke had called them, probably got used to people sliding away from their touch.

Tran wanted to recapture the easy conversation of a few minutes ago. Why had he mentioned Luke anyway? Luke already got in the way of everything he did, everything he wanted. He didn't have to conjure the ghost himself. He decided to tell Soren about his experience of last night.

"Do you know Jay Byrne?" he asked.

Soren's gray eyes flared. "That creep! He tried to pick me up at the Hand of Glory once—actually offered me *money* to pose for some dirty pictures, as if I needed his money. I only considered taking it for a second, because I knew it would make my ancestors roll over in their graves, and I like to do that whenever possible."

"What do you mean?"

"Well, see, the Byrnes are a mixture of old money and new money, which is death in some circles. And they say the old money they *do* have is cursed. His mother is a Devore, but she also comes from a line of swamp trash, as my family would say, right up through the nineteenth century. Her great-uncle was Jonathan Daigrepoint."

"Who's Jonathan Deg—"

"Daigrepoint. I thought every kid who ever grew up in New Orleans would've heard of Jonathan Daigrepoint."

"Versailles isn't exactly New Orleans."

"Well, this didn't happen in New Orleans, either. Jonathan Daigrepoint lived in Point Grosse Tete, deep in the bayou country south of here. His family were Cajun fishermen and trappers. Jonathan didn't go out drinking and dancing as his brothers and sisters loved to do. He never had much to say, never married or had a girlfriend, and no one took any notice of him until they found the abandoned boat shed where he'd killed fifteen little boys. Most of them were still in there—cut up with a hunting knife, it looked like, though there was really too much decomposition to tell. Some were black children from the next town over, and he probably could have gotten away with that, but some were Cajun kids, and one was a runaway from New Orleans. They brought him here to stand trial. The court had to hire an interpreter because the Daigrepoints spoke only French, and swamp French at that. This was in eighteen seventy-five."

"Wow." Tran made a mental note to tell Soren about the decapitation of Jayne Mansfield out on Chef Menteur. Right now, though, he wanted to hear the rest of this tale. "So where does the old Devore money come in?"

"Louis Devore was twenty-one when the trial was held. He got called as a juror. The whole Daigrepoint clan had come up from the swamps to watch their son get crucified. During the long hours in court every day, Louis took a fancy to Jonathan's sister Eulalie, who was just fifteen. At the end of the trial, Louis voted 'guilty' with the rest of the jury, but he and Eulalie were in love. His family threatened to disown him if he married a miserable piece of swamp trash with killer's blood in her veins, but they didn't. At least she was the right gender, I suppose.

"Louis and Eulalie married a fortnight after Jonathan was hanged for murder, and they started making little Devores, and one day a Devore married a new-money Byrne from Texas. And that's where Jay came from."

Tran shook his head. For the second time in ten minutes, Soren had poleaxed him. "How do you know all that?"

Soren shrugged. "People talk a lot in old New Orleans families. But look, I hope you're not mixed up with that creep."

Tran felt suddenly protective. Jay was odd company, all right, but he hadn't been a creep. If anything, he had been rather kind. "So he comes from a weird family, and he wanted to take your picture once. Why does that make you hate him?"

"Oh, Tran, I don't *hate* him. I *hate* Pat Buchanan, Bob Dole, my grandfather . . . not poor old Jay Byrne. He's nothing but a harmless Kodak queen, I suppose. He just seems . . . I don't know . . . *slimy.* There's nothing really wrong with him on the outside, but I can't imagine ever wanting to touch him."

"Well, I can." To hell with it; he wouldn't be ashamed. "As a matter of fact, I spent last night with him."

It was fun to watch Soren's mouth fall open and his eyes grow rounder. "You didn't," Soren breathed. "You *did?* What did he . . . I mean . . . what was it *like?*"

Tran had intended to confide the whole strange experience: Jay's last-second refusal to fuck him, the bizarre sterility of the bathroom, maybe even the bag of human hair. But now he didn't want to tell any of it. Soren obviously loved to gossip, and Tran had no desire to give him ammunition against Jay. So he just let a little smile drift across his face. "Oh . . . you know."

"Did he take pictures of you?"

"We never got around to that."

"Oh, my." Soren was actually clutching the sides of his head, as if trying to force the knowledge into his brain. "You really *like* him, don't you?"

"Believe it or not."

"Jesus. Luke . . ."

"What about Luke?"

"Nothing. He'd freak if he knew, that's all."

That nagging suspicion again. "How come you know what Luke would think about everything? I never realized you two were such good friends."

"Well . . . we've gotten to know each other better since you broke up, it's true."

There was no way Luke and Soren could be a couple, not that Tran would care. Luke only liked white boys if they were slender, dark-haired, dark-eyed, and fine-featured—in short, as Oriental-looking as possible. Soren was slender and fine-featured, but as Aryan as they came. And he was a child of clubland and cyberspace, neither of which Luke found remotely interesting.

Tran remembered that his longest conversation with Soren prior to today had been about computers and telephones. Specifically, about hacking and phone phreaking. All at once it dawned on him. "You're part of the radio station, aren't you?"

Soren's eyes were disarmingly clear. "What radio station?"

Tran barely heard him. "Sure you are. It's the only way you two could stand each other. You saw Luke just last night, didn't you? Or do you call him *Lush?*"

"I have no idea what you're talking about."

"Soren, do you think I'd turn you in? I know what you're doing is illegal. Do you think I'd put you all in jail just to hurt Luke?"

Soren stared at Tran, then seemed to come to a decision. "I don't know you that well, Tran. We haven't spoken twenty times before today. I wasn't going to gamble what we have left of our lives on trusting you."

"Do you trust me now?"

"I guess I have to. You're queer and you might be positive. You're pretty much our target audience. But I worry about Luke, and you have a lot of reasons to hate him."

"I don't hate him. I did for a while, but not now."

"He still loves you."

"That's sick."

"He's sick."

They sat for a few minutes in silence. The little restaurant was cool and empty, the shadows of a late autumn afternoon beginning to lengthen in the corners. The waitress dropped off their check, which came to just over $10, and smiled at Tran. She was close to his age, the sort of girl his parents would have liked. Tran barely noticed her. He was wondering how Luke could still claim to love him after cursing him and hurting him and wanting him to die.

"Look," said Soren as they drove back across the bridge, "do you need a place to stay? I don't really like having company, but if you're sleeping on the street . . ."

"Don't worry, I have money. I'll find something. Thanks anyway."

Soren glanced over at Tran, then shrugged. They were at the midpoint of the Crescent City Connection, where the view included a crystalline cityscape and a vast housing project, a velvet expanse of swampland and a weal of factories. Far below the span, the Mississippi curved away in a long arc on either side. "Are you afraid I'd tell Luke where you were?"

"Well . . ." Tran shifted in his seat. "He's gotten crazier, hasn't he?"

"Oh, definitely. Do you listen to the show a lot?"

"I used to," Tran admitted. "It started up in, what, spring of this year?"

"May."

"That wasn't so long after we broke up. I still had this bitter obsession with Luke. When I turned on the radio one night and heard his voice, I thought I'd finally gone crazy. By the time I figured out it was real, I couldn't turn it off."

"I run his voice through an encoder."

"Doesn't matter. I loved the guy for two years, and I loved to hear him talk. I know his inflections, his phrases, even the way he clears his throat. Haven't you ever been in love?"

"No."

Tran turned in his seat. "What?"

"No. I've had a lot of flings. I've had a couple of relationships. But I can't honestly say I've ever been in love. Now there's a good chance I never will be. No matter how ugly things got between you and Luke, I can't help envying what you had."

They came off the bridge at the Camp Street exit and drove through downtown, back toward the French Quarter. There was a huge abandoned building among others near the elevated roadway, an empty warehouse with hundreds of broken windows. Late afternoon sunlight slanted through this building, illuminating the shards that remained in the frames, the dust that sifted down from the high ceilings. Tran stared at it and wished he could live there. No one would ever know where to find him. He would spread a blanket over the broken glass, wash himself with dust, roast bats and locusts over a tiny fire late at night.

Even then, no doubt, someone would envy him something.

11

J ay stood at the butcher block slicing andouille sausage for
jambalaya. He was using the same knife he had employed on
Fido, its heft and whisper-sharpness reassuring. Everything
else in his world was in tumult. He couldn't imagine why he
loved it so.

Meeting Andrew had made the universe yawn wide for him
somehow. It was like discovering that your innermost fires and
terrors, the things you believed no one else could fathom, were
in fact the basis of a recognized philosophy. Some part of you
felt intimately invaded, threatened; some other part fell to its
knees and sobbed in gratitude that it was no longer alone.

They had spent that first day in bed, but little of their contact was sexual. Andrew claimed that his HIV status made his
bodily fluids dangerous. Jay didn't care. He remembered the
taste of Tran's come burning its way down his throat, the tight-
ness of Tran's ass around the head of his condom-swathed
cock. It wasn't as if he had never taken the risk. But sex with
Andrew seemed almost beside the point, something they
could contemplate later, after the torrent of words had slowed.

They talked obsessively, their conversations spilling over

each other. They bathed in shared knowledge. Neither of them had ever been able to discuss his passions. Andrew had had his diaries, which Jay wished he could read. Jay had had nothing. Now they could not stop comparing, exulting, marveling.

"But why do you eat their flesh?" Andrew had asked. "What do you get out of that?"

"You've never tasted it?"

"Only blood. And I like the look of that more than the taste."

"Blood . . ." Jay shrugged. "Blood is fuel. It's all right, but it's not what they're *made* of."

"Do you want them to become a part of you? Is that it?"

"Partly," Jay admitted. "It took me a long time to feel they were staying. I'd eat their meat and it would become my meat and I'd be alone again. After a while, though, I started to feel them."

Andrew nodded. His dark eyes were reflective, but he looked as if he understood. At last he said, "Is there any other reason?"

"Because they taste wonderful," Jay told him.

In the languorous days that followed, they came back to this subject again and again. Andrew spent most of his hours wandering around the house, entranced by all the comforts Jay took for granted. Jay would come upon him in the library, paging through oversized folios of art and photography, reading bits of novels like a starved man; or in the parlor, with an assortment of CDs on infinite shuffle; or in the bedroom, lounging indolent on silken sheets and soft pillows. He was a man of sublime taste and culture who had been deprived in every conceivable way, and his renewal made Jay feel strangely alive.

In the evenings they dined out. Jay found himself rediscovering the city's great restaurants, tasting rich concoctions he hadn't dreamed of in years. It was embarrassing to sup at Broussard's or Nola with some ragged guttersnipe he planned to kill later, who would invariably slouch in his borrowed jacket poking at his food: *What's this stuff?* Andrew knew what he was eating, and savored every mouthful. But occasionally he would catch Jay's eye over a plate of pompano en papillote, a dollop of daube glacé, or a succulent morsel of cedar-plank drum, smile his dark smile, and ask again about the taste of boys' flesh.

The rice had been cooking down with onions, garlic, tomatoes, and celery, and the jambalaya was almost done. Jay added the sausage, stirred in a bowl of shelled shrimp, dosed the pot with Crystal sauce, and left it to simmer while he loaded the dishwasher. When the shrimp had had time to cook through, he forked up a mouthful of the steaming rice. It tasted nearly perfect: peppery, savory, redolent of seafood and smoked pork. But he thought it could use a little more body. A little more *meat*.

He opened the refrigerator and took out a plate covered in Saran wrap. The plastic looked as if someone had partially unwrapped it, then hastily put it back. Had Andrew lingered over this plate, wondering but unable to take the first bite?

Jay began shredding the meat with his fingers. He hesitated, breathed the fatty aroma rising from the plate, then put a piece in his mouth. Beneath the gamy-sweet taste lay a hint of foulness. It was still fresh, but not as fresh as Andrew ought to have.

He served the jambalaya as it was. Andrew tucked into it with his usual impeccable table manners and voracious appetite. Jay ate sparingly, absorbed in Andrew's descriptions of certain back rooms and starless alleyways in Soho. When he paused to sip his cold Dixie, Jay said, "Why don't you just go ahead and try some?"

Andrew raised his eyebrows. "Some . . . ?"

"You know you're curious. I saw you licking your lips that first day in the slave quarters. You swallowed molecules of a human body then. Why not try enough to taste it?"

"Why not, indeed?" Andrew poured the rest of his beer into his glass, centered the bottle back in its wet ring of condensation. "I've thought of it every day since we met. I thought of it before, too. Back in London, as I cut up the bodies for disposal, I'd occasionally muse on that final taboo. I'd say to myself, *Andrew Compton, you've sucked their cold mouths and cocks; you've licked their blood from your hands by the bucketful; you've boiled the flesh off their skulls, then used the same pot to make curry. Why not just fry up a few tender bits and see what it's like—perhaps with a nice egg?"*

"What stopped you?"

"I suppose I was afraid. Keeping them beside me in bed for a few nights was one thing, but I was unnerved by the thought of waking alone in the dark and still feeling them with me, in my very cells. Does it ever frighten you?"

Jay smiled. "Before I met you, Andrew, it was my only comfort."

After Jay's exquisite dinner, we strolled through the residential backstreets of the French Quarter, avoiding places of human congregation, lingering in stillness and shadow. The dark streets were pleasantly sinister after the cozy golden glow of Jay's dining room. A chill breeze whispered through verdant gardens; a lone saxophone wailed somewhere far away. For the first time since I'd left England, I remembered that it was November.

We stopped for a nostalgic nightcap at the Hand of Glory. For some reason the place was packed with a young Gothic crowd tonight, resplendent in their monochrome regalia, the myriad textures of teased hair, torn lace, fishnet, and crushed velvet more fascinating to the eye than colour. I remembered a Goth boy I'd brought home once. He had bared his white throat to me willingly, as if meeting a lover whose touch he'd awaited for years.

When I told Jay about this, he frowned in puzzlement. "Didn't you want to draw out his pain? Wouldn't it have been interesting to see if he still welcomed it?"

"Well, I suppose he might have done. But what if I'd spoiled his experience of death? He seemed to have been looking forward to it all his life."

"They're always afraid at first. The ones who have never experienced terrible pain start out calmer, because they have no concept of how bad it can be. When they discover how much their bodies are capable of hurting, they're astounded. When they realize it isn't going to end quickly, they crumble under the weight of their own fear. The ones who have known pain are terrified from the start. But either way . . ." Jay groped for the words to express something that had obviously long intrigued him. "After you've been going for a while, after they've begged and screamed and vomited and realized none of it is going to make any difference, they pass into a kind of ecstasy. Their flesh becomes like clay. Their insides cleave to your lips. It becomes a collaboration."

"But surely they're just trying to get it over with faster?"

"I don't know." Jay's eyes were dreamy. "I think once the body realizes it's definitely, irrevocably going to die at your hands, it begins to work with you. You might be choking a boy, or cutting or burning him, or your fingers might be knuckle-deep in his guts, but at a certain point his body not only stops resisting—it falls into your rhythm."

He reached for my hand across the table; it was the sort of bar where you could do that. His fingers were damp where they had held his beer bottle, slightly bony, very strong.

"So you've engaged in this soul-deep collaboration," he went on. "The boy has surrendered everything to you: his fear, his agony, his life. What would you do then?"

I settled into the pleasure of memory. "I'd wash the body, rinse off the fluids of death: the blood, urine, saliva. I'd leave him in a cold bath until the wounds coagulated. Then I'd powder him, and the talc would enhance the pallor until he looked almost blue. We'd lie in bed together. I'd fall asleep holding him, stroking him."

"And the next day?"

"I disliked the stiffness that developed as rigor mortis set in. Sometimes I'd wait until it passed and keep them another day or two. More often they'd begin to smell and stain my bed, and I'd have to dispose of them."

"One-night, two-night stands," Jay said dismissively. "You can prolong the parting, and you can stave off decay. But in the end it all catches up with you. Why not savour them every way you can? While you were wiping and powdering, I'd be enjoying the first of several sumptuous meals."

"Tell me again how you prepare them."

"In general, or blow by blow?"

"Blow by blow, with all the trimmings, of course."

Jay returned my smile, faintly mocking: my obsessive ambivalence on this subject amused him. Then he began to talk, and his eyes narrowed and darkened with pleasure as he described his culinary prowess.

"I cut them into manageable pieces and flay the meat off the bones. This was really messy at first, but I improved over time. Now my cuts of meat look better than the ones at Schwegmann's. I wrap them in plastic. I save some of the organs—the liver if I haven't torn it up too badly, and the heart, which is quite tough but has a bitter, intense flavor. I tried to make soup stock out of some bones once, but it tasted awful. Human fat is just too rancid to eat. Usually I tenderize the meat and roast or fry it with very little seasoning. Each part of the body has a distinct flavor, and each body tastes subtly different."

"Of course. Human lives are much more varied than those of swine or cattle."

Jay smiled. "Exactly. You have an instinct for this."

"Hello, Jay."

We looked up, startled out of our reverie. A honey-skinned, glossy-haired form had materialized out of the pale matte-dyed crowd. Naturally thinner than most of his compatriots in black, he too wore silver ornaments in his ears and dark rings of makeup round his eyes—Oriental eyes like elongated chips of obsidian, jaded beyond their years. The rest of his face was very, very young.

I could see the possibilities of the situation flickering through Jay's mind. He had a good deadpan gaze, but not good enough to fool me. Whoever this little chappie was, he obviously knew and fancied Jay. This put Jay in the awkward position of wondering *(a)* if he introduced me to his friend, would I be jealous; *(b)* would his friend also be jealous and say something to make me more so; *(c)* would he endanger my anonymity by introducing us?

I almost enjoyed watching Jay squirm, but only because I gleaned new knowledge from every facet of his character, and until now I had not seen him genuinely uncomfortable. But I could not leave him to suffer for long.

"Good evening," I said in my suavest voice, nudging Jay's leg under the table. "I'm Jay's cousin Arthur. I'm in New Orleans on holiday."

"Uh, hi. My name's Tran."

As the boy shook my outstretched hand, a startled look passed over his face, for my fingers had very briefly slid up and encircled his wrist.

"Are you from London?" he asked, recovering.

"Got it in one."

"Do you live near Whitechapel?"

"No, actually. Kensington." (This was a lie; I'd never lived in a posh area. People paid too much attention to their neighbours in posh areas. Of course, in the end even my neighbours in Brixton were driven to complain.) "Why do you ask?"

"Oh, you know . . ." He shrugged, a movement made charming by the slightness of his shoulders. "I've read about Jack the Ripper."

"Really? Did you know he arranged his murder sites in the shape of a cross?" Tran shook his head, so I went on. "If you mark the sites on a map of London, you'll see that all save the last one form quite a regular cross shape. The odds of that happening at random are extraordinary."

"What about the last one?" Jay interjected.

"That was the one where he just freaked out," said Tran.

"He shredded the girl and tore out all her organs. He would've had to be covered in blood, but nobody saw him leave the building."

"It was the only one he did indoors," I pointed out. Jay glared at me. "Sorry. You tend to absorb these things living in London."

"I think it's interesting." Tran slid into the booth beside Jay, who looked more pained than ever. "I like to read about killers. I like to think about how their minds work."

I smiled across the table at him. "Any theories yet?"

Jay banged his beer glass down on the scarred tabletop. "Look, I'd love to sit here and talk about perverts all night, but we need to get going. I think I left the coffeepot on after dinner."

You did not, I thought. If Jay wanted to drag me away from such a beautiful, acquiescent boy, I knew he must have his reasons. But getting up and leaving was the last thing I wanted to do. I'd gotten a good look into this boy already, and he was fairly begging for our attentions.

"Oh, I won't keep you. I'm just here looking for some customers. Midnight Sun's playing later, and you know, this crowd . . ." Tran touched his forefinger to his tongue. "You need anything, Jay?"

"No."

"Well . . . see you later. Too bad you can't stay for the band."

"Are they very good?" I asked.

"I love them. I'm just going to get drunk and dance and stumble back to the Hummingbird at dawn."

"Bit of a long, lonely walk, isn't it?"

Tran shrugged. "It's cheap. They don't ask for ID—I registered under the name Frank Booth. And who knows? Maybe it won't be so lonely. Maybe I'll meet a mysterious stranger tonight." He gave Jay a last longing look.

"Be careful," I told him. "You never know who's out there, do you, Jay?"

Jay could only shake his head.

"I'll try. It was nice meeting you, Arthur. See you around the Quarter?"

"I hope so," I told him.

We crossed Jackson Square on our way to the grocery before we went home. A pearly gibbous moon rode high in the curdled purple sky. The cathedral's spire soared upward, lacy as a New Orleans sepulchre, stabbing at veins of cloud. On the cobblestones below, the ragtag nighttime denizens of the square drank, sang, ranted, or simply slept.

"We must have him," I said with utter confidence, "and we *shall* have him."

Jay shook his head violently. "I already told you there's no way we can. Tran's a local kid."

"It is of no consequence. I want him. I want to *eat* him, Jay."

"Andrew . . ."

"He is the ideal victim."

"He is not. He's the worst possible victim."

"From a practical standpoint, perhaps. But in the practical details you lose sight of Destiny. *That boy is meant for us, Jay, and we will have him.*"

"Absolutely not."

We traversed the urine-scented alley that ran along one side of the cathedral and emerged near the A&P on Royal Street. I held the door for Jay as we went in. He took a plastic basket from a stack of them and moved through the narrow aisles, selecting mustard, capers, a sort of hot sauce he hadn't tried before. I followed silently, smiling to myself, biding my time. Jay was buying no real food, only condiments. I knew I would be able to make him see things my way.

The checkout girl held up a jar full of a chunky, viscous reddish substance. "What is this stuff?"

"Chutney," Jay told her.

"What you do with it?"

His mouth quirked in a half-smile. "You serve it with meat."

How completely I loved him in that moment! The conscienceless depths of his eyes, the lank straggle of his blond hair on his pale neck, the carnage of secrets contained within the noble dome of his skull. I knew I was smarter than Jay; though he did not lack intelligence, his sphere of awareness was the narrowest I'd ever encountered. He was so keenly focused on his world of tortures and delicacies that he had trouble concentrating on anything outside that world. It made him seem a bit ephemeral, like a spirit stuck in the earthly plane, obsessively repeating one action over and over, trying to get it right. In my previous life I had always been able to support myself, keep body and soul together, if sometimes just barely. I could not imagine Jay working for a living. Yes, I was better versed in the ways of the daytime world. But in that moment I knew Jay was the supreme animal of the night.

Outside the A&P, Jay stopped to buy a newspaper from a crippled vendor. The corner of St. Peter and Royal Streets seethed with varieties of French Quarter nightlife. A black a cappella group performed across the street, dark voices scatting in unison. A man in a filthy, tattered army jacket and a drool-slick gray beard berated the empty air in front of his face. A policeman pulled up on a little motor scooter, looking bored.

Jay and I headed down Royal Street. We had gone less than a block when a thin dirty-nailed hand slid out of a patch of darkness at the mouth of an alley. "Spare some change, fellas?"

We turned to look at the boy sitting hunched against the iron gate that separated the alley from the street. Ratty clumps of long ginger hair hung down over a face that might have once been strong-boned, but now looked hollowed, starved. His eyes were his most arresting feature, ice-blue irises rimmed with a thin circle of black. Though the night was damp and cool, the boy wore no jacket, and I saw that his inner forearms were scarred with a mixture of razor slashes and needle tracks, some half healed, some fresh enough to ooze.

"Sure, I think I have some change." Jay reached into his

pocket, came out with a crisp fiver. The boy's pupils dilated at the sight of it, but he did not reach for the money until Jay held it out to him. One grubby hand came up and scraped his hair away from his face as he tucked the bill into his shoe. He did not smile, but gave us a long, grave stare that communicated his thanks. Jay and I exchanged a look and came to a decision.

"How would you like to make some more money?" Jay asked.

"What'd you have in mind?"

"We live just down the street. If you'd care to join us for the rest of the evening, you could have a shower, something to eat . . ."

"How about the money?" He spoke quickly, rather glassily, and I sensed that this was the junk talking. I knew a thing or two about young street junkies; they would do almost anything for cash, but they always wanted to know how much they were going to get.

"Well . . ." Jay pretended to think about it. "I could give you a hundred for the evening."

I saw a flicker of elation in the boy's eyes, but he only said, "Fair enough. I'd like to see a friend first, though."

Jay's brow creased in annoyance. "We don't want to wait around while you cop. Look, I've got some morphine at our place from a back injury I had a few months ago. Will that do?"

"Morphine?" The boy sat up straighter. "What kind of morphine?"

Jay shrugged. "Half-grain tablets. I never used many of them. I think I may have ten or twelve left."

"Yeah, that'll tide me over." He scrambled to his feet, hoisting a dirty backpack on one shoulder. He was taller than I'd expected, but painfully thin, and I wondered whether there could be much meat on those stark bones.

"What's your name?" I asked.

"They call me Birdy."

"Who does?"

"The sad fucks who have any reason to talk to me."

Not your standard tarty come-on; but I could tell that Jay appreciated the irony of the reply. I did, too.

Back at the house, Jay punched in a series of numbers on the keypad of his security system, then unlocked the gate. Motion sensors automatically bathed the courtyard in soft light. Birdy stepped in hesitantly, as if he knew he was going to his death but didn't care overmuch. His ginger hair hung halfway down his back, tangled and frayed. I thought how beautiful he might have been in some parallel universe. Then I reverted to my contemplation of his beauty in this one.

Thirty minutes later, I lay on one side of the bed staring at Birdy's unconscious face. Jay really did have morphine for an old back injury, which he said he'd gotten moving the big refrigerator into the slave quarters. We had watched the boy cook it up and shoot it into his vein with his own needle, our breath quickening in unison as the blood blossomed into the clear solution. As soon as those icy eyes fluttered shut, Jay stretched out Birdy's arms and handcuffed his skinny wrists to the bedposts. The boy muttered a faint, incoherent protest. I unzipped his trousers and yanked them to his knees.

Soon we had him naked, his legs secured by ankle straps lined with sheepskin, which struck me as obscurely comical. I kissed his nipples, his ribs, his concave stomach. When I began to suck his cock, it grew instantly hard and stayed that way, a quality I had always liked in my young junkies. He tasted sweaty and sharp, not clean but intensely *human*.

"I love heroin users," Jay whispered. "As long as they're young enough and not too strung out, their flesh has a faint gingery taste."

"What about the risk?"

"HIV? If it finds me, I accept it with my blessing. Maybe

it's already found me. If so, I welcome it." Jay leaned over the boy's prone body and kissed me, cupping his hand behind my neck, sliding his tongue deep into my mouth. I wondered at his attitude, but could not argue with it; after all, I had never felt better in my life.

Birdy moaned. We glanced down at him. His eyelids fluttered; his tongue scraped over dry lips. When I gave him a tot from the flask of rum on the nighttable, he sucked gratefully at the bottle's neck.

"Jam it down his throat," Jay suggested. "Then we can break it."

I ignored him, sliding my arm under the thin shoulders, cradling the meagre frame. I felt Jay's lips brush the top of my head, a brief affectionate kiss; then his weight left the bed. Immersing myself in the odours and textures of the boy's body, which was now entirely out of his control and mine to handle as I wished, I barely noticed.

Though it owed more to strong drugs than sexual desire, Birdy's passive state made me nostalgic. I beg you to recall that the last two men I'd killed, junior doctor Waring and poor Sam, had been struggling, hurt and bleeding, fighting for their lives. (I refused to include Doctor Drummond in this count— he was not the sort of man I would have chosen to kill, and his death had been uninterestingly easy.) Now here was a scruffy, beautiful boy immobilized and waiting for my blade. It took me back, it did.

All the way back to my first time. I'd been seventeen, shy and spotty, but had managed to talk my way into the fringes of a punk crowd brimming with testosterone and rebellion. Another boy and I broke into a derelict office building—I no longer remember what we pretended to be looking for. He said he would do anything I liked, and I ordered him to kneel before me. When he did, I knocked him semiconscious with a brick and heaved him across someone's forgotten desk. I didn't mind, a little later, when he vomited on the dusty desktop. A good bit of sperm and blood had already seeped out of him, and the fluids mingled warmly on the glass. I rubbed my hands through them, stroked them over my chest and down to the greasy juncture where my cock met his asshole. Though I had already more or less killed him, I didn't consider the possibility that he could be artful enough to kill me too, months or years in the future, in the harsher light of another decade. It was 1977, Sid Vicious was still alive, and no one had a horror of bodily fluids. Vomit was one of the less precious bodily fluids, but after watching our wretched heroes slash their veins, blow mucus out of their nostrils, and void the contents of their stomachs onstage, we could scarcely upset ourselves over a harmless string of bile oozing from a lover's mouth. After all, the musicians vomited onstage to show their contempt for us, their audience. And contempt was surely an expression of love.

Now Jay was padding back across the bedroom, stroking the length of my spine, pressing something smooth and cold into my hand. I lifted my head from the boy's chest. It was a hunting knife Jay had given me, a sleek bone-handled thing with a barbed blade fully eight inches long.

"It was my great-great-uncle's," he said.

"I love you, Jay."

"I can't say that. If I loved you, I don't think we'd both still be alive. But I *know* you, Andrew, and that's something I've never said to anyone else."

"I know you too."

I felt him shiver. "Go ahead. Do it any way you like, but do it now. I want to see him die."

I placed the tip of the blade against the boy's throat, right at the V of his collarbone. It was sharp enough to pierce the skin with very little pressure. A bead of blood welled up, very dark against the parchment-pale skin, then spilled over the ridge of the bone and streaked the left pectoral.

I always have to laugh at writers who employ the phrase

Something snapped inside him as a prelude to violence. The only time I ever felt anything snap inside me was the day I decided to leave prison, a sharp immediate relief like the snapping of an elastic that had constricted my heart for years. But when I saw that first drop of blood—always, when I saw the first drop of blood—something *melted* inside me. Like a wall of earth crumbling and dissolving in a hard rain, like a sheet of ice breaking apart and letting a river run free.

The knife parted skin and muscle, skated over breastbone. When it reached the hollow of the ribs it sank deep into the body. There was no resistance, no indication of agony; Birdy lay motionless in his restraints and let me open him up like a Christmas parcel. As my hand brushed his erection aside, I felt the blade grate against his pubic bone. For a long moment his torso remained intact, bisected from throat to crotch by a narrow red ribbon. Then his wound blossomed open and his contents spilled forth, a cornucopia of rare fluids and stinking scarlet treasures . . .

A sepulchre of disease.

Time slowed to a crawl as we stared at the boy's yawning body cavity. I could not make myself touch it. At last Jay put his hands in the wound and pulled the edges apart, giving us a better view of the soapy-looking nodes and curls of tissue sprouting from the boy's organs, from his very *meat.* The things were everywhere, sinister as mushrooms, obscenely white against the glistening reds and pinks of his inner body.

"What is it?" I asked at last. "Some sort of cancer?"

"Something poisonous . . . from his drugs . . . or the air . . . or the water." Jay stroked one of the pale nodes, then smelled his fingers, which were coated with thin blood and a greasy-looking substance. "We can't eat this."

I took several deep breaths, trying to compose myself. I'd tapped into my murderous slipstream, worked myself up to killing intensity. Now I was afraid to touch the prize. I felt like a starving man led to an exquisitely set table, titillated with luscious smells from the kitchen, then informed (just as the first steaming delicacy is set before him) that the cook has laced the banquet with weed killer.

Jay was kneeling above me, his hands and bare chest and pale hair streaked with blood. He looked delicious. I reached for him and pulled him down, and we grappled in the wetness of the spreading stain. He raked his nails across my buttocks, up over my back, etching my flesh with his own designs. The scratches blazed as if doused with acid. I heaved him over and rolled on top of him, pinned his arms, sank my teeth into his biceps. His skin tasted of sweat and boy's blood. Twisting beneath me, he managed to grab a handful of my hair and yank it until the roots shrieked. Without quite realizing what I was about to do—I had subdued so many boys in just the same way—I gave him a quick, sharp clip on the jaw.

Jay's head reeled loosely on his neck. He fell back on the bed, eyes flickering up to whites. I saw blood on his lips, on his teeth, but couldn't tell if it was his own or our guest's. I pulled his eyelids up, made certain both his pupils were the same size, checked his pulse and breathing. I'd only stunned him. Quickly I removed the cuffs from Birdy's wrists and fastened them on Jay's. I didn't bother with the ankle restraints. I wouldn't mind if he thrashed a bit.

I turned him over, stroked the golden down on the backs of his thighs. When I parted his buttocks and ran a finger down his crack, he made a low protesting sound. I hesitated, then leaned over to get the condom and tube of lubricant I knew I would find in the nightstand drawer. Within seconds I had the rubber on my erect cock, well greased. I gripped Jay's hipbones and lifted him, probed his ass, slid into the tight heat of his lower intestine.

The invasion shocked him into rigidity, which made his inner muscles ripple and constrict. He groaned into the pillow, a helpless, furious sound. I bit the back of his neck hard, a favourite gesture of mine ever since I had seen a lioness do it to her prey on a nature programme. At the same time I pressed the tip of my cock against his prostate and rocked gently. Despite himself, Jay began to melt around me.

"It's all right," I said into his ear. "It's me inside you, it's Andrew. I'm the one who stayed on my own, remember? You need to have me inside you. This way you can keep me with you forever."

Jay mumbled something into the pillow.

"What?"

He raised his head and spoke distinctly. *"Then take off the rubber."*

I stopped fucking him. When he glanced over his shoulder, I saw tears on his face. "I mean it. If you're going to rape me, do it right. Make every cell in my body belong to you."

Our eyes locked and something passed between us, something that changed this from an act of rape to an act of love, more intimate than killing the boy together had been. I pulled out, peeled off the condom, and applied more lubricant to my throbbing cock. Jay's ass opened willingly to me as I slid back in, naked as the day I was born. We moved together as if we had done this a thousand times, came together as if the rhythms of our bodies were perfectly synchronized. As I shot pearlescent poison deep into Jay's entrails, he bit my fingers nearly hard enough to draw blood.

"Hungry?" I asked. "Who decides who we eat next? Hmmm, Jay?"

"You do," he whispered into the palm of my hand.

I cradled him, treasured him. He was still alive, and I respected him infinitely, for now he had acknowledged what we both knew to be the truth.

Jay was indeed the splendid young animal of the night.

But I had tamed him just enough to show who was the master.

12

"**H**ere's a nifty item from yesterday's paper. Shandra McNeil of Gertrude, Loooz-i-anna, was convicted on three counts of attempted murder, which may be upgraded to first-degree murder if any of her victims dies before her. McNeil, who has AIDS, engaged in unprotected sex with several men she met at singles' bars. Three who have since tested HIV-positive brought suit against her. McNeil pled guilty, and said she exposed at least ten men to the AIDS virus without warning them. Her reason: she desperately wanted a child before she died. Shandra McNeil is now five months pregnant.

"Well, if it wasn't for that fetus, I'd say pin a medal on her. She's wiped out at least three breeder assholes, probably a lot more, and all because her biological clock didn't *stop* ticking when the time bomb in her cells *started*. Shandra, you dumb bitch, thanks for your wonderful addition to the human race. The world really needs another digestive tract. Let's just hope the poor kid catches HIV sliding down your diseased cunt, so your stupidity-riddled genes can die off as soon as possible.

"Let's move on to more reputable sources, shall we? Here's

one from the *Weekly World News*. The headline: AIDS KILLER
RISES FROM DEAD! The story: 'Gay serial killer Andrew
Compton died of AIDS on November fourth . . . and on November fifth, he flew the coop! Bureaucrats at Painswick
Prison in Birmingham, England, deny responsibility' . . .
hmmm, big surprise there . . . 'since the homicidal homo disappeared from the morgue of a nearby hospital where he was
being held for autopsy.

"'Compton was arrested in nineteen eighty-eight after a
sex-and-torture spree that left twenty-three young men dead
and dismembered. Shortly before his death, he tested HIV-
positive. HIV, the virus that causes AIDS' . . . thank you,
Weekly World News . . . 'is considered unlikely to survive in
bodies dead over twenty-four hours. BUT IS ANDREW
COMPTON REALLY DEAD? Scotland Yard is reportedly
treating the case as a body-snatching, but offered no comment
about who might want the AIDS-infected body of a vicious
psychopath.'"

Luke paused for a beat, then delivered the punch line he'd
planned around this story. "Well, hell, who WOULDN'T?"

He caught Soren's eye over the control panel. Soren closed
his eyes and slowly shook his head, denoting silent suffering.
OK, so the tabloid story had been in bad taste. WHIV needed
a little comic relief every now and then.

"I think it's about time to take a call," he said. Soren nodded, picked up a cellular phone and listened, then handed it to
Luke, who placed it in a cradle on the console and punched
the speaker button.

"You're on WHIV. Talk to me."

A girl's voice, smug and self-righteous. "I just wanted to
say I think you're a very sick person."

"No shit, honey. I'm on ten kinds of medicine, all of which
are toxic, none of which I can pay for. I've got sores around
my asshole from weeks of chronic diarrhea and cheap toilet
paper. My throat feels like it's full of ground glass and I get big

black spots in front of my eyes when I stand up. Thanks for the diagnosis."

"That's not what I mean and you know it. AIDS is a poison you create in your own blood. You say you hate breeders, but the ability to nurture life is a sacred gift from the Goddess. Whether you know it or not, you suckle at Her breast."

"Well, Her rancid milk hasn't done a thing for my T-cell count. You fucking Wiccans love a secret, and I'll blow it right now: your entire reason for existing is obsolete. You worship an outdated biological imperative. Have a shitty day."

Click. Dial tone.

"Martyr, you're into that moon-hugging stuff. Do you worship a Goddess? Don't tell me if you do. I hate those bitches, all but Kali—at least when she breeds, she eats her young."

Soren had rigged the chip of his cellular phone so that it generated a new ID number each time it was used, and couldn't be traced. As a result, they had a different phone number every broadcast. Reception was often very poor out here in the swamp, but Johnnie kept them close enough to New Orleans to pick up calls. Today they were tied up at one of the many deserted docks they used, which helped a little.

Luke switched over to music mode and played Robyn Hitchcock's love ballad "Queen Elvis" from the acoustic album *Eye*. Looking at the jewelbox, he recalled the lament for a lost lover in one of the other songs. *Even talking is out of reach* . . . It captured the white-hot agony of an affair ended in anger, the silent void left by the absence of the person with whom you'd had the most intensely emotional conversations of your life.

He flipped through his newspaper clippings, stared at the grainy photo the *Weekly World News* had run with its story. Compton was a handsome devil with a shock of dark hair and a slanted half-smile. Luke tried to imagine killing twenty-three boys, found it disturbingly easy. He wondered just how far removed he was from a predator like Compton. Luke thought a lot of people deserved to die, but those were people he hated, either individually or collectively. Andrew Compton had probably felt some kind of love for his twenty-three boys, yet he had murdered every one of them. It was a real pisser.

Just as the song ended, another call came in. *Great,* Luke caught himself thinking, *somebody else to abuse.* An older man by the sound of his voice, faintly hoarse but crisp around the edges. "Mr. Rimbaud, I presume."

"None other."

"Good afternoon to you and your crew."

"Not particularly, but thanks anyway. Wanna talk about something, or is this a social call?"

"Sorry, don't mean to waste your airtime. The little amenities help keep me sane. I'm a fifty-year-old gay man calling from Metairie. I've been with my lover for fifteen years. We have two sons and a daughter."

"Neat trick. How'd you manage it?"

"Straight friends chose us as godparents to their children, and asked us to be legal guardians in the event of their death. They died in a boating accident when the kids were young. There was no family to contest our guardianship, so we got them. Mr. Rimbaud, we went through every kind of hell to raise those children as our own. Their schools sent social workers to spy on us every term, first grade through senior year. Their friends' parents forbade their children to visit our home. Other kids harassed them so often we had to start them all in karate lessons before they reached their teens.

"We raised three heterosexual kids who understand what it's like to be gay, who'll call the straight world on its homophobia wherever they see it. They're damn good martial artists too, by the way. When I listen to your show, I hear you saying those kids shouldn't exist because they are the product of 'breeders.' By those standards, you and I shouldn't exist either. Your standards are illogical, impossible—yet you express them so fervently, and often so eloquently.

"If you don't think children are our hope, what do you suggest? How would Lush Rimbaud redesign the world?"

Luke took a deep breath, leaned into the microphone, and waited for Lush to start talking. It took him the better part of a minute to realize that Lush had no answer.

"Mr. Rimbaud? Are you there?"

"I'm here," he said in his own voice. "What's your name?"

"Alex."

"Are you HIV-positive, Alex?"

"Thankfully, no."

"But I bet you did some stuff in your flaming youth that made you wonder. Some stuff that kept you on edge until you got those first test results."

"Of course. Didn't we all?"

"Yeah. Yeah, we did. And some of us who flunked the test haven't learned to take life one day at a time or think of AIDS as our spiritual teacher or any of that other happy crapola. Some of us look in the mirror and all we see is a senseless fucking virus that's going to kill us without mercy or dignity. We become sexual pariahs, and we live on stolen time. Every moment we stay alive is a moment we cheat the death a billion right-wing fundamentalists think we deserve. The world shrinks away from us in hatred, terror, and disgust, as well it might—*we're plague victims, and we're contagious.*

"I don't know, Alex, it just . . . gets me *down* sometimes. You ask me how I'd redesign the world. Easy: I'd stick around for another half-century or so. That's all I want.

"My beautiful, stupid ex-boyfriend, with his black frocks and tattered notebooks, he thought death was some kind of romantic figure. He'd burn incense and listen to his Bauhaus CDs and press his frail hand to his wan forehead. *Très gothique,* no? He even shot up heroin with me, because he wanted to TRY IT ALL, TO PUSH THE LIMITS OF EXISTENCE—but mainly he liked it because it gave him a three-hour hard-on.

"Somehow though, after he found out his lover was HIV-positive, death didn't seem quite so . . . *pretty* anymore. His love of death was a sham, because he was twenty years old and he knew in his secret heart that he was never gonna die. Death was for old movie stars, for crack dealers in the 'hood—not for *his* cute little ass.

"And you know what? By the same token, my insistence on living is a sham. I know I'm going to kick it within the next couple of years. All those guys who were never gonna die from AIDS—Michael Callen, David Feinberg, Lake Sphinx—they're all gone. I will be, too. Why not kill myself now and save taxpayers the few grand I would've cost them in medicine, instead of sticking around and bitching about the millions of dollars sucked up by breeders?"

Luke had almost forgotten the caller was there until his crisp voice interrupted. "Because you have something to say, obviously."

"Do I, Alex? Do I really? 'Cause I don't know anymore. I don't want to finish the book I'm working on because it's not good enough to be my last one. The most desirable thing I can imagine is to wake up with my boyfriend one more time, and that's not gonna happen, because I'll probably never see him again. Sometimes I get on the radio and my mind goes blank. I can just hear it in a few more months: 'WHIV, your station for AIDS dementia blackouts! Twenty-five minutes of silence every hour, guaran-TEED!'

"But I'm Lush Rimbaud, and I refuse to shut up or die. And I waste what little breath I have left talking trash about people like you who've made an actual difference in the world. I know I never have and never will. Hell, people probably hate queers *more* because of me. Go ahead, man. Make more humans. Somebody's gonna do it, and most of them are going to raise assholes, idiots, and psychos. If you can do otherwise, you've done better than me.

"Fuck it. Fuck it all. I'm signing off."

He disconnected the caller, removed his earphones, and killed the mike. Soren was staring at him, aghast. Luke couldn't care. He felt as if he had spent the past several years harboring two distinct personalities that had just abruptly merged. The resulting effect on his brain reminded him vaguely of being ass-fucked with insufficient lubricant. He put his hands over his face and closed his eyes.

"Luke?" Soren's voice was soft, cautious. "What's up?"

"I don't know." It came out as a croak, dry-throated and guttural. "I can't do this anymore. That guy was right. I don't want to redesign the world, I just want to take it down with me."

"That guy never said—"

"I'm the one saying it." Luke pushed away from the console and stood. His head spun and his knees began to buckle. Soren was there, catching him, sliding wiry arms around his chest and hugging him tight.

"What are you saying? You really don't want to do WHIV anymore?"

"I *can't.*" Luke let his head sag against Soren's chest. Soren lowered him back to the chair, but didn't let go of him. "I'm just so fucking tired . . . and I know I'll never finish my book . . . and all I really want is to be with Tran."

"You know you can't."

"But if I die without trying again, I'm a coward. I don't mind having regrets about stuff I've done. It's the regrets about stuff I *haven't* done that bother me."

"I understand. But you've *been* trying to get back together with Tran, and it hasn't happened. You have important work to do, Luke. Or would you rather spend the rest of your life chasing a dream?"

"Yes."

"So you're quitting the station?"

"Soren . . ." Luke could see defeat in the set of the younger man's shoulders. WHIV was easily the most important thing in

Soren's life. "That support group you go to. Do they ever talk about the role emotion plays in sickness?"

"Of course."

"In the past six months I've gotten angrier and I've gotten sicker. Now I feel like there's nothing left inside me but broken glass and rusty nails. I don't want to spread that shit around anymore. There's one thing I know will make me happy if I can get it, and I mean to try. Or would you rather watch me drown in my own vitriol, just because it sounds so damn good on your pirate radio station?"

"I thought you were as committed to WHIV as I am. I thought you fed off the anger in a way I couldn't understand. You *are* responsible for your own emotions, Lucas."

A part of him knew this to be true. Another part wanted to rage against it, to claim that those emotions had been forced on him by chemistry and circumstance, but this went directly against the insistence on free will that helped him maintain a margin of hope. He wondered when he had become such a miserable, self-pitying wretch.

"You're right about everything," he told Soren. "And I'm sorry to walk out on you. But this is what I have to do."

Soren nodded and started putting some of his equipment in a cardboard box. Luke couldn't tell how angry he was. Maybe hearing an admission of wrongness and an apology from the lips of Lucas Ransom had stunned him into temporary acquiescence.

Johnnie Boudreaux had been listening to their conversation from the deck. Now he eased his tall body into the cabin and pulled up a crate next to Luke's lawn chair. Slowly he rolled a joint of some sticky green pot one of his few remaining friends in the swamp had grown. When he fired it up, Luke noticed a fresh KS lesion near the corner of his mouth, dark like a bruise in the match's flickering shadow.

Johnnie exhaled blue smoke, then asked, "Y'all really mean to shut it down?"

"I don't want to," Soren said. "But we can't do it without Luke. Nobody could replace him."

"Somebody could replace me, though."

"What do you mean?"

"Hate to tell you now, but I plan on checkin' out myself. Not just quittin' the boat, I mean, but . . ." He made a gun of thumb and forefinger, gestured at the side of his skull.

"Why now?" Luke asked.

"Well . . ." Johnnie's hands twisted together in his lap, white and strong, with a thin but permanent black line of engine grease under each nail. "My brother died two days ago."

"Brother . . . ?" Soren glanced at Luke, who was equally mystified. "We didn't know you . . ."

"Had a brother, yeah. Etienne was a lot older than me. Lived at home when I did, but he made a lot of trips into New Orleans." Johnnie chuckled thinly. "To the French Quarter."

"Was he gay?" Soren asked.

"Why'd you think our parents kicked us both out at the same time?"

Soren sucked in his breath, and Luke said, "He gave you AIDS?"

"He was the only person I'd ever been with."

"He molested you?" Soren again.

Johnnie shrugged. "Do you call it molestin' if I always liked it? Anyway, he's dead now. Came down with the pneumonia again and there was nothin' we could do."

Luke thought of something. "Who took care of him while you were on the boat?"

"Our sister. She's twenty-two. She'd leave her kids with her husband and come over to our place. Tell him she was goin' to see our folks. You can bet if our folks ever happened to stop by while she was out, she'd get her ass kicked good, prob'ly by Jo-Jo *and* our daddy."

"Jo-Jo?"

"Her lovin' husband. The one who threatened to break my

arms and Etienne's legs if we ever came near their house again."

Luke imagined the life of this woman, twenty-two years old with children in the plural and a husband who must be every bit as stupid as his name, watching her brothers die of a strange and sickening disease she'd probably only heard horror stories about, unable to tell anyone. Maybe there *were* some hells worse than his.

"I told her I was goin' to break the news to you guys, then do it out here in the swamp, so she wouldn't have another body to mess with." Johnnie grimaced. "We buried Etienne ourselves. It was pretty awful.

"So I figured if you wanted to keep the station runnin', you could leave the boat tied up here. Y'all know how to row the pirogue and how to get back to your car from here. This dock is as close to safe as you can get. Or you could learn to drive the boat—it's easy."

Soren shook his head. "I'm shutting down. I can take my equipment out in two pirogue trips. WHIV is dead."

"Do you want us to go?" Luke asked Johnnie.

The look he gave them was almost shy. "Would you stay with me? I know it's a hell of a thing to ask. But I'm scared I'll do it wrong. I don't want to lie here hurtin' . . . and . . . well . . . I saw Etienne die. I want somebody to see me."

Luke and Soren looked at each other, then agreed, trying not to show their reluctance. It wasn't a thing you ever wanted to do for a friend. But when asked, you pretty much had to.

Johnnie exchanged a fierce hug with each of them. Then he took the pearl-handled revolver from his coat pocket and walked out onto the deck. Luke and Soren followed.

"Johnnie?" said Soren. "What should we . . . *do* with you?"

"Roll me over the side and say a prayer for my soul."

"But . . ." Soren's hands sketched frustration in the air; *what about the smell, what happens when your bloated corpse floats to the surface next week;* all the dreadful questions he couldn't ask.

"You worried about *body disposal,* Soren?" Johnnie threw back his head and laughed, the first time Luke had ever seen him do so. "City boy, don't you know they got big-ass *gators* in this swamp?"

Soren looked sick.

"I hope I give the fuckers AIDS. Damn gator killed my dog once." Johnnie looked forlorn for a moment; then a shadow seemed to pass from his face. "Bye, Luke. Bye, Soren."

He lowered himself to the deck, tipped his head backward over the edge of the barge, and took the gun barrel deep into his mouth. Luke had barely registered the muffled *pop* when blood exploded from the top of Johnnie's head, cascaded out of his mouth and nostrils, painting the wasted flesh of his throat, fountaining into the water.

Luke and Soren had gripped each other's hands without thinking. Now their fingers were knotted together painfully. Luke extricated himself and knelt by Johnnie. The dead boy's eyes were half-open, unblinking, unlit. His features were slack, his mouth relaxed around the gun's barrel as if around a lover's softening cock. Johnnie had asked them to say a prayer, but Luke had none at his disposal. He planted the sole of his boot against Johnnie's hip and rolled him over the side of the barge. Johnnie's body made a small splash from which grew a pattern of concentric ripples. His blood traced bright threads through the oily dark water.

Soren turned away. "Can we go now?"

"Wait." Luke shaded his eyes, looked toward the far bank of the bayou. Was that a prehistoric shape detaching itself from the clumps of water weed and cypress root that grew in the shady boundary between morass and land? Was that a pair of gold reptilian bubble-eyes gliding across the still water toward the boat?

"Luke. We don't want to see this."

"I do."

A pair of long snaggle-toothed jaws yawned open like hinged boards studded with hundreds of nails of varying lengths, driven in at random deadly angles, smacked into Johnnie and clapped together with a sound like a rifle report. Luke heard bones crunching. Johnnie's body was pulled under so quickly that it left a little swirl of blood on the slick surface. The gator made a sinuous trail in the water as it swam for its lair. Luke had heard they would keep a corpse in the root caverns under the bank for days, letting the meat soften and grow rank in the stagnant mud.

"Let's go," he said. But Soren was already in the deckhouse dismantling his equipment, refusing to look at the water, or at Luke's eyes when he came in.

Soren had misjudged the weight of the gear; three trips in the pirogue were required to get it all back to the dock where his car was stashed. Luke had caught a ride with Soren, and he was glad of it. He didn't feel well enough to drive the thirty miles back to New Orleans.

By the third trip in the overloaded little boat, the shock of Johnnie's death had dissipated somewhat. They were hot and sweaty, beginning to get on each other's nerves. Soren kept making bitchy little comments designed to hide his sorrow at tearing down the station. Luke, calmer than he'd been in weeks, tried to ignore these barbs. But as they climbed into the car, dirty and exhausted, Soren asked, "What are you going to do when Tran won't take you back?"

Luke felt his temper resurfacing, a distant flare. "You don't know whether he will or not."

"He hasn't before. He certainly isn't going to *now*."

Something about the stress on that last word made Luke suspicious. "What do you mean, *now?*"

"Well . . . what if he's seeing someone else?"

Soren inserted the key in the ignition. Luke grabbed his hand, prevented him from starting the engine. "You know something."

"Don't be silly. How would I? Tran and I hardly know each other."

"First you tantalize me, then you overexplain yourself. Cut the bullshit. You've seen Tran. You know something. Tell me."

"Luke, let go of me."

He gripped Soren's wrist harder, enjoying the sensation of small bones shifting in his grasp.

"You bastard, you're hurting me. Tran was right."

"Yeah? Right about what?"

"You're a crazy fucking sadist."

"Probably. When did Tran bestow this pearl of wisdom upon you?"

"Last week. The same day he told me about his new boyfriend."

"Who?"

Soren was silent. Luke tightened his grip again, then twisted.

"Oh *Christ*—Luke, that *hurts*—"

"Give me a name."

"Jay Byrne."

Luke let go of Soren's wrist. Soren hauled off and socked him in the shoulder. Protected by his leather jacket, Luke barely noticed. He was trying to place the name, which seemed familiar in a vaguely unpleasant way.

"Jay Byrne? Who the hell is that? Isn't he some kind of French Quarter chicken hawk?"

Soren nodded. "I think he's a creep. Tran seems to like him well enough."

"What else do you know?"

Nothing loosened the lips of a nelly fag like a little well-timed violence. Soren spilled the whole story, from finding Tran asleep in Jackson Square to dropping him off at the Hummingbird Hotel. If he wasn't still registered there, Soren guessed, Tran would be at Jay's house. No, he didn't know Jay's address, but he did know that it was an extremely well-secured private residence on lower Royal Street, and he had had occasion to observe that the finials of the wrought-iron gate were shaped in the likeness of pineapples.

"OK." Luke tried to make himself calm again. "Thanks for the information."

"Oh, you're *so welcome.* I mean, it's not as if you *intimidated* me into talking about it or anything."

"I'm sorry if I hurt you. But you know you'd been wanting to tell me."

"Am I that obvious?"

"Yes."

"Then why can't you tell . . ."

"What?"

"Will you do something for me? Since I gave you the information?"

"What do you want?"

Soren's voice was almost a whisper. "Come home with me."

Luke couldn't believe it. He'd had no idea Soren was attracted to him. He'd had no idea *anyone* would be attracted to him in his present state: he felt wasted, caved in, so ugly.

"I know I'm not your type," Soren went on when Luke didn't answer. "I mean . . . my hair is naturally brown, but I've bleached it for so long, you may as well call me an Aryan. Hell, I don't even own a wok."

Luke couldn't help cracking a smile. Soren returned it tentatively, then reached over and took Luke's hand. Luke saw that Soren's wrist was circled with the deep red marks his fingers had made. He touched them gently, brought Soren's hand to his lips, kissed the knuckles, the ball of the thumb, the fingertips.

"Let's get going," he said.

Soren's hand shook as he turned the key. Luke supposed it had been quite a day for the poor kid. Quite a day for everyone, come to think of it.

They didn't talk much on the way back to New Orleans, but

it was a comfortable ride, the sunset bathing them in warm light as they drove through the swamp. Luke dozed and awoke with a hard-on, thinking of Tran, then remembering it was Soren beside him. He sat up and looked out the window. They were just pulling up to Soren's house in Bywater, a tatty bohemian neighborhood between the Faubourg Marigny and the Industrial Canal.

Soren started making out with him as soon as they were inside. "It's been so long since anyone touched me at *all,*" he explained breathlessly, "and I keep having these fantasies about you, and I never thought you'd be interested, and oh *God* Luke you turn me on . . ."

It was amazing how these things worked out sometimes. But even as he marveled at the sad irony of it all, Luke found his tongue exploring Soren's mouth and his hands straying to Soren's ass.

The bedroom was a soothing expanse of white and ecru in various textures. They fell onto an enormous feather bed and made love for three hours: curious at first, then tender, then passionate. Luke had thought he would be too distracted by his knowledge of Tran and Jay to enjoy himself. He was happy to be proved wrong. Soren was a master of calculated passivity, presenting himself for ravishment in a hundred pretty ways, emitting his pleasure in obscenely elegant phrases and long throaty cries. It was great fun, and at Soren's insistence it was all done safely, since no one knew the effects of repeated infection.

Eventually Soren's breathing deepened and his body relaxed into sleep. Luke eased out of bed and walked silently to the living room, where a cordless phone was placed in the center of an immaculate coffee table. He dialed information, scrawled a number on the back of his hand, dialed again. A surly male voice answered. Some sort of party or drunken brawl raged in the background. No one named Tran was registered at the Hummingbird Hotel.

He wasn't surprised that Tran's parents had kicked out their firstborn. It seemed the natural result of freeloading off them and lying to them for more than three years. Like other Oriental sons Luke had known, Tran tried to have it both ways, keeping up a facade of propriety for the folks while living an exaggeratedly queer and raunchy life of his own. This wasn't the first time Luke had seen such a situation blow up in someone's face, or even the first time he'd helped cause it.

Either Tran was registered under a false name, or he was with his new boyfriend. Once the second possibility had taken root in his mind, Luke gave no further consideration to the first.

He got dressed and let himself out of Soren's house. It was after ten now, not such a great time to be walking around Bywater alone. But Luke had his leather jacket and a razor in his boot and a hollow, burning stare. No one bothered him. And it was only a couple of miles to the French Quarter, where Jay and Tran unwittingly awaited his arrival.

13

As soon as Andrew let him up from the bed, Jay started packing Birdy's body for disposal far away. He didn't want the diseased thing in the house or the slave quarters. It was an omen of the worst kind, an urgent telegram from the universe, a warning that things were not as he had believed; perhaps things were not even as he could imagine. Luckily, in case he had any trouble reading the entrails of the universe, Andrew was right there to help him along.

Birdy appeared to have died of shock or exsanguination. His face was white, slack, drained of what little animation life had given it. Jay lifted the corpse off the bed onto some garbage bags, wrapped it, secured the package with long strips of silver duct tape. When he had finished, Birdy was tightly doubled up in several layers of heavy black plastic, an awkward lump that seemed too small to be a boy. Jay wrestled it into an army-surplus duffel bag he'd picked up in a Decatur Street junk shop and saved for just such a purpose. The bag was large enough to hold two of Birdy.

Andrew was lounging in the blood-drenched bedclothes,

watching indulgently. "Do you want to go for a ride in the swamp?" Jay asked him.

"I didn't know you had a car."

"Well, I don't. I mean, I hardly ever drive. But there's one at my disposal when I need it."

"Nice, this wealthy life."

Jay shrugged. "It leaves me free to pursue my interests, that's all."

"I should say it does!"

Jay collected the car from a nearby garage, swung back down Royal Street to pick up Andrew and Birdy, then headed west on 61, the Airline Highway. Seedy thrift stores and motels gave way to used car lots, abandoned shacks, the encroaching darkness of the swamp. Highway 61 traversed a narrow strip of mud between Lake Pontchartrain and the Mississippi River. The land out here was soft, wet, overgrown, sparsely inhabited. They passed through the whole of St. Charles Parish and into St. John the Baptist, a rural parish seeded with poisonous pockets of industry. The night was illuminated only by the occasional faraway flame of an oil refinery.

Forty miles outside New Orleans, Jay exited the highway, drove north on a state blacktop, then turned onto a gravel road and bumped along until he came to a locked gate in a chain-link fence that stretched away into scrubby woods. Bolted to the steel mesh, a panic-orange sign read PRIVATE PROPERTY— NO TRESPASSING.

Jay got out of the car and unlocked the gate. He drove through, then got out again and locked it behind them. The gravel road led into more woods, beyond which loomed a featureless building of corrugated metal.

"A secret spot for that weekend getaway?" Andrew asked.

"Yes, of sorts."

They lifted their unwieldy parcel from the trunk and carried it to the building. Jay had the key to an unmarked door. Stepping inside, he touched a switch on the wall. There came the brief hum of a generator, and fluorescent track lights in the ceiling flickered on.

The building was full of poison pyramids, towering stacks of steel and plastic drums sloshing with the chemical leftovers of a decade or more. For years the foremen of Byrne Metals and Chemicals had paid various teams of "waste disposal experts" to haul the drums away, shunting them off to the lowest bidder and breathing a prayer of relief as the trucks disappeared down the winding swamp road. No one had any idea what became of the drums after that, and no one was required to know.

But those were the good old days, and long gone. Now it was not even worthwhile to pay the "waste disposal experts," but more expedient to let the drums stack up in forgotten warehouses like these. When a warehouse was full, there was always the swamp.

Jay had explained all this to Andrew on the drive out, and now Andrew was silent, perhaps lulled by the toxic miasma that surrounded the place. Jay upended the bag and let the parcel slide out, then pulled a box cutter from his pocket and slit the black plastic. Retrieving a screwdriver, a prying tool, and a pair of elbow-length industrial gloves from a nearby shelf, he levered the lid off a blue fifty-gallon barrel. A noxious smell filled the air, part chemical, part rot. Donning a second pair of gloves, Andrew helped him lower Birdy's naked corpse into the barrel ass first, so that it ended up in a tight fetal position.

"What's this we're putting him in?"

"Hydrochloric acid."

"Eats right through the bones, does it?"

"It has before."

They hammered the lid back on, gathered their traces, and left this remote archive of poison as orderly and silent as they had found it. On the way back to New Orleans, Jay stopped to toss the bloody garbage bags into a Dumpster behind a Popeye's fried chicken outlet. They returned to the French Quarter as if to a womb, crawled into a freshly made bed just before dawn, and slumbered for most of the day.

Jay got up once, around noon. He put in a call to the Hummingbird Hotel, asked for "Frank Booth," and was connected with a very sleepy-sounding Tran.

"Did you meet a mysterious stranger?"

"Who is this . . . wait a minute . . . Jay?"

"How many other men have your number?"

Tran laughed. "You must be kidding. Nobody even talked to me last night. I think they smell my desperation."

"I feel partly responsible for your desperation."

Tran was silent; a passive indictment.

Jay thought of Andrew, asleep down the hall, dreaming, hungering. He closed his eyes and took the plunge from which there was no turning back. "I'm sorry about all that. It's been a long time since I had such an intense experience with anyone." (*And let them live,* his mind amended.) "My cousin enjoyed meeting you, and I'd like to see you again. Why don't you join us for dinner tonight?"

"Well . . ." Jay could picture him all rumpled and morning-eyed, trying to sort out this unexpected situation. "I . . . I'd love to."

"Good. Around eight?"

"Uh . . . sure."

"See you then."

Jay hung up, feeling a strange mix of terror and elation. His world was careening out of control, but instead of panicking as he would have done a short while ago, he found himself fascinated by its destructive path.

He slid back into the warm bed, molded his body to Andrew's, and slept again. In a few hours he would have to conjure up something for dinner, something simple but exquisite, some toothsome delicacy.

Something suitable for a beautiful boy's last meal.

·   ·   ·

Upon awakening, Jay made a pot of coffee and sat at the kitchen table sipping it, paging blearily through the *Times-Picayune* he'd bought at the grocery last night. In the pre-Thanksgiving food section he read a detailed description of an edible creature newly invented: a gastronomic miscegenation composed of a turkey, chicken, and duck, deboned and nested from smallest to largest, each filled with a different savory stuffing.

This appealed greatly to Jay, and he phoned the delicatessen where they were made. Above protests that the shop did not normally deliver, and in any case could not do so by this evening, Jay named a discreet sum. Dinner, he was told after a hurried consultation at the other end, would arrive at his gate by seven; he need only reheat the thing for an hour.

He woke Andrew with a mug of steaming sweet black coffee and sat on the edge of the bed watching him drink it. There was something severe about Andrew's face despite the tousled spikiness of his dark hair, the clear hypnotic blue of his eyes, the handsome regularity of his features. Perhaps it was a shade of nose length or a wry twist of mouth, the things that made his face seem essentially English. Perhaps it was cruelty.

Andrew blessed him with a dark smile. Jay wondered what would be different between them when this night was over.

Jay had to remind me twice that my name was supposed to be Arthur, though it hardly seemed to matter now. By the time Tran rang at the gate, we were already pleasantly sloshed on cognac. This may have been our first mistake. In the interest of retaining some modicum of our faculties, we should have stayed sober until after dinner. But we were feeling an odd elation, perhaps at the sheer finality of what we were about to do. And we both knew we wouldn't be hungry at dinner.

Tran arrived promptly at eight carrying a bottle of chilled champagne. I wondered where the flowers and chocolates were, but said nothing. Tran and Jay had their odd little courtship, and it wasn't my place to meddle. On the contrary, I found it rather sweet. And I was quite looking forward to watching Jay kill something he had, however superficially, cared for.

Soon we had the champagne poured and the strange nested fowls on the table. Jay and I had discussed lacing Tran's food with a sedative, but we feared his prior knowledge of drugs might allow him to detect such a dose. Besides, Jay suspected that it might be easiest to make Tran swallow a pill simply by offering it to him.

As Tran ate, Jay and I swilled champagne, pushed scraps around our plates, and stared at him. A tender rump roast dangling into a den of leopards could scarcely have been more oblivious, or looked more delectable. Though I was unused to the idea of boys as potential nourishment, I had more than a passing acquaintance with them as victims, and Tran played that role so perfectly I almost believed he was doing it on purpose. He was pretty—very pretty—but so were loads of other boys. This one had something extra. How could a single person fulfill all the mannerisms, distill that vital blend of insecurity and insouciance, exude pheromones that so clearly begged *cut me, fuck me, lay me out cold and have your way with me?* It was as if all the boys of my past had been swirled into one exotic, dangerous cocktail, which Jay had (somewhat reluctantly) served to me with the appropriate garnishes.

When the champagne was drunk and the dishes cleared away, we adjourned to the parlour. It felt like nothing so much as a polite stopover en route to the bedroom. We were all crackling with sexual energy; you could smell it in the dusty parlour air if you breathed deeply enough. Jay offered Tran a snifter of cognac. The boy accepted it, and I saw their fingertips touch, Jay's index finger extending to slide over Tran's knuckles. Tran looked at him, looked at me, drained half his cognac.

"You're meant to sip that," I said.

"I'm not as drunk as I want to be."

Jay caught my eye and shrugged. Maybe we wouldn't have to sedate him with pills after all.

By his second cognac, Tran was sprawled on the Oriental rug with his head tipped backward, resting on my knee. I was seated on a slippery love seat done in rose-coloured satin, Jay beside me, close but not quite touching. Suddenly, without warning, he leaned over and planted a wet kiss on my mouth. His lips tasted of cognac. In my peripheral vision I saw Tran watching us, a drunken sexy smile contorting his fine features.

As Jay ravaged my mouth, Tran turned over and ran his hand up my leg, then fumbled at my zipper. By the time he got it undone, I was hard enough to ache. He ran his tongue over the head of my cock and in a slow spiral down to my balls, gripped my thighs, and took me deep into his throat.

It felt heartbreakingly good. I gasped into Jay's mouth, gripped his shoulders, arched my back. Tran kept swallowing me, elbows splayed, head buried between my legs. Jay put his hand on the back of Tran's head and pushed down. The tip of my penis clicked past his tonsils and slid deeper into his throat, which seemed to go into peristalsis around my swollen flesh.

I felt orgasm lurking, drawing near. Then it was sinking its teeth into the back of my neck just as I had done to Jay last night. Not until it had overtaken me, mauled me, and spit me out half-alive did I realize that my hands had gone round Tran's throat, choking him as Jay forced his head onto my cock.

I fell back on the love seat. Tran flopped off of me, long strings of saliva and spunk trailing from his open mouth. Only Jay's hand tangled in his long hair kept him upright. He took a great wet gulp of air, then another. I could see that his eyes had partly rolled back in his head, but I could not tell whether he was conscious.

Jay stood, pulling Tran upright with him. Tran wobbled on unsteady feet but did not fall. "Come on," Jay said. "Let's get him to the bedroom."

By the time we had Tran spread-eagled on the bed, he had begun to mutter incoherently. I pulled his jumper over his head. His hair came out of its ponytail and spilled around his bare shoulders, a luxuriant black tumble. Jay unzipped Tran's loose bluejeans and tugged them down his skinny legs. He was naked beneath, his body wonderfully smooth, his cock half-erect.

Jay and I looked at each other. His eyes asked a mute question.

"He's yours," I said.

Jay's cold gaze shifted to the boy on the bed. He undressed slowly, touching himself every now and then as if to ascertain that he was still made of solid flesh. Only by the slight tremor of his hands could I tell how drunk he was. He knelt beside Tran and stroked the boy's flat belly with reverent fingers, bent and kissed one of his puckered brown nipples. Tran stirred but did not open his eyes.

Jay leaned over to remove an object from the nightstand drawer. For a moment I thought it was some sort of arcane sex toy. Then I saw that it was a Phillips screwdriver in quite a large size. He took the blade in his mouth, coated it lightly with spit. Then he pulled Tran's legs up, exposing the tender crack between the silken buttocks, and he jammed the screwdriver into the centre of that crack. At the same time he bent again and bit deeply into Tran's left nipple.

Tran's body convulsed in a long shudder of pain. Jay gave the screwdriver a final shove, a nasty twist, then yanked it out and held it dripping with blood and shit before the boy's wide-open, terrified eyes.

Tran lashed out and knocked it from his hand. Before Jay

could react, he was up and off the bed, lunging for the door. I grabbed for him, caught a handful of flying hair, smashed his head against the door frame. He left a smear of blood on the white paint. But the force of the blow had been insufficient to drop him. Revived by terror, Tran tore away from me and charged down the hall.

We almost caught him in the parlour. I was an arm's length behind, Jay right on my heels. Tran raged through the room, grabbing at lamps, vases, anything he might hurl at us to slow our progress. Jay snatched up a glass paperweight and sent it flying at Tran. It glanced off his skull, snapping his head forward. Still the cursed brat would not fall. He ran into the foyer, yanked at the door, opened it and stumbled into the courtyard.

In three great bounding steps he crossed it. Then he was hammering at the gate, which was impenetrable from the street side, but required only the push of a button to open it from the courtyard. A serious flaw in Jay's security system, I thought; only two days ago I had pointed it out to him. The gate slid soundlessly open and our Tran was through the widening gap in a flash, naked and bloody, but free.

I followed Jay back inside. "I'll go get him," he was saying, more to himself than anything. "Got to put on some clothes and get some cop insurance. Yes, I'll get him."

He walked quickly to the bedroom, threw on shirt and trousers, shoved his slender sockless feet into loafers of exquisite black Italian leather, retrieved his wallet from the dresser and had a quick peek inside. As always, the wallet contained a fat sheaf of bills. Cop insurance.

"Well, bring him back alive," I said as Jay turned to go.

"Don't worry," Jay told me. "We're not done with this one yet."

14

His first thought was that the French Quarter had never looked so dark.

Here and there he could make out blurry rectangles of light that might be windows. An early string of Christmas bulbs twined through the ironwork on a high balcony, blinking gold, red, gold; a wavering gas lamp, ghostly in the deserted night. But for each point of illumination there were ten impassive brick facades, ten rusty gates that hung ajar on blackness.

Every nerve and chemical in Tran's body was telling him to be frantic with terror, and his brain could barely remember why.

He was cold. Dimly he realized this was because he was naked, but he couldn't quite remember why that mattered, either. This was the French Quarter; he'd worn almost as little on these same streets last Mardi Gras, with Luke beside him. He was hurting, and that *did* seem to matter more with every step he took. His head pounded like a huge heart; his bitten nipple throbbed as the cool air teased it erect. But those pains were nothing compared to the cramping in his gut, like a steely hand clamping onto his intestines and *twisting* . . .

He couldn't recall what had happened exactly. He had thought Jay was interested in him again, and it had made him horny enough to get drunk, to lose his fear of getting burned a second time. He remembered watching the cousins make out, then sucking Arthur's uncircumcised cock, intrigued with the texture and pliability of the very clean foreskin. But beyond that was oblivion, then the rending pain in his asshole and nipple. Pure instinct had sent him hurtling off the bed, and he had only the faintest memory of Arthur, face contorted with rage, smashing his head against the door frame. Now he was out here. None of it made any sense.

A few more steps and the pain doubled him over. He leaned against a wall, retching but unable to bring anything up from his damaged system. He felt a cold sick sweat springing up on his face, along his spine, under his balls. For a moment the pain in his head threatened to blot out the others, and he welcomed it; it was easier to bear than the gaudy blaze of pain in his gut.

Then suddenly hands were on him, pawing at his bare shoulder. *Jay. Arthur.* Tran jerked away, curled, fell to the sidewalk.

"Hey buddy—hey, you OK—"

He stared up into a blurry black face. Big pale-palmed hand reaching down to him, long shape slung over the guy's shoulder—a gun? no, an instrument case. Street musician on his way home. This guy would know his way around the Quarter, could help him get somewhere safe.

Tran tried to move, to take the man's hand and pull himself up, but everything felt so *heavy,* even his own hand far away at the end of his arm. He registered the locust buzz of motors pulling up nearby, the pounding of hard soles across concrete. Then the musician was grabbed from behind.

"Getcher ass up *against* dat wall—"

"Motherfuckin nigger pervert—"

The first remark came from a fat white cop, the second from a slight, slender black one. Their absurdly tiny NOPD scooters idled at the curb. Their hands were, variously, gripping the back of the musician's neck hard enough to dimple the skin; on the back of the guy's skull, shoving his face into the rough brick wall; yanking his arms behind his back, handcuffs ready.

Tran tried to say something, some wonderful crime-tale cliché like *Hey, you got the wrong guy,* but he could not make his mouth work. He swallowed, trying to moisten his raw throat. His saliva tasted of blood and come. Some of his teeth felt loose. Worst of all, he was still drunk.

He couldn't think of a single reason to stay for the rest of this scene, so he closed his eyes and invited blankness into his head, and blankness accepted his invitation.

By the time Jay rounded the corner of Barracks Street, a small crowd had already begun to gather around the bleeding boy on the sidewalk. The cops had released the musician, who stood rubbing his sore neck and glaring at them. A pair of tourists from Alabama wandered by, lost in search of Bourbon Street, and stopped to watch the action.

"Looks lak somebody needs to call a ambulance," one of them remarked.

"That won't be necessary," said Jay, coming up quickly, getting between Tran and the cops, but not too close to the cops. "He lives with me. I'll take him home."

Jay knelt beside Tran and pulled him into a sitting position against the wall. Tran's eyes fluttered open. For a long moment he stared at Jay. *If he starts screaming, I'm through,* Jay thought. But there was no sign of recognition in Tran's pain-dulled eyes. After another moment they slid shut again.

"He lives wit' you, huh?" asked the white cop. "What's he doin' bare-assed out on the street?"

Jay met the cop's rheumy gaze with unwavering honesty. "I'm afraid he had too much to drink. He's not used to it, and we argued. He ran out before I could stop him."

"What's his name?"

"John Lam."

"How 'bout you?"

"I'm Lysander Byrne. I live up on Royal."

"Lemme see some ID."

Jay handed the cop his driver's license with two bills folded discreetly under it. Catching the flash of green, the other cop waved an imperative hand at the onlookers. "Y'all go on, now. Nothin' to see here."

"That boy's hurt," the musician protested. "Look, he's just a young kid—"

"He's twenty-one," interrupted Jay.

"Looks about fifteen to me," one of the tourists said.

"Got blood on him," the other pointed out.

Everyone looked at Tran. It was true: though not immediately noticeable in this half-light, several dark smudges of blood stood out against the pale skin of Tran's face, chest, and legs.

"Mr.—" The white cop consulted Jay's license. "Mr. Byrne? Know why he's bleedin'?"

"I saw him fall as he was running away. Probably banged himself up then."

The black cop bent to examine Tran more closely, then straightened up and pointed to the bite mark on the boy's nipple. "He did that to himself, too?"

Jay shrugged. "I did that. I'm not responsible for his sexual proclivities, but I do try to indulge them."

The cops glanced at each other. Utterly unlike in every other way, their faces bore twin expressions of distaste. The white cop handed Jay's license back, scissored gingerly between thumb and forefinger. Apparently he was willing to take his chances with the money. "Mr. Byrne, I suggest you take your, uh . . . *friend* home and keep him there until he sobers up. I see him on the street in this condition again, I'll arrest him."

Jay nodded, smiled. Someone else might have found this performance humiliating. He was savoring the cops' cluelessness, their utter belief in his act. "Thank you, Officer."

"Hold up a minute!" The musician gestured at the cops, at Jay. "That kid looks hurt bad to me. I say he needs an ambulance."

"Zat right, nigger?" The black cop took two steps toward the musician, pushed his skinny face into the older man's seamed one. "Well, I say he *doesn't*. And I say you need to get your black ass outta here while you still got the chance."

The musician looked at the other cop, at the limp form of Tran, at Jay who met his gaze without sympathy or rancor. He looked around for the two tourists, but they had done a quick fade. At last he hitched up his instrument case on his shoulder and walked away toward Decatur Street, shaking his head in disgust.

"I'll just take him home now," said Jay.

Luke blazed through the streets of Bywater and Marigny, past Victorian cottages and camelbacks and shotguns, old houses mostly rickety but painted a spectrum of colors. Here and there a house was boarded up and ravaged with graffiti. But as he approached the Quarter, the streets took on more of a genteel-homo air, a rainbow flag or windsock fluttering from every other porch, a pink triangle or a SILENCE = DEATH sticker on every other car bumper. In these lovingly renovated, tastefully appointed homes, people were making dinner, having sex, getting dressed to hit the bars, dying of KS and PCP and CMV and crypto and toxo and a hundred other incomprehensible horrors the rest of the world just called "AIDS."

Or living with those horrors. Soren liked to stress that distinction: *Are you dying of AIDS, Luke, or are you living with it?* He'd always had a sarcastic comeback. Tonight he would answer the question truthfully, one way or another.

He had no idea what he meant to do. Assuming he could even find Jay's house, how was he going to get in—ring the doorbell? *Uh, good evening, Mr. Byrne, sorry to disturb you at this late hour, but after all the horror stories my ex has probably told you about me, I'm sure you're real eager to let me in so I can rip your fucking THROAT OUT* . . . No; what then? Forced entry? What the hell did he think he was *doing,* anyway?

He wished he had kept Johnnie's gun.

He wished he had a needle and a ready vein.

For a moment Luke thought of bypassing Royal Street, going instead to a certain bar or two, looking up one of his old acquaintances, the kind of old acquaintances who always hang around junkie bars mopping up the tears of fallen angels. He had money in his pocket; he could score enough heroin to keep him high for days, to stop his heart. *Let it go,* said something in him. *Let Tran go where he will. Leave them alone. Show yourself some mercy.*

But the stronger part of him—the part that had been angry all the time for more than a year now—would not allow it. Junk was too easy. Tran was his rightful lover in this world. He had shucked the ballast of WHIV, and he no longer cared whether he finished his novel. This was the real story, the only one whose ending he still cared about.

He crossed Esplanade into the Quarter. This end of Royal Street was dark and empty. The air smelled of wood smoke, a lonely autumn scent. As he walked, Luke checked the finials of every wrought-iron gate for pineapples. In this way he happened to catch sight of the commotion taking place halfway up the block on Barracks.

Police scooters at the curb, their whirling bubble lights lending the scene a sick stroboscopic quality. Two blue backs, one broad and one narrow, both topped by small round heads that sat atop their shoulders without the interruption of necks. A tall, coolly handsome blond man gripping the arm of a naked boy whose long black hair hid his face. As the blond man pulled him upright, the raven sheaf of hair fell back, and Luke saw that the boy was Tran. Which must mean that the blond man was Jay.

His heart clenched. Pain corkscrewed through his chest and down into his belly. He hadn't eaten in two days, so his bowels probably weren't about to turn traitor on him, but the familiar cramps wrung his gut anyway. He hadn't known what he was going to do before; what the hell was he going to do *now?*

The cops were getting on their scooters. They were going to let Jay have him. This registered in Luke's mind more clearly than the dark smudges of blood on Tran's skin, more fully than the shock of seeing Tran naked and helpless on the street: *They were going to let Jay have him.* And Jay could not have him.

Luke leaned against a building and gathered his strength. He'd been awake since dawn; he'd watched one friend blow his brains out and had strenuous sex with another; he'd walked two miles in a highly pissed-off state of mind; he'd missed three doses of various medications. He was tired. Anyone would be.

Even so, he pushed himself away from the building and walked as quickly as he could up Barracks.

Jay saw Luke coming and recognized him at once. He'd never seen Luke before, but the leather jacket and battered boots, the badass stride, the ghastly-handsome face left no doubt as to the identity of this new character. *Luke always carried a razor in his boot,* he recalled Tran saying. *After he got sick, he said if anyone fucked with him, he'd slash his wrist and throw blood in their eyes . . .*

Jay wasn't afraid of a little blood. Razors didn't worry him much either. But what if Luke took Tran away? Andrew would be disappointed, maybe even angry. Maybe even angry enough to leave. And Tran would remember what they had done to him; perhaps his injuries would require medical attention. Doctors would ask questions, and talk to cops, and these two cops would remember him and find out he'd lied . . .

Silently he calculated the contents of his wallet. He'd given the cops fifty dollars each. Would another fifty make them turn a deaf ear to anything Luke might say? Jay thought so, but he wasn't sure. Better make it a hundred more apiece. He put his hand on his back pocket, not taking his wallet out, just letting the cops know it could happen.

"I know that boy," Luke said. He was out of breath, and his eyes looked quite insane. "What'd you do to him? What's wrong with him? Tran?" He moved forward, reaching for Tran. The white cop put out a meaty arm and blocked his way.

"You know this guy?" the black cop asked Jay.

"We've never met, but I've heard about him. He and John are, uh"—Jay coughed discreetly into his free hand—"a thing of the past."

That look of distaste passed between the cops again. *Give them something they don't want to hear,* Jay thought, *and they won't listen as carefully.*

"His name's not John!" Luke yelled. "It's Vincent Tran! Dammit, I *know* him!"

"Oh yeah?" the white cop asked. "How come he ain't actin' like he knows *you?*"

"Can't you see something's fucking *wrong* with him? Tran, it's Luke, baby, come on, Tran, *look* at me . . ."

Jay had been supporting most of Tran's weight with one arm; now he wrapped the other around Tran's chest, protective new boyfriend confronting psycho-obsessive old one. "He's fine, Luke. I'll take care of him. Why don't you just try to take care of yourself?"

He saw a flash of pure murder in Luke's eyes. This man was not someone to underestimate. There was madness there, obvious and gaudy. Jay turned back to the cops and took out his wallet. "Look, do you want to see some ID?"

"We alr—" The words died on the white cop's lips. "Yeah. Lemme see your driver's license."

Sleight of hand wasn't one of Jay's strong points, but he tried to fold the two hundreds under the license with a modicum of discretion. Luke, of course, missed nothing. "You goddamn filthy crooks. You'd lick this pedophile's ass for another hundred." He tried to shove past them, his hands clawing for Tran. The cops moved simultaneously, quick as snakes, pinning Luke's arms behind him and wrestling him up against the wall. It had to hurt, but his furious expression never changed, and his burning eyes never left Jay's.

The white cop bent to speak in Luke's ear, though he didn't lower his voice. "You got any more smart mouth to give us, asshole? 'Cause if you do, you get to take a ride in the cruiser with some of our buddies. Now we're gonna give these gentlemen an escort home, and you're gonna turn around and walk the other way. Understand?"

Luke remained silent. The black cop gave his pinned wrists a jerk. *"Understand?"*

"No, I don't understand." Luke ground his face into the wall. He was nearly sobbing. "I don't understand how you can find a kid naked and bleeding on the street and give him back to the guy who probably did it to him. I don't understand how you can take a bribe from that freak and forget about the kid's safety. I don't even understand what he's doing with Jay instead of me."

The white cop jammed a knee into Luke's back. "Faggot, if I hear *one more word* outta you—"

"He's just upset," said Jay. "Please let him go."

The cops, remembering where the grease on their palms had come from, dropped Luke's arms and stepped away from him. Luke remained against the wall, his face pressed into the cold bricks.

Jay wanted to get Tran back to the house before he began to come out of his stupor. "Shall we?" he asked. The cops mounted their scooters and puttered off so slowly that even with Tran in tow, Jay was able to stay a few steps ahead of them.

As his peculiar entourage turned the corner of Royal Street, Jay glanced back over his shoulder. Luke was flattened against the wall, gripping it with both hands, holding himself up by the fissures in the brick. His shoulders heaved convulsively. Jay could still hear his sobs.

He almost felt sorry for the man.

Tran awoke to a world of pleasure and pain.

The last thing he remembered was being out on the street, naked and cold. A hazy memory of Luke's face tantalized him. Had Luke been there? He thought so, but the whole scene seemed so unreal, a distant nightmare that was quickly eclipsed by the present one.

His wrists and ankles were tightly bound, and there was a wide strap across his midsection. The restraints felt like greased leather. The surface beneath him was metal, slick and cold. Every breath he took filled his lungs with a hideous smell, something sweetly rancid, worse than fish guts rotting behind a grocery in Versailles. His head hurt dreadfully. The bars of fluorescent light overhead branded themselves into his corneas. He had a hard-on, which was as deep in Arthur's throat as Arthur's had lately been in his own. Jay was staring down into his face, blond hair stringy with sweat.

Tran tried to speak but found his lips dry and swollen. Jay offered him a sip of water from a nearby cup. When Tran lifted his head to drink, his brain throbbed in protest. It felt as if blood vessels were bursting in there.

The water trickled down his throat, deliciously cold. When it hit his stomach, there was a dazzling burst of pain. He swallowed again and found himself able to speak in a hoarse whisper. "Jay . . . what are you doing?"

"Killing you." A ghost of a smile touched Jay's lips, but not his pale eyes.

"Why?"

"Because it's what we do. And because you're beautiful."

"Have you always done this?"

"Since I was younger than you."

"How . . . how . . ."

"How many? I've lost count. How do I do it? Various ways. Is there anything special you want?" He stroked Tran's cheek with a bony finger, and Tran realized he was absolutely serious.

"I don't want to die."

Arthur stopped sucking Tran's cock, raised his head and stared into Tran's eyes. "You're lying."

"I'll scream."

"We know." Jay laid gentle fingertips on Tran's temples, bent and kissed his forehead. "When you get too loud, we'll gag you."

A wave of terror swept over him, threatened to drag him into its mindless depths. They meant it. They meant to tear him up alive, and he was trapped. There was no way out. The only time Tran could remember feeling remotely like this was when he found out Luke had tested positive. That was the first time he had ever really believed he was going to die. Now he found that he did not fear death as much as he feared the pain that would precede it.

Bile rose in his throat, hot and bitter. Jay saw him choking and forced his head to the side. Thin vomit trickled out of the corner of his mouth onto the table. Jay wiped it away with a damp cloth, then wiped Tran's sweaty face with another.

The gesture brought Tran no relief. With his head at this new angle, he was able to see the shelves that ran along the back wall, and their contents. The objects were distorted by perspective and fear, but he could make out bones, flowers and candles, jars with strange floating contents.

He focused on a single jar, and was barely able to grasp the meaning of what he saw: eyes in bloody water, staring out at him or past him, twenty pairs or more, as large and cloudy as pickled eggs. He realized what the awful smell was. In that moment he knew he was going to die, here and now, though he did not accept it; that would come later, and harder.

Jay let go of Tran's head and moved to the foot of the table, beside Arthur. They stood together for a moment, gazing at him. Tran looked back at them with something beginning to resemble awe. They were, after all, his destiny. Luke had tried to claim that role falsely, and failed. These two men had taken it by force, simply because they wanted to. Through his terror, through his sorrow, something in him loved that.

But it was going to hurt like hell. He knew he probably could not yet conceive of the pain they would put him through before he died. He had no frame of reference for it; up till now the worst pain he'd ever experienced had been a busted ankle in a high school gym class, courtesy of a redneck who liked to call him a commie gook.

Thinking of school made him think of his family. He imagined how his father would feel when he found out about this: guilty and grief-stricken, yes, but also vindicated in his beliefs. This was the sort of end his father expected him to meet, a dirty painful death . . . but, for the family, so much faster than watching AIDS devour him in stages. Maybe his father would view Jay and Arthur's intervention as a stroke of divine mercy, a bifurcated arm of God descending with scimitars to lop off a malformed twig. Tran wondered if he were insane for having these thoughts, wished he were insane, tried to will himself there but could not.

Hot tears spilled from the corners of his eyes and dripped into his hair. He had never felt so helpless. Surreptitiously he pulled at his restraints, which gave less than half an inch. Jay Byrne knew how to trap a boy so he could never get away. Jay deserved his reputation after all, and more. Tran wasn't really surprised. But then he wouldn't have been surprised to find out Luke had killed somebody, either.

Now Jay was crossing the narrow room to a rack on the opposite wall, a sturdy metal affair fitted with all sorts of hooks, clamps, and compartments to hold tools. Tran saw an electric drill, an awl, a claw hammer, more screwdrivers, a hacksaw, pliers, surgical implements, an assortment of knives. The stark light made the stainless steel glitter like diamonds. As Jay selected a number of items, Arthur squeezed Tran's hand reassuringly.

Jay returned with the tools and set them somewhere out of sight. In his right hand was a single hemostat, scissorslike blades minutely serrated, large enough to clamp an artery or hold a fat joint. He took Tran's uninjured nipple between thumb and forefinger, rolled it gently back and forth. Even now Tran couldn't help responding to Jay's touch. His skin shivered with gooseflesh; his nipple hardened. Jay pinched up the sensitive tissue and closed the hemostat on it.

This new pain was immediate, intense, and crushing. It robbed him of breath. He knew he could not bear it. But he had to, and worse yet to come. Even as he formed this thought, Jay clamped a second hemostat on his left nipple, the one that had been bitten nearly through. Tran found his breath and shrieked, a desperate sound that ricocheted off the long, low walls.

"We'd better gag him," said Arthur. "It's only going to get worse."

"You're right." Jay's hand forced something round and slick into his mouth, smoothed his hair back and fastened something behind his head. Tran tasted latex, felt his tongue being pushed into the shallow well at the back of his throat, scant millimeters from triggering his gag reflex. He wondered if he would choke, then realized it would be a mercy. But he did not choke; he was not blessed by asphyxiation or catatonia; he remained excruciatingly aware of everything.

Arthur's strong hands gripped his hipbones; Arthur's erect cock prodded the cleft of his ass. "Jay, do you mind if I—"

"Fuck him? Sure, go ahead."

"It won't get in your way?"

Jay smirked. "Your dick's not *that* long."

"Oh, aren't we the clever one!" Arthur's grinning face hung over him, blue eyes alight. Arthur's fingers lubricated him, spread him. Then Arthur's cock was sliding into his damaged rectum, a brand-new world of pleasure/pain unlike anything Tran had imagined, searing, soaring, sickening, teasing his prostate and ripping open his wounds.

As Arthur fucked him, Tran was aware of Jay unbuckling the wide strap around his middle, allowing him to breathe a little easier. He pulled air in through his nose, rolled his head back and forth on the table. The pain felt as if it were reaching some sort of crescendo, but perhaps it was capable of attaining infinite peaks.

Jay trailed spidery fingers along Tran's collarbone, his chest, his ribs. He laid his hand on Tran's belly and palpated gently, as if testing the ripeness of fruit. Tran felt his organs constricting in dread, cramping under Jay's palm.

When he saw the next tool Jay chose, he shut his eyes tightly. Too soon he felt the knife's tip at the base of his breastbone. Then the long fillet blade was sliding through his flesh, a shuddery cold sensation like the sick shock of a paper cut multiplied a thousand times. At the same moment, Arthur thrust deep into him and ejaculated. The sperm burned like bleach and salt on his torn inner tissues.

Tran raised his head. Jay had made a long shallow incision from his breastbone to his crotch, neatly parting the skin. Tran could see the layers of fat and muscle beneath. Arthur stood at the foot of the table, his cock and thighs smeared with Tran's blood, his pubic hair matted with it.

Jay thrust the knife into the incision again, and Tran's head fell back. The cold blade twisted inside him, severed some tough membrane with an agonizing *crunch,* sank into vital softness. Tran heard his own blood pattering onto the table, felt it pooling warmly beneath his back and buttocks. Blood filled his throat, welled past the gag and trickled out the corners of his mouth.

Jay unfastened the gag and pulled it out. A freshet of blood and bile followed it. Tran coughed, retched, tried to scream. It sounded like someone attempting to gargle boiling water. Jay put the knife down, leaned over and cradled him, kissed his bloody mouth, licked his chin, his throat, his swollen nipples, the edges of his incision. Tran felt consciousness beginning to slip away, merciful blackness fogging his brain at last.

He was yanked back by the white heat of Jay's teeth in his belly. Not just in his skin or even his flesh but down in his *guts,* pushing back the edges and thrusting deep inside, ripping something out of him. The pain was a wire of infinite length vibrating at an unimaginable speed. Rabid jaws churning slippery tubes. Stinking acids of digestion. Meat in Jay's mouth, dangling, dripping. Arthur feeding from Jay's mouth, their lips purpled with dark blood, their jaws chewing the stringy flesh in unison. His own dear flesh.

He saw them through a haze of red. The pain began to recede. He felt dreamy, weightless, very cold. The thought that it was nearly over soothed him like a lover's touch. Tran closed his eyes and did not open them again.

The wall started to hurt his face after a while, but Luke couldn't move yet. The cops' casual malice, Tran's indifference, and Jay's smug command of the situation had paralyzed him.

At last he felt he could let go of the wall without collapsing. He brushed crumbs of dirt and brick off his wet cheeks, but he could not wipe away his last image of Tran: face bloody and blank, eyes utterly without recognition. Tran had looked straight through him and had not known him. How could that be? Last he'd heard, Tran was scared of him. It didn't make sense.

Jay must have done something to Tran; he'd looked drunk and hurt. Maybe Jay was into rough stuff. Tran had never been opposed to a little rough stuff. But maybe this time it had gotten out of hand.

Luke knew two things: he was still going to find Jay's place, and he was going to get to Tran somehow, if only to make sure Tran was all right. But he couldn't go there yet. If Jay had given the cops a large enough bribe, they might cruise by his house a few more times to make sure Luke didn't turn up. If he did, Luke had no doubt they'd arrest him in a heartbeat.

He set off in the opposite direction and walked until he saw the muted neon of a bar. It was a suitably dark and sordid place, populated by grizzled old androgynes and a few gaudy creatures who might have been hookers or particularly inept drag queens. Luke's abraded, tear-stained face caused no comment in this joint. He ordered a double shot of whiskey straight up. The house brand was rotgut. It was what he was used to, and it went down easy, sloshed once around his empty stomach, and melted warmly into his bloodstream.

Cleaning himself up in the restroom, he noticed that his eyes were bloodshot and his gums a sick grayish-pink. Soren must have been desperate. Was he crazy for imagining Tran could ever want him back? Probably, but it hardly mattered anymore. Now he had a score to settle with Jay as well: for hurting Tran, for humiliating him in front of Tran, for leading Tran away naked in his arms.

Luke left the bar and walked back up lower Royal Street, checking the finials of each gate. When he saw the cast-iron pineapples, he crossed the street and stood in a recessed doorway to get a good look at the property.

Built on a wide, deep lot flanked by three-story townhouses, most of it was hidden behind a high brick wall topped with iron spikes and glittering coils of razor wire. Through the bars of the gate he could see one corner of the house, a vaguely Roman affair in whitewashed stone or stucco, the scalloped arches of its porch reminiscent of a mausoleum. The walkway that ran alongside the house to the rear of the property was a black rectangle lit only by the tall wavering flames of two gas jets enclosed in hurricane lamps. Beyond these eerie wisps of light, Luke could see nothing.

Cautiously he moved to the gate and peered through the bars. The yard was overgrown with ferns, gnarled vines, and a large oak tree, several of whose branches overhung the sidewalk within easy, tempting reach. But there was no way he could go in through the front. He'd already noted the video camera at the top of the gate. The sides of the property looked equally impenetrable: even if he could somehow get on top of one of the townhouses, the drop into Jay's yard would kill him.

He wrapped his hands around the iron bars for a moment, staring into the darkness. It was difficult to leave knowing Tran was in there. At last he made himself walk away from the gate, to the next corner, and around the block to Bourbon Street, which ran parallel to Royal.

Far from the sleazy tourist drag, this end of Bourbon was closely lined with the well-preserved homes of gay men in their forties and fifties. He found what he hoped was the property directly behind Jay's. Given the rabbit-warren nature of French Quarter architecture, there might be two or three small buildings wedged in between. But if he was lucky, the two lots would share a back wall.

The Bourbon Street property was a massive stucco house with an adjoining alleyway to the rear courtyard. The gate leading to the alley was about eight feet high, made of curly wrought iron with lots of boot-sized gaps, topped with twisty little iron spikes that didn't look particularly formidable. Maybe he could get over it. Maybe, if they didn't have a motion sensor, or a dog, or . . .

There were a million possible obstacles. Luke had to forget them all. He tried the gate to make sure his luck hadn't suddenly changed. It hadn't. He took off his leather jacket and swung it over his head, trying to snag its lining on the iron spikes.

He had to repeat this several times, stopping twice when cars passed. Finally the jacket snagged on the gate and held. Luke tugged it, yanked it hard, let his knees sag until all his weight hung from it. The jacket was caught tight.

He pulled himself up as quickly as he could, grabbing on to the ironwork, easing himself over the top of the gate, using the heavy leather to protect his hands and his crotch from the spikes. When he was over, he clung to the inside of the gate with one hand and carefully freed his jacket with the other. Then he let himself drop into the alley and waited to feel ravening canine jaws sink into his ass.

Nothing. No dog, no alarm that he could hear. He crept along the alley, stopped when he reached the cobblestone courtyard. It was softly shadowed by lights at the base of a gurgling fountain, but otherwise dark. There were no other buildings on the lot.

Luke approached the rear wall. Perhaps ten feet high, of slippery concrete topped with more spikes and razor wire, it would be harder to scale than the gate had been. Yet scale it he must, with no time to waste. He closed his eyes and said a prayer to whatever might be listening, and he *ran* at the wall, hurled himself at it, flung the jacket as high as he could.

For a sickening moment he felt himself falling backward, and fully expected to snap his spine on the damp cobblestones. Then the jacket snagged again. He almost lost his grip on the sleeve. Retaining it through sheer force of will, he hauled himself up and onto the top of the wall.

For several moments he lay there, panting with the exertion, swooning in and out of consciousness. The night swam with psychedelic designs. He wondered if his heart might just give out right now. No, he was damned if it would. He forced himself to move his head and look around. There was a slanting rooftop just a few feet below him, some kind of shed or slave quarters. In the distance, through foliage and shadow, he could barely discern the spectral shape of Jay's house.

The spikes were beginning to gouge through his jacket. Soon they would draw blood. With one last convulsive heave Luke pulled himself over the wall, yanked his jacket off the spikes, and dropped onto the rooftop. He lay with his cheek pressed to the cold slates, resting.

Then, very faintly, he heard a sound from inside the building. A low, bubbling, hopeless scream. Like someone trying to gargle boiling water.

He recognized the voice.

Luke scrambled to the edge of the roof and dropped the last eight feet into the courtyard. Moldy statuary seemed to spring at him as the yard flooded with light. *Motion sensor. Fuck!*

The sound came again, even fainter. Luke wrapped his jacket around his head and shoulders and hurled himself at one of the black-painted windows. He felt glass and ancient wood splintering; then he was kicking the frame away, clawing his way in, throwing the jacket aside and staring at the impossible scene that confronted him.

Jay Byrne and a dark-haired stranger, their pale naked bodies smeared with more blood than Luke could imagine coming out of someone as small as Tran. Yet there was Tran on a wheeled metal table, his body split open by an enormous deliquescent wound, his head thrown back in saintlike agony, his bound limbs convulsing as his back arched in the spasms of death. The tabletop and floor beneath him were awash with blood.

Jay raised his head as Luke came crashing through the window. Long strings of glistening red flesh dangled from his open mouth and dripped from his chin. The stranger was chewing something too. Luke saw all this in the split-second it took him to regain his footing and slide his fingers into the top of his right boot. His momentum carried him toward Jay. He was already flicking open the silver V of the straight razor.

The stranger moved toward him. Jay moved away, behind the table. Luke clamped the open razor between his teeth, hooked the fingers of both hands under the table's edge, and heaved with all his strength. The rubber wheels skidded sideways. Already top-heavy with Tran's weight, the table began to tip. Jay tried to scramble out of the way, but the heavy slab of metal and the body strapped to it came smashing down on his ankle, pinning him.

Luke flung himself across the table. The razor was in his hand again. He was on top of Jay like a lover. Jay clawed at his eyes. Luke twisted his head, caught Jay's fingers in his teeth, and bit down hard. Jay yanked his hand away, but not before Luke had tasted Tran's blood on those bony fingers.

With his left forearm he forced Jay's head back. Jay choked, spat out gobbets of half-chewed flesh. One landed on Luke's upper lip, and he licked it away without thinking. Jay grinned up at him, eyes corrosive with madness. There was a hideous familiarity in that grin. "I don't know you," Luke sobbed as he jammed the blade behind Jay's left ear and dragged it along the path of Jay's jugular.

A thin red line appeared in its wake. *I didn't cut him deep enough,* Luke thought dumbly, *I fucked up, and any second now his friend's going to bury an axe in my head.* Then the line widened into a lipless crimson chasm, and a hot geyser of blood bathed Luke's face, stinging his eyes and blinding him.

15

And so, at what was to have been the moment of our greatest communion, Jay and I were separated forever. There was no chance for anything as formal as good-bye; I barely reached his side in time to see the last of the life pump out of him. His body gave a great shudder and his eyes began to cloud. I was left clutching at that most poignant and useless of regrets: if my lover had to die, why couldn't I have been the one to kill him?

Luke had rolled out of the way as Jay's blood sprayed his face. (I didn't know he was called Luke then, of course, and didn't find out until later.) For a long time I could not take my eyes off Jay. I was afraid of missing anything, any subliminal message his eyes and nerves and skin might convey to me as he descended. Luke could easily have crept up and finished me off with his razor, for I scarcely remembered that anyone else was alive in the room.

Jay had no message for me, only a mad grin frozen on his face, only an exquisite marble pallor caused by the rapid draining of blood. I cradled him, held him to me. His head sagged backward; the jellied edges of the great raw wound in his throat ripped; the ends of his hair trailed in a pool of his own gore. There seemed to be nothing more I could do for him, nothing more I could learn from him.

Gradually I became aware of the other party in the room: his sweaty living scent, the deep and constant anger that ran through him like an electrical current. I turned to face him. He was crouched against the wall, arms wrapped around his knees, hollow eyes fixed on me.

"You're Andrew Compton," he said.

I had expected anything but that. "How do you know?"

"Because I saw your picture in the paper, asshole. I can't believe the *Weekly World News* got something right."

I considered this. Doubtless my picture had appeared in a great many papers; yet no one had shown me the slightest sign of recognition since I left the hospital morgue. You may recall my assertion that murderers are blessed with malleable faces. Yet there is always that person in a million who will know me not for the distinction of my features, but by the predatory kinship in my eyes. I never doubted that Jay had seen it the night we met at the Hand of Glory, although he had not comprehended its meaning at first. Now this interloper could see it too.

I wondered whether I could bring myself to kill him.

"So kill me, Andrew. I recognize you. I can turn you in. Kill me."

I realized I need not kill him. This man would never go to the police. He wished to die a quick and violent death, not to be held in some cell, embroiled in sordid murder, forced to cling to his own miserable thread of a life. And he *was* dying; I could see it in his sallow face, his sunken embers of eyes. But slowly, fibre by fibre, going ungently into a night that did not look good to him at all.

Reminding myself that the separation was only temporary, I extracted myself from Jay's congealing repose. I stood over Luke and smiled down at him. Though I was naked and he was clothed, though he still held a weapon and I had only my flesh, I felt his world's foundations tremble as he realized that he was in the presence of a creature worse than himself.

I paced before him, still smiling. I picked up the fillet blade we had used to open Tran, whetted the blade with my thumb and thrust the resultant gash under his nose. When he failed to flinch away, I knew what he was dying of.

"Are you afraid to die?" I asked him.

"Aren't you?"

"Of course. I've done it, and it's terrifying."

He stared up at me, eyes full of blood and hatred.

"And yet"—I showed my teeth in what I hoped was an ingratiating manner—"it can also be addictive."

His dry whisper saddened me with its pointlessness: "Fuck you." He might be a fellow predator, this one, but unlike Jay he was a puerile one. He did not wish to learn anything from me, and I suspected he had little left to teach me.

I offered him the knife. I directed his attention to the wide range of implements upon the walls. I invited him to simply crawl into the freezer and pull the lid down on himself; I promised him I would not open it again. At this comforting suggestion he only shuddered and buried his face in his hands. I tired of taunting him and left him to his grief.

Jay's skin was sticky with drying blood. I curled around him again, licked his shoulder, traced the curve of his throat to the edge of the mortal wound. When my tongue slid into it, the taste was like nothing else had ever been. At the same time it was like coming home.

I decided Luke could go hang; for all I knew he would do just that, though I rather hoped not, for I enjoyed the thought of his continued suffering. I gathered Jay into my arms and lifted him. He seemed very light, as if something more substantial than spirit had left him. I carried him through the floodlit garden and over the threshold into the house.

I bathed him in the tub, washed the blood from his stiffening hair and his white, white skin, dried him, and laid him gently on the bed. And I had my time with him, this new Jay who did not and could not resist me, who never protested when I tore new holes in him, who minded not at all when I swallowed one of his testes like a salty raw oyster. It was sweet still, better than it had ever been with any of my boys. But it was almost beside the point.

I took a wide strip of meat from his right flank, carefully peeling the skin away. I felt a pang at cutting him so deeply now that I was not making love to him, but the cutting of this strip of meat was essential to both of us.

I fried it lightly in butter, tucked it between two slices of fresh bakery bread, and wrapped it in cellophane for the trip.

Before I left the house, I had a look at myself in the bathroom mirror. My body felt strong and lean; my colour was better than it had been since I left Painswick. I felt different now I'd been recognized, as if there was something I should do. But I could think of nothing else to do here.

When I carried Jay back out to the slave quarters, Luke was gone. I laid Jay down beside Tran, arranged his arms around the boy's torn and stinking body. Then I sat beside them for a long time, unable to take my leave. At last my legs began to cramp, and I pulled myself up and returned to the house.

I dressed in a loose sweater of Jay's and the trousers I had bought in Soho on Guy Fawkes' Day. Out the front, I hailed a cab and crept away down Royal Street behind a mule-drawn carriage, anonymous as any tourist, back the way I had come.

Upon my Greyhound-borne arrival, I had noted that the bus terminal doubled as the train depot. Here you could purchase tickets on trains whose names were magical mystery tours unto themselves: Southern Crescent, Sunset Limited, City of New Orleans. Paying with Jay's cash, I reserved a private compartment on a train that shot straight out into the American desert, a land I imagined as arid and relentless as my own heart.

I had hours to wait. I spent them watching the door, secure in my anonymity, not in the least intimidated by the occasional policemen passing through. At last my train arrived, a long string of silver bullets with their functions painted on the sides: DINING CAR, OBSERVATION, SLEEPER. I was a SLEEPER. My compartment was miniscule and orderly, exactly the sort of shell I craved.

As the train pulled out of the station, I stripped naked, folded down my bed, and crawled between clean rough sheets. There I unwrapped and ate my sandwich. The meat was quite tough, with a flavour balanced somewhere between sweet and tangy, itself made up of all Jay's boys.

Adrift in the dark rocking silence, I listened to the workings of my body. My lungs pulled in air and pushed out poison; my stomach and intestines milled Jay down to his essence; my heart marked time. For thirty-three years I had lived in this prison alone.

Once again, I slowed my pulse, my breathing, my involuntary functions to nearly nothing. I had not known if I could do it a second time. As I slipped under, I felt a vast relief. The desert was days away. This time I did not need or want to pass for dead. I wanted only to keep Jay's meat in me as long as I could, to process and assimilate as much of him as possible. When I awoke, he would be with me always, and all the world's pleasures would be ours to revel in.

This time I was not corpse, but larva.

Epilogue

Late in the year, New Orleans still has its hot days. In the slave quarters, Jay and Tran blossomed like the giant stinking carrion-flowers that grow in humid jungles. Their ravaged abdomens swelled and burst like red-black petals, a jubilee of rot. Their putrescent fluids pooled on the concrete floor and in the hollows of their disintegrating bodies.

Luke pushed the plunger on the hypodermic and sent a luscious flood of brown Mexican heroin into his vein. He let himself fall back on the dirty motel sheets, the needle still hanging from his arm, his heart taking a slow dive. His memories receded into a nightmare blur. He was still caked with blood and French Quarter filth, but as the drug coursed through him, he felt himself becoming clean and pure.

Their faces, cocks and balls grew into shapeless masses of blackened flesh. Swollen tongues like ball gags forced their jaws wide. Organs tumbled out of their bodies like distended winebags. From their decomposition rose wisps of steam and soft wet sounds of gaseous intimacy.

. . .

Luke awoke with dirty sunlight in his eyes: he had forgotten to pin the gap in the curtains before he nodded out. His throat was sore. His mind was utterly undrugged and lucid, and he could not bear this.

He was able to reach the bottle of whiskey on the table without getting all the way out of bed. He lay back on his wadded pillows and guzzled rotgut, trying to illuminate everything he had seen and done in the Quarter. He could smell death on himself. He had lines of rotting blood under each fingernail. Nonetheless, he would attempt one final piece of propaganda: he would understand how it had all happened, and he would grope toward why; he would convince himself that he had a book to finish and another year to live.

He fixed his eyes on the ceiling and began to talk.

Tran fell out of his binding straps and melted slowly into Jay's ribcage. A large, viscous, faintly iridescent stain ate up the concrete floor around them. Their eyes were black caverns. They gave birth to worms, generation after generation, until their bodies were covered as if in a living blanket. Soon they were picked clean, their bones an ivory sculpture-puzzle shining in the dark, waiting to tell their mute love story.